Living Ink : Ascension

Praise for *LIVING INK: ASCENSION*

"Curiosity and a hunger for slow-burning intrigue propel you through this mysterious and incredibly original story. The stellar world-building and rich characters will leave you turning pages until the very end."

—**Ryder Hunter Clancy**, bestselling author of *MYSTIC INVISIBLE*

"With *LIVING INK*, Deans has crafted a truly compelling, original story that evokes creepy feelings through a powerful use of well-developed atmosphere and tension. The sense of mystery and foreboding is palpable. This tale keeps you on the edge of your seat . . . fearful of the shadows and unable to stop turning pages. I highly recommend this fascinating and memorable novel."

—**Michael D. Britton**, - whose fiction is featured in *Fiction River Magazine's* Superstitious edition, the Joyous Christmas holiday special, and the Chances romance collection. His latest tale, *Predict THIS*, appears in *Pulphouse Magazine* #14.

"In *LIVING INK*, Deans has wonderfully constructed a tense, chilling, atmospheric tale of horror and intrigue reminiscent of *Event Horizon*. An abandoned ship mystery that is a welcome addition to any horror or science fiction shelf. The reader is drawn down the cold, foreboding corridors of the tale to meet an antagonist as frightening as any in the genre. An auspicious debut from a wonderfully creative pen."

—**Burke J. Grooms**, award-winning author

LIVING INK
ASCENSION

a novel

R.H. DEANS

NEW YORK

LONDON • NASHVILLE • MELBOURNE • VANCOUVER

Living Ink : Ascension

A Novel

© 2023 R. H. Deans

Published in New York, New York, by Morgan James Publishing. Morgan James is a trademark of Morgan James, LLC. www.MorganJamesPublishing.com

Publisher's Note: This novel is a work of fiction. Names, characters, places, and incidents are either products of the author's imagination or used fictitiously. All characters are fictional, and any similarity to people living or dead is purely coincidental.

Proudly distributed by Ingram Publisher Services.

A **FREE** ebook edition is available for you or a friend with the purchase of this print book.

CLEARLY SIGN YOUR NAME ABOVE

Instructions to claim your free ebook edition:
1. Visit MorganJamesBOGO.com
2. Sign your name CLEARLY in the space above
3. Complete the form and submit a photo of this entire page
4. You or your friend can download the ebook to your preferred device

ISBN 9781631959530 paperback
ISBN 9781631959547 ebook
Library of Congress Control Number: 2022936050

Cover and Interior Design by:
Chris Treccani
www.3dogcreative.net

Front and Back Cover Illustration by:
Ryan Guest
dropofcreativity

Morgan James is a proud partner of Habitat for Humanity Peninsula and Greater Williamsburg. Partners in building since 2006.

Get involved today! Visit MorganJamesPublishing.com/giving-back

Acknowledgments

I would like to acknowledge all those who helped me bring my story to fruition. I feel very blessed to have so many who encouraged me: Calliope Writing Coach, where I learned how to perfect my writing, beta readers that gave me essential feedback, my rockin' editors, my agent for being so excited to work with me, and Morgan James Publishing for taking a chance on a new kid. Last, but certainly not least, I would like to thank my family for sacrificing with me every step of the way.

Prologue

mmersed in the intoxicating aroma of the only other being she knew, Bubaé drank in the sweet smell radiating from the alien's flesh—Terren's flesh. Her senses swam in the savory fragrance as she nestled her slug-like body further into the alien's warm embrace. Lacking any limbs with which to return the gesture, she did the only thing she could. She sat like a lump in the being's comforting maroon arms.

Bubaé considered the female alien, wrapping her in a lethargic hug. She sensed a growing fondness for the lower life form, a type of bond—maybe something like a friendship. However, the fleeting feeling kept her from being a true friend. At the same time, her apathy didn't cause her much concern. She closed her black, buttonlike eyes and drew in Terren's sweet scent swimming in the air.

Her mouth watered.

A soft whimper escaped Terren's lips and clung to the gloomy night. Bubaé cringed and waited to see if the weak plea alerted passersby outside the quarters. Minutes ticked away as the two remained motionless in the middle of the floor. She sighed with relief. No one seemed to be coming. At this hour, the only witnesses of her anticipated deed would be the extensive array of framed military awards and the room's meager furnishings.

The perfect chosen time for the perfect chosen task.

With the pair lumped together on the cold floor, Bubaé's head—if you could call it that—nestled into the nook of Terren's neck. Her short, razor-like teeth sank deep into the female's soft, supple skin, giving Bubaé more of a solid hold. Meanwhile, her beige body cascaded down the torso of the seasoned veteran, leaving her stubby tail to end near Terren's waist. Her clammy skin dampened the alien's clothes with a clear gel that caused a type of paralysis. Terren's obliviousness to her current predicament sealed the night's transpiring even further.

The faint tapping of Terren's tears sounded on the floor nearby. The slow, rhythmic drip pulled at Bubaé's heartstrings as she sensed Terren's entity sobbing on the inside. Picturing the alien's copper eyes, she imagined her vacant stare into space and the streams of salty liquid running down her silky cheeks.

Almost choking up, Bubaé swallowed hard.

She tried to downplay her part in Terren's predicament, but Bubaé couldn't deny her role in the alien's deteriorating physical state and mental detachment. With a mouthful of Terren's sweet flesh still sinking between her teeth, she started feeling something. She struggled with the odd sensation . . . an emotion: sadness. A sting formed somewhere behind her eyes, and her black orbs began misting with tears.

Bubaé mentally turned toward an established telepathic link she shared with Terren. She intimately sensed the female's thoughts and emotions. An invisible sphere of energy sat at the end of the connection—a mental prison Bubaé created around the female's consciousness. She tried drowning out Terren's thoughts, but they called to her from inside the unconventional cage. It wasn't possible to shut them out altogether and keep the linked sphere active, so she continued listening to the gentle weeping.

Terren's thoughts came between sobs. *Where am I? . . . Why can't I see? . . . Why do I feel so cold?* Her obliviousness persisted.

As Bubaé waited for the perfect moment, her first encounter with the female drifted into her mind. She remembered being nothing more than an egg floating in frigid space. Terren had scooped her up and tucked her into a nook in her spacesuit. The warmth from the artificial life support penetrated her shell as Terren brought her onboard.

Bubaé basked in the memory.

She sensed Terren's motherly care even during her incubative state. The female's inner warmth reminded her of a solar flare's cradling heat that soaked through her shell. She remembered hatching and seeing Terren's face for the first time. The alien's maroon features etched themselves into her mind as the most exquisite creature she had ever laid eyes on. Terren even gave her a name.

Bubaé's stomach rumbled.

Terren never could quite figure out what to feed her.

The female squeezed Bubać in a weak hug. The affection cast doubt over her course of action. Her hunger and physiological urge to morph to maturity pressured her to continue. She felt almost overpowered by her nature—almost. Visions of a bliss-filled future danced in the recesses of her mind, compelling her to carry out her adolescent merge into adulthood. To achieve her ambitions, she would need a vast amount of energy. Her thoughts focused on Terren's enveloping embrace—about the same amount of power concealed within a single, high-functioning life force.

Bubaé sensed something changing from within.

The small window of opportunity she waited for presented itself at last.

Her vision split as the process began.

In a blink of her black, buttonlike eyes, Bubaé saw two separate but coexisting planes—the physical and spiritual realms. Both Bubaé's and Terren's bodies encased their luminous spiritual essence, much as a crunchy shell would hold a tasty nut. She gazed down. Her own spirit glowed a pale blue. She looked at Terren, whose soul shone a golden yellow.

The dual vision took its toll on Bubaé, drawing on her energy and stealing power from her life force. The time to finish her dark deed was now or never. She pressed against her physical shell to break free from it. Wiggling and worming, she burrowed through the tough membrane. As her soul emerged from its physical husk, she accessed a type of dimensional pocket. Her instincts informed her she could roam around unhindered in the small space but warned that the place wouldn't last forever, not without a massive surge of energy.

Freed from her body, Bubaé glanced back at her now-empty physical form. Her mortal frame remained alive and well in Terren's arms. Just by looking at it, no one would ever guess it didn't contain her spirit anymore. She turned to Terren and started burrowing through the female's physical shell. Inching her way in, she broke through the barrier and latched onto the maroon alien's warm, inviting soul.

A keener sense of Terren's entity flooded Bubaé's awareness.

Terren's white-knuckled grip on life slackened. *What's happening to me?* her thoughts cried out.

Bubaé hesitated.

Pulling back from the deep emotional and mental link she shared with Terren, she relaxed her ethereal clench on Terren's soul.

I have to finish this, Bubaé thought, *but I don't want to kill her.*

"I'm scared. Bubaé, where are you?" Terren's mind called out for her "pet."

Bubaé remembered the sensation of comfort radiating from the maroon alien when she saw her little "creature" at the end of a long day. The uplift had always fascinated Bubaé. She perceived the female's same frantic search for soothing now. Instead of providing relief, though, she continued holding Terren's mind at bay. Her hesitation drained away more energy.

A new thought drifted in. *I am more than just a pet to Terren. She sees me as a friend and loves me. She wants me to be happy. Terren would want this for me* because *she loves me.*

The new belief sank in, cementing Bubaé's chosen course of action. She mentally charged forward and invaded Terren's consciousness in the spherical prison. She flooded the female with a sense of peace and comfort. Inspecting the being's intellect through the link, she perceived Terren's complete pacification.

Bubaé's mental and emotional projection kept the female calm while she bore into the golden, spiritual essence and headed in to claim her prize. Terren's soul stiffened under the strain of the unanticipated invasion.

Bubaé paused.

Her instincts told her that pushing too hard right now could lead to her immediate expulsion. Corralling her nagging urge to continue, she waited. What felt like ages later, Terren's soul began softening and relaxed just enough. With a sufficient amount of pliability restored, Bubaé resumed her plan.

She burrowed her way in, letting intuition be her guide. The treasure she sought radiated searing energy like a blazing beacon in the darkest of nights. The insane amount of power it encased would make it seem like a fountain of pure sunlight—a stark contrast to her own pale-blue, luminous spirit. Terren's sweet, intoxicating scent flooded Bubaé's senses with every inch she gained.

Parting more of Terren's golden spiritual essence, Bubaé squinted as a single flaxen ray blasted her with its light. She had finally happened upon the object of her desire—the epicenter of the female's soul. She uncovered it a little more, and heat radiated from it like a miniature sun. It glowed brighter than Bubaé had ever imagined. The rest of Terren's luminous spirit shuddered and started collapsing around her.

Acting fast, Bubaé seized the epicenter, and Terren's mind screamed from the mental prison.

Terren's soul hardened again in defense—a defense that came much too late to be of any use.

Bubaé ignored Terren's bloodcurdling mental screams and pushed past her few tender feelings. *You're only food. You're only food,* Bubaé repeated to herself.

Bubaé dug into the bright epicenter with her suction-cupped grip.

Terren's mind raced as she searched for an escape from the prison Bubaé had created around it. In her mania, the female's consciousness ran straight into the unseen border generated around her intellect, and she bounced off the barrier. She shook off the force of the impact and started clawing at the invisible boundary.

Bubaé kept the sphere active, denying Terren access to her mental freedom.

Terren's frenzied attack on the prison wall caused her sanity to partially break through the unconventional cage. Bubaé noted the slight breach. A few of Terren's muscles began twitching, flickering back to life, which brought more vigor to her efforts for freedom. The female's body started convulsing on the floor. Bubaé dug in and latched onto the epicenter tighter through the tremors. Doubling down, she mentally regained control over Terren's pained mind. Just like a handler exerting dominance over a misbehaving creature, she forced the female's intellect to be still.

Terren's body calmed.

With Terren's mind bound and gagged, Bubaé turned her full attention to her newfound, glowing treasure. She produced a stinger from her spirit's abdomen and punctured through the brilliant epicenter. The shrieks of Terren's sanity breaking filled the mental prison as she began thrashing.

Bubaé held firm and continued her work. She pushed pale-blue light through her stinger. The golden color of Terren's soul churned with the added hue, and its brilliant luster started fading. At the same time, the epicenter began expanding. With every millimeter of growth, Bubaé felt Terren's vitality weaken.

She pressed on.

Terren's soul bloated and doubled in size. The swelling of the female's core pushed Bubaé back out of the makeshift tunnel she had burrowed—with her still clinging to it. Micro-tears ripped across its smooth surface as it bulged against the insides of Terren's physical shell. The spiritual center barely held itself together. Bubaé found herself almost outside again but still latched onto her prize.

Terren's life force started slipping away.

"Goodbye, my closest companion," Bubaé told Terren through their link as she forced even more of her gelled light into Terren's bloated core.

"What?" A fluttery thought came from the mental prison.

Terren's spirit buckled under the pressure, and her life force exploded. Bits of spiritual matter splattered across the small, dimensional pocket that encompassed Terren's quarters, and Bubaé went flying with them. She flew against the dimensional wall, and the brunt of the blast pinned her in place. The shock wave from Terren's death surged through her like a searing bolt that wouldn't discharge. Torture swallowed her whole as she slid in a heap to the floor.

In time, Bubaé's misery began to fade.

Coming to her senses, she looked around the room. Through her lingering daze, she could tell she was still in the small, dimensional pocket. As she became more coherent, she searched for the telepathic link she shared with Terren. The endeavor proved quite fruitless, just like she thought it would.

Terren's lifeless body lay on the floor. Sadness pierced Bubaé's heart as she gazed at the maroon female's remains that still cradled a beige slug in its arms. Terren's copper eyes held the blank stare of death. With no soul left to generate its power, the mortal coil was already growing cold.

Bubaé looked down at her blue, glowing spirit. Two nubs had grown from the top of her luminous torso. *Limbs?*

As the permanence of the dimensional pocket solidified around her, slight twinges of guilt prodded her. The memory of losing Terren stuck on replay in her mind. Her despicable actions left her soul-wrenched. Just as she succumbed to the idea of being a monster, a thought worked its way in from the recesses of her mind—a sufficient trade-off for her dismal deed.

Don't worry, Terren. Bubaé grabbed hold of the comforting sentiment. *You won't be forgotten. I will call myself by your name. It would be my honor.*

With her guilt finally hushed, she took a deep, relieving breath. An intoxicating smell stirred in the air. She suddenly realized that her transformation into adulthood would soon start. The newfound aroma beckoned to her. She took in another long drag of the scent, filling her senses to the brim. Incandescent drool dripped from her tiny mouth, and a grumble sounded from her glowing stomach. She finally found food that would satisfy. Hunger urged her to feed on the nourishing meal.

Bubaé scraped some of the nearest spiritual mush off the dimensional plane's floor with one of her still-growing nubs. She brought the fragrant substance to her mouth and touched it to the tip of her tongue. Sweetness gushed in. The rich, creamy texture melted in her mouth as she devoured the rest of the tasty morsel. She wandered to the far corners of the dimensional pocket to ingest her meal and put in the extra work of collecting the remains of Terren's precious soul. None of it went to waste. With every warm mouthful, she gained a strength she never knew before—a vigor far beyond her previous comprehension.

Pure energy pulsed through her veins.

Her blue hue glowed with exquisite brilliance.

Bubaé opened her mouth for the remaining bite of her meal, but a yawn snuck out instead. She covered it with a growing nub then gulped down the last glob of spiritual mush and licked the residual flavor from forming fingers at the end of her limbs. She opened and closed her developing hands, feeling a little in awe over the glowing wonders.

She yawned again, and her mind felt heavy. Her slug-like body beckoned for her return. Her spirit glided toward her empty physical shell. Like a droplet returning to its pool of origin, she merged with it. Her stomach felt comfortably full and made her wish she possessed lips so she could smile.

Another yawn snuck out.

Bubaé pushed sleep's nagging requests away and clung to the euphoric moment. Her clammy skin started spinning a threaded cocoon around her. Terren's stiffening embrace became engulfed in the silky strands.

She resigned herself to the chrysalis her body busily spun, and the energy she consumed continued to strengthen the dimensional pocket she created. Nature intended her to flourish. She knew her kingdom might be small at first. Still, with enough time and energy, she could cultivate this raw material into something magnificent, something breathtaking, something almost as beautiful as her cherished memories of Terren.

Bubaé's black, beady eyes fluttered shut.

She accepted slumber's invitation.

Drifting off to sleep, she envisioned a glorious future—one full of adoring subjects hailing her as their queen. She dutifully ruled over them. A bliss she never knew before washed over her, and she slipped into hibernation.

She made no more excuses.

She accepted what she was.

Chapter 1

Brian's awareness began to rouse.

The hiss of a stasis pod sounded from somewhere that felt far away. Brian's waking consciousness drifted from one half-thought to another. He could almost sense every single electron firing to life as his drowsy receptors ping-ponged energy back and forth. The beat returning to his heart pumped liquid warmth through his veins. His lungs started taking in the cryonized air swirling around him.

The short time it took to wake felt like ages.

The mechanics of Brian's pod sighed as the lid finished its ascent. Stuffy air from his room rushed in to greet him. The swirling chemical-filled vapor churning inside his pod danced against his chilled skin, leaving a sweaty fog on everything it touched. The wispy mist acted like a milky swamp where his mind sunk in with every muddled turn of its cognition. He braced himself for what came next, completing the transition from cryosleep to animation.

A full-body ache rolled in, settling in Brian's joints.

His breath quickened.

The agony intensified to the point that he wanted to cry out, but his still-thawing jaw remained clamped shut. His torment peaked and stole his breath away. He forced an exhale, and the pain began subsiding—just like it did every time he thawed. His breathing slowed to normal. He worked his stiff jaw. As relief washed over him, he waited, and like clockwork, his stomach lurched.

Always the nausea! Brian bolted into a sitting position, which sent his mind into a spin. *Even with all our technology, we haven't found an easier way to travel.*

Trying to slow the orbit of the room, he cradled his head with his cryo-weakened hands. The lingering ice crystals in his short hair wet his fingers as they melted. The spinning of his mind slowed, and the nausea began to fade. He climbed out of his pod. His lethargic muscles spewed bitter complaints at him. He stood and stretched his tired, grouchy limbs. Waking from stasis had been much easier in his youth.

Residual grogginess sat on his mind, and he tried rubbing its heaviness from his eyes. The vapor continued its feathery descent down the stasis pod's worn, metal sides. The chilly haze billowed around Brian's feet on the hard floor but quickly evaporated into the dry air. Condensation from the reanimation made his clothes cling to his sticky, wet skin. He brushed past his discomfort and smiled. It always felt so good to return home from deep space. Brian took in a sweeping glance at his quarters.

His smile faded.

The room appeared almost exactly the same as when he went into stasis—almost. A tarnish covering the metallic walls snuffed out their shine. The blankets on his bed still held their crisp corners, but age had drained them of their vibrant color—as though Time himself snuck into his quarters and stole away their zeal while he slept. He could have mistaken them for antiques.

Fewer puffs of wispy fog floated around the stasis pod as it powered down.

Brian noticed dust on everything. His feet left prints in the layer on the floor. Larger gatherings of the fluff clumped together like gray cottontails, hiding under the furniture and in corners. Some even clung to the middle of the walls, defying the ship's artificial gravity. The tiny particles dried out the air and made his eyes itch.

His dresser, which held his meager belongings, rested next to his bed. The elaborate piece of furniture had come to him through inheritance, an almost outdated practice. Few of the wooden beauties existed anymore. He noted the customary picture sitting in its usual spot as he crossed the room.

The familiar holographic photo accompanied Brian on every voyage. He picked up the glass-encased hologram. The technologically advanced still frame seemed a stark contrast to the rest of the aged room. It displayed him and his wife, Grace, frozen eternally in each other's arms. His bride of many years fared better in the aging department than he did. She looked as though she frolicked around the fountain of youth—perpetually ageless. In the photo, she rested her temple on his shoulder. Her bouncing, chocolate-colored curls engulfed her shoulders and tiered down her back. Her playful grin only enhanced the wisdom that he knew hid behind her exotic teal eyes. He envisioned her waiting for him to disembark.

The thought brought a half-smile.

He looked at his own image. Unlike his wife, a sophisticated gray made its appearance around his ears. Matching spots grew down his sideburns and even adorned his goatee. Despite the minor signs of age, he thought he still held a refined attractiveness. He tipped the picture from side to side. The three-dimensional background shifted around the handsome couple inside.

He wiped the dusty picture's surface. Its shine returned in the streaks he left behind. He reseated the holographic keepsake and ran his finger along the dresser, dragging the digit toward himself and leaving a long line in the filth. He scrutinized the build-up of grime as he examined his fingertip.

"BRIAN." Callie's voice from the room's comm jolted Brian from his contemplations.

"Callie?" Brian addressed his first in command and rubbed the grime on his finger away with his thumb.

"I'M GOING TO NEED YOU TO LOOK AT THIS." Callie's silky voice boomed through the comm.

Brian cringed and covered his ear. "Where?"

"THE SHIP'S BRIDGE."

"Urgency level?"

"ROUGHLY SEVEN. IT'S NOT AN EMERGENCY—YET."

"I will be there shortly."

"THANK YOU." The transmission ended.

Brian slightly lowered his hands from his ear. "Computer!"

The computer chimed once, indicating its activation.

"Lower volume setting to level four."

The computer chimed twice in acceptance of the command.

Brian glanced across the room. *What's going on?* he wondered.

He spun potential scenarios in his mind about what Callie's concern might be and opened the top dresser drawer for a black uniform. He turned to a lower cabinet against the wall and grabbed his footwear from inside. His boots still held their polished shine. Stowing them kept them cleaner, but he prided himself on his detailing skills. Brian changed out of his damp clothes and tossed them into his recycle bin. He gazed at himself in a long, dust-covered mirror and smoothed his well-groomed goatee. He straightened his captain's pins and burgundy cuffs, then headed out.

The dim lighting that met him in the hall seemed to multiply the shadows. He slowed to a stop. "Computer?"

The computer chimed once.

"What level is the lighting?"

"Level ten," came the monotone reply.

"Is there something wrong with the system? This doesn't look like a level ten."

"All systems are functional." The computer chimed twice, ending the inquiry.

This isn't right. Brian took in a sweeping glance across the corridor as he slowly continued. The oxidized, metallic walls matched the ones in his room. Dust covered every square inch of the place. A particular storage compartment caught his eye, and he abruptly changed course. Many panels, each holding useful tools, ran down its length. He pressed a sequence on one panel's display pad, and it slid open, revealing a small, disk-like robot.

"Activate," Brian ordered.

The robot glowed a soft green and zipped into the air, hovering an arm's length from Brian. He gave the open cubby a tap, and it slid closed on its own. He tapped his chin while he debated about the bot's modes.

"Light cleaning protocol," Brian ordered.

The robot jumped into action, scanning the entire hall. A grid flashed across the corridor and disappeared just as fast. The bot projected a fanned, neon-green beam across one portion of the wall it had sectioned out. A low-frequency hum sent shock waves that reverberated through the place and pulsed through Brian's very core. Eyeballing the little machine, he took a step back. The cringeworthy stench of seared grime began wafting in the air.

As the bot finished cleaning the section, it systematically moved to another portion of the hall. Brian stepped up to the spotless wall, inspecting the bot's performance. The metal gleamed with a polished shine that freshly manufactured platinum would covet. He turned on his heels and continued down the corridor, leaving the robot to complete its work.

He came across a set of footprints in the dust, the same size and length of stride as Callie's. He fell into step alongside them. Soon, another set of wider prints appeared that looked like Derek's. Brian followed the pair of impressions to the entrance of the bridge. The door slid open upon his approach, releasing the pervasive odor of new carpet, plastic, and a dash of chemicals. The scent accompanied most of the command centers he encountered, regardless of the vessel's age.

As usual, the place felt inviting. Nothing seemed out of the ordinary. Customary computer consoles filled the room. His particular ship's interior held a certain roughness, but what the vessel lacked in extravagant design, it made up for in dependability. *The Gabriel* had never left Brian, or his crew, stranded.

Callie stood at her computer. Her stark white hair swayed about her delicate frame as she collaborated with the mainframe. Her slender fingers danced across the surface of her console, and interchanging holograms hovered above her computer. With her expertise, she breezed through any software program like wind blowing through trees—or as quickly as the Traverse-Pike Virus spreads from one hot spot to another—as the saying went.

Brian detected a minute choppiness in Callie's movements and a slight squint in her eyes, the two biggest signs of her frustration. Her hair down, instead of pulled up into an intricate braid, confirmed the notion even more. The console chimed and flashed a red light at her in complaint of her prodding. She brushed away the eruption of detailed code from the holographic image and continued grappling with the software.

"Report." Brian crossed the room, weaving his way through the consoles.

Callie stopped probing her computer and acknowledged Brian with an annoyed sigh. She cocked her white brow and tipped her head down toward her slender hands. Her fingers blitzed into action with gestures that formed silent communication. *"Not . . . malfunction . . . pretty."*

Brian raised both hands in a request for her to slow down. Perceiving her silent communication as an attempt to exclude someone from their conversation, he scanned the room. He couldn't find Derek but knew the sign language must have been to keep him out. Brian let Derek's whereabouts fade to the back burner. *"Go slower, please. You know I can't keep up with you when your fingers are flying at warp speed,"* he signed.

Callie began articulating her words with her hands in a slower, more pronounced way—and with a slight huff for having to do so. *"Something's not right! Either there's a malfunction in the navigation's mainframe, or we're pretty lost! I was the first to be revived. Then I woke everyone else, or at least I tried to. The computer is being uncooperative, and I've had some difficulty reanimating the crew."* Callie glared at her console as her gestures slowed to a stop.

Brian touched his goatee as he absorbed the information.

A squeamish look washed over Callie's face.

Catching her expression, Brian tipped his head and cocked a brow, indicating his desire for her to disclose the information.

"The computer also says we've been in stasis for a long time," Callie signed. *"A very long time."*

"Are you sure? How long does it say?" Brian gestured and leaned to inspect the readouts.

Callie lowered her eyes.

"Is that why there is so much dust?" Brian prodded.

Callie met Brian's gaze, and her hands flew back into action. *"I believe so. There is a high correlation between the two. It looks like the computer malfunctioned somehow right after we went into stasis . . . But there's something else—"*

"You know," a gruff voice bellowed from nearby, breaking the silent exchange. "I'm trained in sign language, too!"

Chapter 2

Brian and Callie looked in the direction of the voice. Brian leaned a little, and Derek came into view—part of Derek, anyway. The bottom half of the burly man extended from a computer console. Circuit boards, wires, and unique tools spewed around him on the floor near his hips and thighs, barely within his stocky arms' reach.

"I didn't want to bother you with the details, especially when we don't have all the facts yet, Derek," Callie said.

Derek started un-wedging himself from inside the console. "Aye, it's not like I can't tell things aren't going too well." An accent twisted the inflection of his voice. His gruff tone and embellished articulation always made him seem charismatic, no matter his actual mood.

While Derek sat up, his flaming red hair flattened as it smashed against the underside of the console. His stand-on-end locks bounced right back into their frizzy place as soon as they cleared the computer's edge. Orange strands peppered throughout his crazy mane, and the whole mess carried an electrified quality—as though the electronics he dabbled in had given him a recent shock or two. Brian knew this look to be deceiving, though. Derek's love for his industry left little room for carelessness.

A pair of goggles rested snug across Derek's eyes, and his baby blues peeped through their thick, bottle-bottom lenses. Monocle-like layers stacked in front of each glass, magnifying his cobalt orbs a dozen times bigger than their actual size. "The computer chimes sure give a lot away." He winked with an oversized eye and gave a toothy grin.

Callie hung her head and tucked a strand of hair behind her pointy ear. She then ran a finger along the edge of her computer.

"I can't take you seriously with those goggles on." Brian suppressed a smile.

Derek chuckled. "You know they help me tear into the hardware. Plus, from where I'm sitting, you're the one that looks funny—"

"Hey, this is serious," Callie said, interrupting.

"Yes, but *how* serious is the real question." Brian stood a little straighter. Covering his growing grin with his fist, he cleared his throat. "Let me take a look at your console."

Callie stepped aside, and Brian took her spot. He started with a systematic inquiry and explored the computer's program. His hands skipped across the console's display, extracting more information as they went. His fingers didn't go as fast as Callie's, but his efficiency almost outdid hers. He batted at several holographic images while he worked. Not finding anything noteworthy, he squinted and dug even deeper.

"Welp! As a side note, the ship's main filtering system is down." Derek repositioned himself in front of the open panel he had worked on just moments earlier. "It's kind of an important side note, but whatever."

"How fortunate." Callie gave a slight eye roll as she watched Brian work. "This couldn't get any better."

"If you liked that, you're going to love this next part, then." Derek's echoic voice sounded from within the computer's belly as he wedged himself back inside. "Pull up a chair!"

"Just spit it out." Callie sighed. She shifted her weight to one hip and rested her hand on its slender curve, staring in Derek's direction.

"We're running on what's left of the backup power. As you know, the system slows regular functions to conserve energy, and we don't have the materials I'm needing to fix it. Everything seems like it's a million years old. I can't believe the ol' girl's still running—it's so bad! And the dirtiness. It's everywhere!" Derek tried muzzling the buildup of a sneeze.

Brian's hand's paused midair. He peered at the bottom half of his comrade sticking out of the computer's base. "That would definitely lead to the dust buildup."

"ACHOOO!" Derek's booming sneeze filled the room, followed by sniffles.

"I'm not sure how much we can trust the readouts," Callie said, "but from what they say, we never hyper-jumped as a result of a computer malfunction after we went into stasis. It looks like we've been drifting ever since. All the systems went into conservation mode around that time, at least from what I can tell. If the readouts are correct, then we've been in stasis for more than a . . . a millennium."

Derek jerked, and a circuit board dropped out from the confined space where he worked. His top half became more visible as he propped himself up on an elbow. His big, blue googly eyes glared at Callie from his awkward perch. "More than a thousand? Years? It wasn't supposed to take us that long to get back to base. The readouts have to be wrong. It's just not possible. We couldn't have survived. If that were true, we should be dried-up mummies still sitting in our pods, and we would have run out of fuel ages ago. Not to mention the being frozen part. A bunch of frozen blocks of mummified dust is what we'd be. I tell you . . ." Derek's complaints faded into a stream of grumbling.

"Derek's right. That couldn't be possible," Brian added. "I can see why you don't trust the readouts."

"Surviving this long isn't entirely impossible," Callie replied. "It's just profoundly improbable. If the ship slipped into conservation mode shortly after we went into stasis, I guess we could have drifted for a millennium."

"So, basically, we don't know how long we've been in stasis," Brian said.

Callie shifted her weight to her other hip. "Yes."

"Well, flib-jib," Derek bellowed.

Brian recognized *flib-jib* as a word Derek made up to skirt around policies prohibiting the use of derogatory terms.

Derek sneezed again. "Ugh, this dust! Are we at least back to base yet? It probably looks crazy different by now."

"That's another thing." Callie winced. "The computer readouts say we're not back to base. They say we're . . . we're . . . Well, I don't know where they say we are."

"We don't know where we are?" Derek balked. "FLIB!"

"Calm yourself, Derek." Brian continued his search of Callie's computer.

"Lost? That's pretty rich for an exploration ship!" Derek lowered his voice, grumbling in quieter tones as he reclined in the console again.

Callie shrugged. "Now you can see why I didn't want to say anything yet."

Brian's thoughts shifted to his wife. How long had Grace been waiting for him to come back home? His hands flew across the computer's display with more purpose. Just as he swiped a hologram out of the way, the computer chimed and flashed red at him. He brushed away the burst of code that followed but more kept coming.

With a sigh, Brian stopped interacting with the computer and rubbed the back of his neck. "None of this makes sense. Yet, here we are. From what the readouts say, we are in uncharted space, and we've been in stasis for some time. We've probably missed our rendezvous." The gravity of their dilemma sank in as he admitted it out loud. He imagined Grace's disappointment when she found out he wasn't on course to come home. He began wondering if she was even still alive. His heart sank at the thought.

"We've missed our rendezvous?" Derek laughed. "That's quite the understatement!"

"We've missed our rendezvous?" A deep voice boomed from the doorway.

"Ah, Sivien," Derek said. "So nice of you to join us."

Sivien's appearance brought Brian back to the present. He looked at the half-man, half-lizard towering in the middle of the doorway. Green scales covered every inch of the gigantic man's face. His particular subspecies lacked a tail, making him look more humanoid than not. He tossed his rugged, damp hair out of his eyes with one of his clawed hands. A few of the dark locks stuck to his cheeks and jawbone from the tousling.

"Still damp from reanimation, huh?" Brian asked.

Sivien looked at him. "You guessed it."

Brian sighed. "Well, welcome to the party anyway."

"Even though we have no idea when and where this party is," Derek added.

"I don't like those kinds of parties." Sivien's black, forked tongue slipped through his lips while he spoke. His face scrunched to one side, showing his detest for the new information.

"I like parties!" Zella, the last crew member, said as she popped out from behind Sivien's hulking body.

"Zella!" Sivien jumped, grabbing his chest. "I didn't see you there!"

A Cheshire smile spread across Zella's furry face, and her elongated canines peeked over her bottom lip. Her wild mane held a bounce, and her long bangs parted just enough for her green-eyed gaze to sneak through. Perky cat ears poked out from the unkempt hairdo.

"Hey, I thought we called a truce!" Sivien whined.

Untucking herself from behind Sivien, Zella worked her way around him in one smooth move. Her long tail wrapped around her waist several times like a belt, accenting her uniform. The entire length of the whiplike extremity was at least as long as she was tall. She began twirling the tuft of fur on its end.

Sivien held a steady eye on her.

"If you didn't make a truce so darn appealing to break, *maybe* I could stick to one." Zella cocked her head and laughed. She grabbed an unruly lock of her auburn hair and tucked it behind her furry ear. The triangular lobe twitched reflexively, bouncing the strand right back to its original placement. She didn't even seem to notice. "Besides, I get paid for blending into the scenery—literally. *And* it's always good to practice."

21

Brian sighed and stared at the code still spewing in the holographic imaging of Callie's computer. "Derek, did you check this one's hardware already?"

"Aye," Derek replied. "There's nothing wrong with it, at least not from what I can tell."

"Can you come and take a look at this?" Brian glanced at Zella. "It's not cooperating with Callie or me. Three heads are always better than one, or two in this case."

"Of course." Zella held a sly eye on Sivien while she strutted into the room, leaving him standing alone in the doorway.

Once Zella broke eye contact with Sivien, a mischievous smile spread across his face. He rushed up behind her and elbowed her in the back. The playful nudge sent her flying several feet through the air. Never one to be caught off guard, she turned the momentum into a somersault. With the agility and grace of her feline ancestors, she landed on her feet in a defensive crouch—ears twitching. "Hey! I thought you wanted a truce." Her eyes narrowed, and the devilish grin spreading across her face promised a few light bruises.

"Um . . ." Brian raised his finger in objection to the impending retaliatory shenanigans.

Sivien smirked. "I didn't mean to shove you so hard. You're just such a lightweight."

Zella stood tall and straightened her uniform, even though it didn't appear in disorder. She casually strolled toward Sivien, and her hands drifted to the serpentine tail hugging her curves. She began twirling the short fur at its end again.

Sivien squirmed in place. "Truce," he squeaked.

As much as Brian liked the playful banter among his crew, the seriousness of their predicament weighed on him. He opened his mouth to give a cease-and-desist order.

"You know," Callie said, beating Brian to the punch. "We have no idea where in the multiverse we are."

"Oh!" Zella gasped. She dropped the end of her tail and stopped in her tracks. She looked at Callie. Her mischievous grin had vanished, and a perfect O shape replaced it. She looked at Brian, and her fuzzy brows furrowed.

Brian shrugged. "It's true."

"I didn't know." Zella started across the room again. Sivien trailed behind her. "When did this happen?"

"Well, if you two could knock it off, we might be able to figure things out quicker," Callie said.

"True enough." Brian gave Sivien and Zella the sternest disapproving captain's look he could muster, knowing full well it wouldn't deter their antics for long. Neither of them held their promises of a cease-fire very long.

Brian returned to his battle with the displayed projections. A slew of pop-ups kept coming, and he began brushing them away. Suddenly, he spotted something odd in one of the bits of data. Grabbing the air, he eased the image back. Sure enough, he found something small and blinking in the background. He knew the semi-transparent sensor represented something much bigger. He reached through to the back of the hologram and touched the flashing beacon. The new image of the surrounding solar system that burst into view replaced the other projections. Derek plucked himself out of the computer and headed over to get a better look.

Brian stared at a black dot in the center of the miniaturized holographic galaxy. "There seems to be a spacecraft within range."

Callie looked at Brian. "That was the other thing I was going to mention."

Chapter 3

Brian pressed more buttons and manipulated the holographic cosmos. He smoothed his goatee as he studied the black blemish. "Let's take a closer look, shall we?" He winked at Callie and grabbed the air around the small dot with both hands. Pulling his fists apart, he simultaneously opened his hands. The hologram zoomed in, instantly expanding the small blemish.

A perfect, three-dimensional model of a black ship hung heavy in the air. Brian folded his arms and examined the vessel. Zella, Sivien, and Derek joined Brian and Callie at the computer. The crew silently stared at the peculiar craft in the middle of the miniaturized solar system.

Brian reached out and gave the image a soft swipe. The motion activated the program and sent the projection into a slow spin. The bulk of the ship's structure seemed like most others—an elongated cylinder shape—not exactly new. However, towers spiked from both ends of the vessel and randomly dotted its body, creating a jagged and harsh look—something very new.

Callie leaned across to her computer's interface and touched a few of its buttons. "That's not just a ship. That's a complex space station. It looks like it's composed of some sort of black metal. I've never seen a ship constructed in such a manner."

"Neither have I." Brian touched his goatee.

Sivien wrinkled his nose and cast an untrusting glare at the ship. "It sure looks unwelcoming."

Brian thought back to the engineering courses he suffered through during his training days and puzzled over the station's structure. "No one in their right mind would construct a vessel without a sleek, aerodynamic build. A ship like that wouldn't make it very far off the ground, let alone have the capability of exiting an atmosphere. Either the engineers of this monstrosity lost every sane brain cell during its creation, or their brilliance exceeds known understanding." He wondered which case proved true. Weighing the facts of their current predicament, he wagered the latter might just stand a chance. It wouldn't be the first time he saw advancements that dumbfounded reason.

At some point, Derek lifted his goggles to his forehead. "Look at all those sharp spikes sticking out everywhere. It looks as inviting as a black dowager spider's legs!"

"Black dowager?" Sivien scoffed. "What's that?"

Derek's brows jumped, almost touching his goggles. "You don't know what a black dowager is?"

Sivien shrugged.

"Oh! You're kidding. They're just about the nastiest spider you could ever run into. You know, speaking of spiders, down on the planet Captagru, there is a species that grows bigger than your noggin." Derek motioned at Sivien's sizable head. "That spider lays its eggs in your skin, too, making you the first meal for her hundreds of bundles of joy! I mean . . . that is . . . as long as she doesn't eat you first. To top things off, they are also quite venomous."

Brian looked around at the horrified expressions of the other crew members. "Maybe now isn't the best time to bring that up, Derek." He gave a cordial nudge to his comrade's shoulder.

Derek looked up at Brian. The furrow of his bushy, red brows expressed his deep confusion.

"I'm sure there are no spiders on the station." Brian peered down at Derek, trying to cue him in, seemingly to no avail.

Zella sighed. "I wish it *were* one of ours. Um, without the spiders, of course." She glanced at Derek and shifted in place.

"I wish I could have my ignorance back," Sivien said, more to himself than anyone else.

"There's no way." Brian leaned toward the floating image. "It couldn't be one of ours. We've got to be several megaparsecs away from any charted territory. Plus, I've never seen a ship constructed in such a manner."

"Megaparsecs? That far?" Derek gawked at Brian.

"Maybe." Brian shrugged. "At this point, who knows?"

"Well, maybe it is an ally ship." Zella grabbed the image with her furry hands and expanded it even more. She scrutinized the craft as she manually rotated the projection. She suddenly stopped and pointed to one of the station's spiked towers. "This monstrosity might actually be one of ours. It's got our seal right there."

Brian leaned closer. The other crew members did the same, trying to catch a glimpse. Sure enough, right where Zella pointed, he found a seal displayed on one tower, marking it as an allied ship.

Callie glared at the savage-looking station. "How did it get out here?" Suspicion oozed in her tone.

"Anything is possible. Why it's so creepy-looking is an even better question." Derek shuddered.

"Well, we know better than to base our judgment on how things look," Brian said. "Many situations are not what they appear to be. Some things that look good can turn out bad, and some things that look bad can actually turn out good."

"Maybe," Sivien piped in, "they've been here for a while, and we're just lucky enough to find them."

"The odds of that kind of luck are very slim," Brian replied.

"The odds of that are incalculable," Callie added.

Brian looked at Callie. "You know I don't fully trust in calculations. I trust in opportunity. And that craft is ripe with it."

Derek's face brightened. "Maybe they have fuel and parts and can tell us where we are. Maybe they can help us find out what the heck happened to our ship and how we got clear out here."

"Perhaps." Brian tapped his chin.

"How fortunate that there's an incidental space station so conveniently close." Callie shifted her weight and placed her hand back on her hip. "That station just happening to be here feels more like a setup than anything else."

Sivien looked at Brian. "What's our course of action?"

All eyes fell on Brian. His duty as captain instantly weighed on him. Making the wrong decision could prove fatal for any or all of his crew. He'd survived tight spots before, but none of them left him feeling so corralled into only one option. He racked his mind for an alternate solution. Finding none, he gave in. "Clearly, our ship isn't functioning properly, and we're too low on fuel to make it anywhere else. We need help. The most natural course of action is to seek assistance from the space station. After all, it *is* an allied ship."

"Naturally." Callie sighed.

"Maybe they *do* have supplies and *would* be willing to share with us," Sivien said.

Zella folded her arms. "Well, we can't just stay here in this floating tin coffin. Eventually, we'll run out of food and air."

Derek gave Zella a cheesy smile. "We'd run out of fuel first." He straightened as though his added knowledge made him somehow superior to Zella—his odd way of showing off.

Zella glanced at Derek in confusion.

Brian cocked a brow. "Derek, that's not something to be excited about."

"Oh, yeah." Derek grimaced.

Callie's shoulders slumped. "Are there no other alternatives?"

"It doesn't look like it." Sivien brushed his damp hair out of his eyes again. "Besides, if they were an enemy, they've had plenty of time to attack us—and they haven't."

"Fair points," Callie conceded.

Brian sighed at his crew's input. "It's settled, then. We'll contact the station. We are, after all, an exploration ship. Let's explore. Zella, establish a communications channel. Callie, get a visual of the station on screen."

Zella set off to her station.

Brian headed to his captain's chair near the middle of the room, and Callie shifted back to her computer. She powered up the paper-thin screens blanketing the walls and ceiling. The canopy's sheer surface created the illusion of the room disintegrating around them, and a crystal-clear view of the breathtaking expansion of space outside replaced the tarnished metal. The lights dimmed from the draw on the ship's energy.

Glancing around the room, Brian noted the power disruption. "At least we can trust the computer readouts on one thing. We are definitely low on fuel."

"Not to worry. It's all under control." Callie wrung her hands. She jumped to work on her computer. Within seconds, she restored the lights to their original brightness. "See, no problem. Just needed to reroute energy."

Brian gazed at the black speck in the distance on the screens. "We're going to fix this. Somehow, it's going to be okay. We're going to make it through just like we always do."

Zella shot Sivien a sly look as she finished crossing the room. *"I'm going to get you back for that little shove,"* she promised him in sign language.

A squeamish smile briefly swept across Sivien's scaly face. *"Truce?"* he signed back.

Brian hid a smirk. He knew full well that Zella's answer would be a resounding *no* after the shove-stunt Sivien just pulled. He pictured Callie behind him at her station, giving a slight eye roll to the silent exchange.

Sivien took his seat next to Brian at the command. Between side-glances at Zella, he began operating the ship's navigations.

Their vessel started sailing through the breathtaking solar system.

Zella cocked a brow at Sivien and eased into her chair. He squirmed. In compliance with orders, Zella swiveled and got to work. She interacted with her computer more like a cat pouncing on a ball of yarn than a skilled professional working with sophisticated machinery. Her hands sprang from one spot on the display to the next.

Derek moseyed back to the mess he'd left on the floor, snickering at Sivien's expense. He started reassembling the console's innards. Brian's mood lightened somewhat as he watched his crew's interactions. The lingering promise of impending mischief always brightened even the most dismal times.

The black space station grew on the screens. The orbiting planets nearby wallowed in the darkness beyond. Decorative moons, icy meteors, and brilliantly colorful nebulas nestled in the blanket of the all-encompassing abyss that surrounded their vessel. Rich, creamy darkness pooled around the other heavenly bodies while, in return, they bathed in the sea of space's thick twilight. The accompaniment of distant stars glittered like dancing lights in the expansion.

Sailing past the particles of rock and ice of a nearby planet's multi-layered rings, Brian's ship entered within range of the black space station. The towering mass began filling the screens of the entire front of the bridge, overshadowing most of the ceiling. The large towers sticking out looked like needles that Chaos itself randomly pin-cushioned into the vessel. Brian's mind filled with apprehensive wonder as he gazed at the sight. He shifted in his seat as a chill crawled up his spine.

"We're within range." Sivien cut off fuel to the forward thrusters, sending the ship into a calculated drift.

"Zella, open a channel," Brian ordered.

A hush settled across the bridge. Zella's furry hands pounced across her computer, creating a communication link between ships. Her movements abruptly stopped, and her finger hovered over the final button to establish an open channel. Zella looked at Brian and waited for his signal. He gave an affirmative nod, and Zella's finger touched down. She nodded back.

"Greetings!" Brian announced into the open link. "We are *The Gabriel* of the Tansunee Fleet from the Botaniel Quadrant."

He waited for a reply.

No response came.

His crew exchanged glances.

Brian repeated his greeting, and the absence of any reply continued to fill the open channel with its nothingness. Giving sufficient time for the other ship to respond, he tipped his head toward Zella—requesting an analysis.

Zella's fingers pounced on a few more buttons, and then she turned back to Brian. "All the readouts show they are receiving our transmission."

Brian eyeballed the station overshadowing his bridge and repeated his message another time.

Silence still hung heavy in the air.

Brian turned to Callie. "Are there any life signs on that ship?"

Callie pored over her console's display. "I can't tell for sure, but I can see that all the ship's functions are online."

Derek stopped fiddling with the computer panel he was wrestling into place and popped his head up. His blue eyes sparkled with excitement through his goggles. "Maybe it's abandoned, and we can help ourselves to any goods we can find." His toothy grin spread across his face.

Brian reclined in his chair and tapped a finger on the armrest. The notion of a vessel that size going unclaimed didn't sit right with him. "I don't think we can just ransack the ship for its goods, Derek. Someone has to be operating it to keep it functional."

The excitement faded from Derek's animated features. "Aw, shucks." He snapped his fingers and went back to wrestling the panel cover.

"There might be signs of life," Callie said. "I just can't get a straight readout."

Brian leaned forward. "Derek, have you checked Zella's console yet? Is it working properly? Maybe it's saying we've established a link when we haven't."

Derek dropped the panel he muscled, leaving it at a tilt. "I haven't checked that one yet." He picked out a few tools from the floor and crossed the room to Zella's station.

Zella swiveled her chair out of the way.

Plopping one of his gadgets onto the computer's display, Derek plugged its cord into the accommodating slot on the side of the console. He waited for the collaboration between the two networks to reveal any malfunctions from within. He glanced down at Zella and shifted in place. Then he gave her an awkward smile.

Zella stared up at him, blank-faced.

"Uh . . . Hi. Fancy meeting you here," Derek joked.

Zella rested her chin on the furry backside of her hand, looking quite bored. "Indeed."

Derek glanced around and drummed his fingers together while he waited. Zella's gaze settled on his device lying on her computer. She leaned forward, locking it with a harsh stare.

Derek took note of Zella's newfound interest. "Don't push it off the edge. I've got enough broken things I'm havin' to fix around here."

Zella adopted a fake look of offense. "I wasn't going to push it off." She placed both of her hands over her heart, as though his words pierced her very soul.

"Yeah, whatever." Derek waved her comment away. "I know how you cats are."

Zella tipped her head, looking as innocent as a kitten.

Derek finished receiving the code from his device and snapped the tool back out of the panel. "Welp. Everything seems to be working like it's supposed to on our end. It's not our hardware creating an issue—as far as I can tell, anyway." He crossed the room to finish his previous undertaking.

Brian signaled Zella. She cleared her throat and repeated his original greeting, using a different alien language.

Several moments passed.

Brian sighed. "Try one more time."

"Greetings," Zella switched to another alien language. "This is *The Gabriel*—"

Crackling static cut her off.

The transmission broke and reestablished itself several times. Brian tapped his chin and listened to the choppy connection. He slid to the edge of his seat, not quite sure what to expect.

"Greetings," a distant-sounding male voice said through the thick static. It spoke in the language Brian had used during his first three attempts.

All eyes went to Brian, waiting for his response.

Chapter 4

"**G**reetings," Brian said hesitantly and sat forward in his chair. "We seem to have run into problems with our ship. We're low on fuel and need parts. We also need navigational information. Would you be so accommodating as to help us, your fellow voyagers? After all, you appear to be one of our allied ships."

The staticky channel continued cutting in and out.

Brian shifted in his seat as he waited for an answer. "We might have valuable goods we can trade for your generosity, and your kindness would be greatly appreciated." He tried to sweeten the deal.

"You may proceed . . . dock sixty-three, you . . . there." A man's voice barely cut through the static as it granted permission to dock.

Then the link cut out altogether.

"Wow! That was bizarre," Callie said. "I've never heard such a ragged transmission before."

"You'd think a ship like that would have better communication techs," Sivien added.

Derek gawked wide-eyed at the image of the station engulfing the bridge's screens. "Aye! If I was one of their workers, I'd resign. The quality of that transmission is an abomination." His accent shone through his grump.

"We're receiving a docking signal," Callie said.

Derek reseated the panel covering back into place with a kick. "Seriously? Did you hear how awful that sounded?—A space station like that monster should be jam-packed with the best of the best!" He glared up at the massive craft on the screens.

"You're right, Derek," Brian said, "but there seems to be a lot of interference from what Callie picked up. Maybe the transmission's bad because of that."

The logic seemed to defuse Derek's grumpiness a bit.

Brian leaned toward Sivien. "Take us to dock sixty-three."

Sivien nodded.

The forward thrusters kicked back to life under Sivien's care. Their ship started sailing toward the docking platform that gave off the signal. As they approached the sizable station, it loomed over their small capsule even more. Brian gazed up at the beastly-looking vessel. It seemed more like the size of a dead Unabér star overshadowing their ship.

As they moved closer, the tiny details of the station became clearer. Lighting showed through windows in the hull, and the metal's texture seemed more rough than smooth. They rounded a tight angle at the base of a jagged tower, and the chill seeping through Brian's bones reminded him of the frigid atmosphere on the dark side of a moon. A shiver streaked down his spine, and goosebumps pricked his skin. He liked the place even less up close than he had from a distance.

As their small vessel continued traveling to the appointed landing, Brian's thoughts drifted to his wife. The probability of losing her to time sat bitterly on his mind. The idea of never holding her again crushed him. He already missed the sound of her contagious laugh, and the realization of all the missed mornings waking in her tangled embrace made his heart ache even more. Even her fragrance somehow lingered in the air, making it seem as though she stood unattainably nearby. He sighed, unable to reconcile with reality. He imagined her wasting away into oblivion while he cryoslept.

A bitter sting formed behind Brian's eyes. He bit back his sorrow and tried to keep the salty liquid from swelling in his eyes. He pushed his thoughts of Grace aside, vowing to deal with them at a more appropriate time. Right now, he needed to keep his wits about him.

The sting behind his eyes began to subside.

He tipped his head back and blinked a few more times, trying to work more of the excess moisture away. A tiny ray of hope lingered in the recesses of his mind that Grace might have gone into stasis. She could be asleep and waiting for him to return home, even now.

Still, the uncertainty weighed on him.

One stubborn tear ran down his cheek, and he quickly wiped the thing away. He glanced at Sivien, wondering if his colleague noticed.

Sivien stared at Brian. "You, okay?" His forked tongue slipped through his lips while he spoke.

"I'll be all right," Brian whispered back and gave Sivien a warm smile, trying to put him at ease, but his cheeks flushed hot from embarrassment. In all the years together with his crew, Brian had never once shed a tear in front of them. He checked to see if anyone else noticed the brief exchange. To his dismay, Zella seemed to take note. She kept glancing over and quickly looking away. The concern etched across her face matched that of Sivien's.

Gazing down at his computer, Sivien clacked the tips of his claws together and began engaging his console using larger-than-life movements. "Well, no time like the present." The theatrical performance of his job created a diversion for Brian to regain his composure in peace.

Zella watched the dramatic display with a smirk. "Careful not to hurt yourself."

Smiling, Sivien made a few more grandiose movements over his computer. "We're approaching the port." He transitioned back to his regular fluid motions.

Brian's cheeks cooled, and he turned his attention to the front screens. As they sailed closer to the station, the mammoth filled the entire ceiling. A passageway leading into the belly of the beast opened. A blue light flickered across the broad chasm, indicating the force field's disengagement in that section.

They coasted toward the gaping hole.

The bridge darkened as *The Gabriel* sailed through the entrance. The more progress they made through the thick hull, the more light they lost from the distant sun of the solar system. Massive panels outlined the path. Between the metallic slabs, various colors sparked through thick wires like lightning. Another flicker of blue from the force field lit the back screens and informed Brian of its re-engagement. Titan-like groans escaped the mouth's mechanisms as it labored to close behind their ship. A resounding boom rumbled from the resealing passageway, sending a shock wave with it. The crew rocked from its force.

As *The Gabriel* cleared the station's hull, the docking area came into view. Brian stared in awe at the massive chamber on the screens. The room's dim lighting outlined countless landing platforms. The symmetrically organized rows filled the expanse on all sides. His jaw dropped as he gazed at the place's geometric beauty. Each level could harbor hundreds of starships twice the size of theirs.

A nagging thought kept tugging at Brian, and he turned to Callie. "Did you notice anything?"

"Yes, several things." Callie motioned to the screens overhead without relinquishing her gaze on them.

"No, I mean something more obvious," Brian said. "This place is huge."

"Yeah," Callie glanced around the bridge, "everyone noticed that."

"With all the magnificence you *can* find in this place," Brian continued, "tell me what you *can't*."

"What do you mean?" Zella's eyes started darting across the screens.

"What's missing?" Brian prodded his crew for the answer. "Something's missing. A lot of somethings, actually."

Brian's comrades searched the screens with more intent.

"I don't see anything out of place," Sivien said.

"It looks similar to other docks we've landed on." Derek scratched his head, tousling his crazy red hair under his fingers. His face brightened. "It's lots bigger?"

"There are no other ships." Callie frowned. "There's only us, even though there is *plenty* of room."

"That's it," Brian said, looking up at the screens. The barren station made him wonder if anyone had visited the forgotten-looking dock in a while.

"Come to think of it," Callie added, "there were no ships outside either."

"No, there weren't," Brian said.

"Yeah," Derek chimed in. "A place this size should be hopping with commerce."

"But it's not." Brian tapped his chin and stared at the screens. "I wonder where everyone is."

"I don't like this place," Callie said. "It doesn't feel right. There's something in the air."

Derek's finger shot up. "It *could* be a ghost ship," he whispered with glee.

"I'm sure it's not a ghost ship," Brian countered. "And that wouldn't be something to be excited about. *If* apparitions existed, running into them right now *wouldn't* be ideal."

Derek's eyebrows raised as he tilted his head. "It *could* be ideal if they were *friendly.*"

Brian's expression flattened. "I'm sure there are other good reasons besides ghosts as to why there aren't other ships in this section. We'll get answers from the station's crew when we disembark."

A red, flashing light bounced off the tranquil scene on the screens.

"That looks like our spot," Brian said.

Sivien nodded and guided their vessel toward the platform from which the signal emanated. Their ship soon rode along the dock's base, sailing a short distance above the bottom of the spacious, mechanized cavern.

"Docking sequence commencing," Sivien announced.

The landing gear started descending, and soft vibrations rumbled through Brian's chair. Sivien gingerly maneuvered *The Gabriel* into place over the flashing beacon. He slid his claws down the power strip of his computer, easing off the power. The ship touched down with a jolt, and the crew swayed.

Sivien clapped his claws together. "Another perfect landing. We *have* arrived." He stood and took a slight bow.

Zella awarded Sivien's performance with a slow clap.

"Docking was successful, and the environmental conditions seem compatible with our biology," Callie said, attending to her computer. She glanced around at the screens. "Breathing suits shouldn't be necessary, and the station's artificial gravity is active. We just have to wait for depressurization. Then we can disembark—which, according to the readouts, could take a little time due to the size of this place."

Brian tipped his head toward Callie. "So, in other words, hurry up and wait." He climbed from his chair.

"Pretty much," Callie replied.

Zella stood and powered down her computer.

Callie turned off the screens. The scene outside the ship instantly vanished, and the walls returned to their original tarnished metal. The room's lights immediately brightened. She turned to Brian and shook her head. Her hair swayed about her delicate frame. "I just have to say that this feels very off, and I don't like any of it." She wrung her slender hands.

"I don't like it much either." Brian sighed. "But I don't feel like we have much choice. We need fuel and parts. We can't head home until we have at least those two things. Maybe they'll have coordinates that tell us where home is and can help us find answers about our ship. As for now, we need to get our gear and some provisions. We'll meet back up in the holding bay for departure."

Callie's shoulders slumped. "I wish there was a different way."

"Me too," Brian replied. "But there doesn't seem to be one."

Callie hung her head.

"We need to stick to our objective." Brian started toward the door with Sivien not far behind. "Let's get fuel, the parts we need, and hopefully some directions so we can go home."

Callie stepped away from her console, and her hands flew to her hair. The beginnings of an artistic braid burst into creation at the end of her nimble fingertips. She made it to the door first and exited the bridge. Derek followed right after.

Sivien bounded past Brian and quickly crossed the rest of the room but stopped short at the door. He turned and looked at Zella. Noticing his halt, she hesitated. With an over-the-top dramatic wave of his arm, he bowed to her. Swinging his arm out wide, he invited her to go first. She smirked and kept a sharp eye on him while she passed. Sivien held his bow for a moment, creating a safe distance between them. Once she had walked past, he stood, then exited as well. Brian stopped at the threshold of the door. He turned and took in a sweeping glance across his bridge, wondering when they would return. With a sigh, he left the room.

The door slid shut behind him.

Chapter 5

The crew went their separate ways to retrieve gear from their rooms. Brian walked the remaining distance to his quarters alone. The echoes of his footfalls bounced off the newly polished metal of the hall, and the smell of seared dust still clung to the air. He glanced up at the lights. At least the bot's hard work had restored the corridor's brightness. He would have patted himself on the back over the machine's headway if it weren't for their dismal situation. Looking around, he couldn't find the little guy anywhere and figured it must have scampered off to clean the rooms.

Brian's shoulders slumped as he entered his quarters. Dust still covered every nook and cranny of the place. A tickle formed in his nose, and his eyes began to itch. He wagered that his quarters showed up somewhere near the end of the bot's cleaning protocol, something he planned to remedy in its programming the next time he saw it.

Brian went straight to the footlocker at the end of his bed. He rubbed the dust off its security scanner and waved his hand over it. It unlocked with a click. "At least you still work." He lifted its lid.

Rifling through the contents, he found his communication device. Its multi-functionality provided a thin force field that came in quite handy against most enemy blasts. He seated the receiver in his ear and attached the small transmitter to his uniform's breast. He set the device to conservation mode, and it chilled to the touch as it pulled heat from his body to power its functions. The piece in his ear grew cold, too. Thermogenic conversion was one of Brian's favorite types of energy repurposing.

His attention returned to the open footlocker. Collecting some of his other treasures, he tossed them onto the bed. He found his fancy leather backpack and placed it next to his small accumulation of goods, then foraged through his stash of rations and examined one of their labels. The ship's current stellar date far exceeded the one printed on the silver packaging. He inspected the bag for rips or tears but found none. He squeezed the bag, and its squishiness made him wonder if the contents had turned into stardust while he cryoslept. Even though none of the wrappings looked compromised, the pesky notion that they might prove to be entirely inedible nagged at him.

Brian shrugged and finished collecting everything useful. He flipped the leather pack open and scooped the small heap into it. Without skipping a beat, he turned to his weaponry. He fiddled with the bottom of the compartment and tripped its secret releases. Latches popped up, and he tugged on them. Lifting the false bottom out, he set it aside. He gazed at his hidden arsenal. Other weaponry lay concealed around the room, but he took these particular pieces with him on every rendezvous. The assortment comprised various ionic hunting blades, his trusted implosion gun, and a couple of explosive devices. His collection sat in neat, organized rows.

Everything seemed accounted for.

Brian's attention settled on his implosion gun. He traced his fingers down its cold, short stock and grasped its antique wooden handle. He pulled the piece from its cushioned placeholder. The memories from his past kills muddled his mind. Seeing an enemy twist and collapse in on themselves could give any man nightmares. He dismissed the haunting horrors as a necessary part of his duty. His survival skills always outweighed his diplomacy training. Sometimes staying alive meant killing enemies before they killed you.

Despite the dismal realities of space, Brian hoped he wouldn't need to use his arsenal during this engagement. Still, his crew's safety always came first. He adjusted his grip, got a better hold on the antique handle, and slid the gun into the concealed holster fold of his uniform. He retrieved his ionic hunting blades and tucked them into the hidden sheaths in his boots and leggings. Then he grabbed a pair of what looked like silver cufflinks and fastened them to the end of each sleeve.

Going for the last of his arsenal, Brian removed a small, emerald-green box from its padding. An intricate gold design adorned its felt-like surface. He opened it and took out a golden disk. The small object reminded him of the circular currency units he had played with as a child, flipping them in the air and catching them. Unlike those, he needed to handle this little gem with care. It held enough power to disintegrate a small star. He inserted the shiny, last-resort device into a secret pocket against his ribs then snapped the lid of the box shut and eased the empty container back into its place. He reseated the compartment's false bottom and closed the footlocker.

It relocked with a click.

Brian climbed to his feet. He flipped the sack shut and slung it over his shoulder in one fluid movement. The foil packaging of the ration jostled around inside. He started for the door but caught a glimpse of his dresser out of the corner of his eye.

He paused, then backed up.

As he picked up the dust-covered picture sitting on the dresser, fond memories flooded in. A smile found its way to his lips, but his current situation held his nostalgia at bay. He started opening the drawers, searching for something—searching for anything, anything that might work.

He rummaged through the drawers, but he couldn't find what he wanted. Finally, in the bottom drawer, he spotted a suitable piece of cloth. He rubbed it across the picture until its glass-like shine returned. His eyes darted to the top of the dresser, and he dusted it off, too. He placed the photo back. He tossed the soiled bit of material into his recycle bin and pushed the drawer shut with his foot.

Straightening his uniform, he headed out.

Soon, Brian found himself in his ship's holding bay. Large, empty metal containers sat in an organized heap in the middle of the quaint room. On a typical trip back home, loading personnel would replace these empty containers with fresh fuel and supplies. He wondered how long the containers would wait here before they returned to base.

Other than the usual freight, he found the room deserted. None of his other crew members were waiting in the receiving area. He headed to the bench against the wall and took a seat. Leaning back, he rested while he waited for his comrades. One by one, they began trickling in.

Zella strolled in first and sat next to Brian. She wore her tail at her side like a coiled rope. Sivien entered a while later, sporting his collapsible ax across the chest of his uniform. The device blended in with the dark material, making it look like a stylish accent instead of a weapon. Callie came in next. Her hair didn't sway about her tiny frame anymore, but a series of braids crowned her head. Decorative pins accented cross-sections of her weaved locks. Brian knew the damage the seemingly innocent accessories could cause. She also wore a mechanized sleeve that covered her entire left arm. Derek waltzed in last. He crossed the short distance of the receiving bay. Taking the only open space left, he plopped down on the end of the bench. A thick, meaty aroma walked in with him.

The entire crew wore matching backpacks.

Derek adjusted the goggles that rested across his forehead, and his lips smacked as he munched on something robust. He started digging into a satchel he had belted to his hip. The large pouch held many of his self-proclaimed treasures—mostly gadgets and snacks. Derek's wafting smell and loud chewing seemed to catch Sivien's attention.

Callie accidentally bumped Brian, stealing his own attention from Derek. She was fiddling with her mechanized sleeve. Ironically, they called it Little-G, which stood for "little gadget," but no one with any sense would consider the device trivial tech by any means. Its mind-based interface made Callie the best one to use it. Most of the crew could barely grapple with its software, if at all.

Zella glanced up at the clearance light. "Still red, huh? Depressurization is taking longer than normal to complete."

Brian gave a quaint nod and decided to change the subject. He cleared his throat, gaining his crew's attention. "I'm assuming everyone has your communications device. We're going to do a quick comms check." He reached up and touched a spot on his transmitter, waking it from conservation mode.

The crew followed suit.

Brian cleared his throat. "Can you hear me?"

Sivien leaned toward him with a smirk. "I can hear you just fine."

"Through your comm?" Brian shook his head at Sivien's old joke.

"Yes," Sivien said with a chuckle. "I could hear you through my comm, too."

Derek snickered. "Aye, mine's working fine too."

Zella hid a smirk. "Check."

"Check," Callie replied with a curt nod.

The crew's voices sounded in Brian's earpiece as they spoke. "It looks like they're all working fine. I can hear all of you, too." He set his device to its active setting, which muted the device unless he pressed the transmission button.

The others did the same.

Satisfied with the functionality of their equipment, Brian once again leaned against the wall, waiting out the depressurization process. Zella started batting at an unruly lock of her auburn hair, and Derek began chewing again. Sivien gazed narrowly down at Derek, but he didn't seem to notice. His lip-smacking actually got louder. Callie took note of Derek too, and her expression soured. She turned and tried to scoot away but didn't have anywhere else to go. She stopped fiddling with Little-G's buttons and twiddled her fingers in her braids instead.

"You outdid yourself with that style," Brian said, trying to distract everyone from Derek by making light conversation.

Callie ran her hand along the thickest braid that crested her hairline. "Nerves. You know that." She continued fidgeting with the weaved locks that circled the crown of her head and disappeared near her neck.

"Don't worry. We're not planning on staying long," Brian said.

Callie's shoulders visibly relaxed, and her fidgeting slowed.

"Callie," Derek said through his chewing. He reached his stocky hand behind her shoulder and gave her an awkward pat. The thick smell of savory meat wafted from him even more while he spoke. "We'll be in and out of there in no time. You don't even need to worry about it!"

Callie's body stiffened under his pat, but she accepted his unpolished encouragement.

Sivien raised a brow. "I thought you were out of all your secret jerky stashes, Smacky-Lips-McGraw. Are those even still good? They could have been sitting around for ages."

"That's not my name. And I only told you I was out so you wouldn't sneak any. Why, do you want one?" Derek squinted an eye in suspicion and looked up at him.

"I told you that wasn't me." Sivien turned his nose up. "I don't eat that nasty crap."

"It had to be someone." Derek tapped his chin in contemplation.

Zella slightly shifted in place and started picking at her nails.

Derek's smile returned as his attention refocused on the piece in his hand. He tore off another chunk. "Well, to answer your question—yes, they're still good! A bit tough, though. You know, it wouldn't be a secret stash if everyone knew about it, now would it? You sure you don't want one?" He raised a brow and continued chewing.

"Ooh, I do!" Zella perked up. Her ears stood on end. She opened her hand, gesturing for a piece.

"Oh, no!" Sivien groaned. "Not you too."

Derek side-glanced at Sivien. "Zella, I appreciate your honesty. I wish everyone had that quality." He began scrounging in the satchel on his hip.

His tongue poked out of the side of his mouth as he searched into the depths of his pouch.

A smile grew across Zella's face.

Derek's eye widened. "Ooh, I found a big one!" He pulled out his prize. With a wide grin, he passed the large portion of jerky to Zella's eagerly waiting hands.

Callie cringed.

"Would anyone else like a piece?" Derek rummaged through his satchel again. "Under the circumstances, I'm offering!"

"No, thanks. I'm good," Sivien replied.

Brian shook his head, and Callie waved the odoriferous offer away.

"All right." Derek tore off another piece. "Suit yourselves. I do have more if you change your minds, but the offer won't last forever."

Callie stared at Derek. "Save some room for later."

"What do you mean?" Derek looked confused.

The light of their holding bay changed from red to green. "Decompression is complete," the ship's computer announced.

"Never mind." Callie shrugged, waving the short-lived conversation away.

A resounding hiss erupted as the ship's seal broke. The ramp started descending just a few feet away. Brian climbed to his feet, as did his crew. A blast of cool, refreshing air rushed in to greet them, replacing the stagnant air in the holding bay with a fresh surge of oxygen. He closed his eyes and took in a long drag. He could have sworn he caught a hint of a salty sea breeze. It reminded him of someplace, but he couldn't quite remember where. The faint smell quickly faded.

"I didn't realize," Callie said through an inhale, "how much air we had depleted."

The ramp boomed with finality against the dock's floor.

Everyone moved to the top of the ramp, sucking in the fresh air. Zella eyed Derek's satchel on his hip. He slipped her another piece of jerky, and she lit up with glee as she snatched it from his hand. She started gnawing on it and took the lead down the ramp.

"Shields up," Brian said, remembering his duty. "We don't know what's waiting for us out there, but we need to be ready."

Chapter 6

One by one, the crew members touched the transmitters on their chests. For a split second, a flicker of blue light engulfed each one of them as their shields activated.

"Remember," Brian said, "shields are—"

"Shields are meant to deflect," Derek interrupted, mimicking Brian's voice. "They're not supposed to take a full, head-on assault."

Brian peered down at his short comrade.

"Yes, yes." Derek resumed his normal voice. "We already know."

"I know. It's just that some of you seem to need reminding sometimes." Brian shot a look at Sivien.

"Who, me?" Sivien shrugged and tried to look innocent. "But I can take most hits with no problem."

"Just because you *can* take a hit doesn't mean you *should*," Brian replied. "Besides, we don't know what kind of weapons are out there anymore. Let's just be more cautious this time, okay?"

"I can't promise I'll try," Sivien said as he shuffled down the ramp behind Brian. "But, I'll *try* to try."

"Well, at least that's a start." Brian took his final step off the ship, and his boot touched down on the station's hard floor. At the same time, a high-pitched sound squealed in his receiver. He squinted his eyes shut and shot his hands over his ears. The unbearable tone ended just as quickly as it started, but a faint static crackled in the background of his device. He shook his head as he made his way out from underneath their vessel.

"My transmitter is a little glitchy." Brian's voice dissipated into the thick atmosphere of the room.

Sivien stepped off the ramp and immediately grimaced, shooting a hand up to cup his ear. "Mine is too." The sound of his voice likewise absorbed into the dense emptiness of the chamber. He began wiggling one of his claws into his ear.

"There might be something disrupting our transmissions." Callie jabbed at her sleeve's buttons.

Brian furrowed his brows. "Is Little-G glitching?"

"No, he's fine." Callie shuffled to Brian's side and glanced around. "Where is our welcoming party?"

"I don't know." Brian looked around. "That's a good question."

Brian wandered a few more steps, soaking in his surroundings. Each level of the docking hangars was detached from the others. He couldn't find access to the other floors anywhere. Only their lone ship dotted the barren landscape of the level they had landed on. He looked at the open expanse to the left, where they came in. He gazed up, trying to see the dock's ceiling, but the place seemed never-ending. The port stretched out above them and faded into the distance. It looked more breathtaking in person than it had on the screens of the bridge.

"This place feels like a cave." The port sucked the strength from Brian's voice right out of the air. "It sounds different, though. Inside a cave, the sound bounces instead of dissipates—for the most part."

Sivien looked at Brian. "What's a cave?"

"Ooh, ooh . . ." Derek's brows jumped high, and his pointer finger leaped into the air, but the explanation of a cave couldn't quite seem to make it out. He removed his finger from its enthusiastic pose and rested it on his bottom lip instead. "Hmm . . ."

Brian understood Derek's difficulty in explaining what a cave was. He wondered how to describe it himself. He thought for a moment, and an idea came to him. He fanned his arms wide above his head. "Just imagine all of this, but not made from manufactured parts. Picture it made from rock, dirt, and years of land erosion instead."

A thoughtful look spread across Sivien's face. He scratched his head with a claw and started surveying the place more intently. Brian reached up and gave Sivien a brotherly clap on his broad shoulder, which sparked blue energy from his shield.

"I wonder what kind of metal this is," Derek said, marveling at the floor. He leaned over and touched one of the intricate, circular designs engraved on its surface and traced his finger along the deep groove. He brought his stubby digit back up and inserted it into his mouth. His eyes widened. "This place is squeaky clean!"

Sivien's lip curled. "Ew gross, Derek. Taste the air like a normal visitor." His black-forked tongue shot out and flicked back and forth in the air.

"You guys are both gross." Zella placed her hand on her hip.

Sivien stopped tasting the air, and his eyes fell to his boots. "Derek's right, though. This place is squeaky clean."

Derek hopped a couple of times, continuing his inspection of the floor. "What is this?"

Callie scanned the black metal with her sleeve. "Its composition is not found in our database."

"I wonder what the engravings mean," Sivien said.

Callie scanned the intricate design carved into the floor. "That's also not in our database, and I'm still not picking up any life signs in my scans either. There seems to be some sort of interference, though."

Zella glanced around. Shifting her weight, she flipped a coil of bouncy hair out of her face. "And still no receiving party?"

Brian looked around. "I guess not."

"Maybe the members of the welcoming party are still on their way," Callie said. "I wouldn't blame them, either. This place is huge! Personally, I'd walk this monstrosity as little as possible. Good news, though. I have found a door leading farther into the station. It's approximately five kilometers in that direction." She pointed past their ship's starboard bow.

"That's not much of a walk," Sivien scoffed.

"What should we do?" Derek asked. "Wait for the station's crew to arrive?"

"Maybe our welcoming party is closer to the door," Brian replied. "I wouldn't want to trek all the way out here either. Perhaps they'll meet up with us there."

"We won't have to walk. There is a teleportation terminal just over there." Callie pointed in the opposite direction. "And there's another one near the door. We can probably get there in a snap."

Brian looked in the direction she pointed. A large pad raised from the floor in the distance. He leaned toward Callie and tried to inspect Little-G's readouts. Callie turned toward their ship but held out her arm so Brian could still see. She pressed a few buttons, and *The Gabriel's* ramp started to close.

Callie lowered her arm. "We've got to keep the old girl safe and secure in our absence. We certainly don't need any more surprises today. We especially don't want something crawling into the ship when we return. Nobody needs that again." She cast a glare in Derek's direction.

A smile spread across Derek's face. "That, um, wasn't exactly my fault." He tipped his head toward Sivien a couple of times.

Sivien caught sight of Derek's disguised pointing, and his brows furrowed. "But you—"

"Never mind that now." Derek waved a hand in the air. "Let's get to the teleport and transport ourselves to the door."

Brian sighed and started making his way to the terminal. His crew trickled behind.

Soon, everyone stood next to the raised black pad. Large, engraved circles outlined individual rings on the portal's dark, glassy surface.

Callie eyed the terminal. "If these teleports make the journey to the door shorter, someone should have been here by now. I don't know why they didn't send someone to greet us."

"I'm sure they have their reasons," Brian replied. "Like you said, this place is huge. Maybe it's just taking them longer than we're used to."

Derek sniffed the air. "Hey! Do you guys smell that?"

Sivien sucked in a deep breath. "The invigorating fusion of nitrogen, oxygen, and some other minute components that, when mixed together, create air?" He looked down at Derek and grinned.

"No, not that," Derek replied.

Zella perked up. "Your jerky?"

"No, not that either." Derek rested a hand on his satchel.

Callie briefly stopped scanning the teleportation pad. "Chemicals?"

"What? No!" Derek said. "I mean like something cooking."

"Like burning?" Zella frantically sniffed the air and looked in the direction of the ship.

"No!" Derek slapped his hands to his face and dragged them down his cheeks. "It smells like food—like cooking food. What's the matter with you guys?"

Zella stopped sniffing the air. "Oh, then no—and I don't smell anything burning either."

Derek shot a look at Brian that pleaded for his validation.

Brian took in a few whiffs of the air himself and grimaced. "I'm sorry. The only thing I can smell is fresh air."

Derek's expression morphed into a mixture of hurt and confusion.

"This darn thing!" Callie repeatedly jabbed her sleeve's buttons, drawing everyone's attention from Derek's scent-based plight.

"Callie!" Derek's mouth dropped open. "Don't do that! He's a tough gadget to fix."

"Something's wrong with it." Callie's frustration seemed to grow with each new flustered jab. "It's not working right."

Brian placed one hand over Little-G and his other on Callie's hand. Her momentum slowed to a stop, but she didn't relinquish her glare on the device. He stared at her in disbelief for her harsh interaction with the device. "It won't locate the access point?"

"Huh? Access point?" Callie blinked a couple of times, and a look of confusion swept across her face as she looked up from her sleeve.

Brian gingerly released her. "Yeah, the access point to the teleports—could you find one?"

"Oh . . . Oh, yeah." Callie's gaze fell back to her sleeve but didn't really focus on the device. "I didn't find one. The teleport's compilation is just too foreign. I don't know how to make it work."

Zella approached the raised pad. "Well, we *are* in the future. Maybe it works just by standing on it and thinking. You know, something like Little-G's technology—that mental link thing. Maybe it just takes you to where you want to go." Excitement rang in her voice as though she meant to try out her theory.

"Aye! Now we're talking." Derek lit up at the suggestion. He drummed his fingers and hurried after her.

Zella lifted her foot to step onto the pad.

"Wait!" Brian held out a hand. The action stopped them in their tracks. "I know you both get excited about new tech, and it might work like that, but we don't know for sure. We also don't know exactly where we're going or anything about this station. It's probably better if we don't use the terminals until we understand this place a little better."

Zella put her foot back down, and Derek spewed a fluster of grumps. Brian could only make out pieces of his counterargument—"a lost opportunity of adventure" and "missing out on a fun contraption."

"Maybe the portal is broken," Callie said, interrupting Derek's huff. "I mean, it's probably not, but I can't think of any other reason their crew hasn't used it to send us a welcoming party."

"Yes, they've had more than enough time to dispatch personnel while we boarded," Brian agreed, "but it doesn't answer the question of why they'd have us land here if they knew they had broken machinery."

"That's true, I guess. Having us land here knowing the teleports were broken doesn't make much sense." Callie's head cocked as she studied her sleeve's readouts. "On a different note, I found something interesting. I'm detecting micro technologies similar to the ones used in Little-G."

"Intriguing." Brian raised his brow. "Which ones?"

"The ones that sustain the mental link capabilities," Callie replied. "Zella's theory of thinking where to go and being transported there might just be how it works."

"Fantastic!" Sivien blurted. "Let's hop on there and think our way closer to the door. We know another teleport is there, and we could just blink and be there."

Brian raised his hand again. "I would love to say yes to that plan, but we know how difficult it is to work Little-G's mind-based interface. Callie's really the only one who can use him. Callie and I might end up where we wanted to go, but the rest of you could end up somewhere else completely—or worse, vaporized." He looked straight at Sivien.

Sivien gulped and tugged at his uniform's collar.

Brian continued. "We really don't know exactly how to use these tele-porters, so I can't permit their use. It would be too reckless."

"What should we do, then? Wait by the ship?" Zella picked up the end of her tail and swung it around, looking rather unamused. She stared at Brian, waiting for him to reply.

Brian sighed. "I don't think waiting around the ship is a great solution either. Callie's right. They've had plenty of time to send a welcoming party."

"You're not suggesting what I think you're suggesting, are you?" Sivien winced.

"I'm sorry, but I believe I am," Brian replied.

"We're going to walk all the way to the door on foot?" Sivien straightened his full height, making him stand even taller and look more intim-idating.

Brian cocked an eyebrow at Sivien and half-smiled. Then he gave an apologetic shrug.

"It appears so." Zella smiled at the exchange.

Sivien groaned.

"Welp. Since nobody is coming to greet us here, we'd better start going to them," Derek said, walking in the opposite direction of the door.

"Derek, that's the wrong way," Brian said.

Without skipping a beat, Derek pivoted on the spot and headed in the right direction. Brian shook his head and followed. Zella and Callie fell in line, but Sivien didn't budge. He stood there, glancing back and forth from the teleportation pad to the departing crew.

"Come on," Zella called.

Sivien raised his arms, looking defensive. "We're really going to walk that far? Can't we, you know, fly the ship and land closer to the door?"

"Low air," Zella responded.

"And low fuel," Callie added. "You should know that best."

"Bah! I do!" Sivien huffed and started jogging to catch up.

Callie slowed and pressed a few buttons on Little-G. A green, glowing projection began hovering near her arm. It detailed a miniature three-dimensional model of the surrounding area. "My scans should show us the way." She hopped back into step with the others.

Sivien caught up and matched the rest of the crew's pace.

The sound of their footfalls became the only thing breaching the thick, empty atmosphere of the docking hangar.

Chapter 7

It didn't take long for Brian to lose some of his alertness on the dull journey. He tried his best to keep on his toes in this unknown place, but the unchanging scenery and their monotonous, hollow-sounding march across the dock made his eyes glaze over. Just as his boredom reached its peak, he noticed Zella lagging behind. Soon, her step slacked even more. He had to turn slightly to keep an eye on her whereabouts. He leaned to Callie and bumped her elbow, grabbing her attention. Her white brows furrowed as she looked at him.

Brian motioned with his head down to his hands. *"Here we go,"* he signed.

Callie's brows wrinkled even more. Brian could tell her mental cogs were turning, trying to glean understanding from his odd message. He tipped his head in Zella's direction, hoping to clue Callie in. She slightly rolled her eyes, but a smirk grew as she studied Zella's movements.

Zella started bending the chamber's lighting around her. Her whole body began shimmering. Then she stepped beyond the visual spectrum and vanished into the thick air. Derek and Sivien remained blissfully unaware that Zella had performed her signature move. Brian instantly lost track of her. The one thing he knew for sure was that Zella stalked her prey—the inattentive Sivien.

Callie snuck glances around and signed back to Brian. *"Should we warn him?"*

"We never do," Brian replied with his hands. *"Besides, he's got his shield up. How much damage can she really do?"*

Sivien suddenly froze in place and rose onto his tiptoes. His dark mouth cranked open in a silent scream. His body stiffly arched, making his huge chest puff out even more. The painful-looking motion left him staring straight up at the ceiling as though he begged the cosmos for sweet release.

Zella's taunting giggle erupted from somewhere nearby. She let the surrounding light normalize, and she became visible again. She leaned snugly against Sivien's side. Brian could barely make out her fingers, clamped around a portion of his underarm, and he wondered how she got through his shield. Her canines peeked through her devilish grin while she held Sivien in an unforgiving pinch.

"I told you I'd get you back," Zella taunted.

It didn't take long for Sivien's abrupt halt to catch Derek's attention. He glanced at Sivien and slowed. He started laughing as comprehension of Sivien's misfortune set in. "Aye! She's got you good, don't she! I don't know how she got through your shield, but that's hilarious!" He continued laughing.

Zella tipped her head toward Derek. "The shields are just another form of light. And, apparently, just as easy for me to bend." Her smile widened.

"I didn't know you could do that," Derek said.

"Neither did I." Zella gave him a wink. "It just came to me."

Sivien stood there, not even twitching a muscle under Zella's lock-tight hold.

Brian slowed momentarily and observed Sivien's situation. The corners of his mouth betrayed his desire to appear neutral on the matter. He pressed his lips together, trying to hide his amusement. He didn't know Zella could manipulate the shield's power grid either. The fact that she figured it out slightly unnerved him. He cleared his throat, indicating that Sivien's punishment for the truce violation should end.

Zella bent the light again and slipped back out of the visible realm. Sivien's entire body slumped. The faint sound of Zella's boots scuffed on the floor as she light-footed away. "There is no such thing as a truce," Zella announced from somewhere nearby. The thick air of the port dampened the volume of her voice.

Brian continued toward the door, and the crew's progression resumed.

"Dang, Zella!" Sivien twisted his arm as he tried to rub its underside. "I think you left a bruise this time."

"Come on, you two." Callie glanced back. "We have a long way to go. Stop goofing around."

"Yeah, Zella." Sivien babied his new injury. "Stop goofing around."

In time, Derek's laughter subsided, and Zella reappeared a safe distance away from Sivien, lessening the chances of retaliation. Before too long, the steady shuffling of the crew's boots on the metallic floor became the only sound again. Brian's shoulders ached from the weight of his pack, and his legs felt weak from the length of their march so soon after reanimation.

"This is so boring and tiresome." Derek broke the silence. His face suddenly brightened, and he looked at Zella. "Can you pinch Sivien again?"

"I don't think so!" Sivien fired back, pulling his arm in tightly. He shot Derek a dirty look. "I mean, I don't mind taking one for the team, but that's a little excessive."

Zella smiled at Sivien. "I should be nice to him. I think he's suffered enough—for now. Besides, we called a truce." She gave a sly wink.

Sivien visibly relaxed and stopped babying his arm a little.

Derek looked confused. "I don't remember hearing you agree to a—"

"Shhh—ut up," Sivien whispered. "That's acknowledgment enough."

Derek's smile faded, and he snapped his fingers. "Aw, shucks. Good thing those don't last very long." His grin returned.

"There it is," Callie announced. "We have a visual on the door."

Brian could make out a wall extending up through the chamber in the distance. He presumed it went all the way to the ceiling, but its detail faded with the room's height. A single door rested at the end of their hangar. He assumed all the other docks led to similar entrances on their respective floors. He examined their access to the station as they continued approaching. The place remained deserted. "That's fairly off-putting." He side-glanced at Callie.

"What is it?" Derek squinted and lowered his goggles over his eyes.

Callie wiped sweat from her forehead. "There's still no welcoming party."

"Maybe they're just inside the door," Sivien said.

"Seriously?" Zella laughed. "You don't really think that, do you?"

"Well, I want to," Sivien replied.

"Why would anyone wait just inside the door to greet us?" Zella prodded. "That makes no sense."

"Chairs?" Sivien said. "Maybe there are chairs inside."

Callie stared at him blankly. "Chairs? You're kidding, right?"

"Some chairs would be nice," Derek said, cutting in. "I could go for at least one of them right now."

"At least one?" Sivien asked. "What would your maximum be?"

Derek drummed his fingers on his bottom lip and looked thoughtful.

"Even if there were chairs, we wouldn't be taking a break right now." Brian sighed and looked at Callie. "How far out can you see with Little-G? Can you tell if there are signs of life beyond the door?"

"Let me see . . ." Callie's pace slowed while she worked with her device.

Brian rubbed the back of his neck, trying to make sense of the ridiculous reasoning behind the station having them land here. "Why did they have us dock in such an empty section?"

"Maybe the rest of them were full." Derek scratched his head.

"Well, I guess we shouldn't rule anything out." Brian moved to Callie's side and watched the images hovering near her sleeve while she worked. "But something tells me that's probably not the case."

"We are here." Callie pointed to the five glowing red dots that indicated their crew in the replica. Zooming forward, she brought a green-glowing, skeletal likeness of the wall into view. "I see no indication of any personnel around that door. As you know, they'd be yellow dots, but there aren't any. My device isn't quite functioning properly, though, so I guess my scans could be off."

Brian glanced at the actual door. As they got closer, he noticed that its dark metal matched the flooring. It seemed bigger than how it appeared in the scans.

Derek perked up and grinned mischievously. "Maybe this section is haunted and that's why it's empty." He gained a few glares for his comment.

"Again, that's not a good thing." Brian shook his head. "And that doesn't even make sense. Why would the station send us to a haunted section?"

"I don't know," Derek stammered. "Oh, you're probably right. That wouldn't make sense."

Brian looked at Callie. "Little-G still isn't working properly, huh?"

"I could swear the amount of interference seems to be increasing," Callie replied, "but our life signs are showing up in the scans, so it's working well enough."

The vast expanse of the docking platform gave way to a well-lit area as they continued toward the door. The oversized entryway stood like a sentinel, guarding the station's inner sanctum against intruders. Another raised teleportation pad sat on its right.

Brian's pace slowed several yards from the large door. He eyeballed the pad to its right. "Any chance you can tell if those teleports were used recently? We need to be sure we didn't miss our receiving party." He looked at Callie.

"I can't promise anything, but I'll try." Callie split away from the group and stopped short of the teleport. She scanned it with her sleeve. "I'm not picking up any energy residue from the power cells. It doesn't look like it was activated recently. It's dormant—just like the rest of this place."

"It's okay." Brian turned his attention back to the intimidating barrier. "We'll just see if anyone is behind this door."

Callie made her way back to the group.

"Even though no signs of life are showing up on our scans," Brian said, glancing at his crew, "Little-G has been glitching, and I'd rather be safe than sorry. I want all of you to be on your guard, but don't *look* like you're on guard. We don't need to start an intergalactic situation because we appeared hostile."

Nods trickled across Brian's crew. He stepped up to the door, inspecting the towering mass. The formidable roadblock's width could fit about a dozen men his size standing shoulder to shoulder and at least double that for height. He imagined Sivien's ease in getting around in the station if the halls matched the magnitude of the door's size. He came within mere inches of the beast.

Any other door would have opened by then.

Brian's stomach twisted in knots. The unsettling feeling of being watched raised the short hairs on the back of his neck. "I wonder how big our no-show alien friends are." He turned and cast a sweeping glance behind him but saw only his crew.

He pushed the silly notion of being watched out of his mind and stepped even closer to the door. He gazed at its rough, ebony surface, wondering what to do next. Taking one more small, tentative step, he reached out and touched the massive barrier. The cold metal stole the warmth from his fingers.

He put both hands against the door. Using all of his strength, he pushed. It still didn't budge. He remembered what Callie said about the teleports using a mind-based interface and wondered if that's how the doors might work. He focused his mind and concentrated as hard as he could. *OPEN,* he commanded it with his mind.

The door didn't move.

Brian's cheeks flushed hot with embarrassment. Taking a few steps backward, he peered up at the titan. "How are we going to get in?" he whispered, mostly to himself. Just then, he could swear he felt a warm gust of air and the weight of unknown eyes resting heavily on his back.

"Aye!" Derek blurted right next to him.

Brian jumped. At some point, Derek had moved to his side.

"Oops, sorry," Derek said with a slight chuckle. "I thought you knew I was here."

"No worries." Brian brushed off his nerves and the persistent notion of being watched.

"Look." Derek motioned to the door. "It's not opening."

Brian's expression flattened. He glanced down at Derek.

Derek lowered his goggles over his eyes and examined the door, seemingly oblivious to Brian's slight irritation.

Returning to his own inspection of the door, Brian tapped his chin and searched for clues as to how it opened. He traced a circular groove etched into the door's surface with his finger. It matched the design on the floor. As he stared at the intricate pattern, he almost lost himself in the rich, artistic beauty. With Derek standing nearby, Brian's stocky friend quickly became the only thing anchoring him from becoming lost in the wonders of the architecture.

Sivien stepped up to the door on Brian's other side. "How do we get it open?" He spread his hands out wide and started pushing.

Brian took a step back. While his crew fanned around the obstacle, inspecting it for themselves, something above the sealed opening caught his eye. He found three words inscribed in bold lettering. "**Space** . . . **Station** . . . **Sirrenia** . . ." He read them out loud.

"Was that there before?" Sivien backed up. His face squinched to one side in confusion. "I don't remember seeing those words when we got here."

"I don't know. I wasn't looking above the door," Brian replied. "Did anyone else notice?"

No one offered an answer.

"At least it's in our language," Callie said.

"Well, it *is* an allied ship," Brian countered.

"Sirrenia, huh? Never heard of ya, love." Derek scratched his head as he stared up at the inscription.

As if in response to Derek's comment, the door began sliding open. The crew froze in place from the sudden movement. As the metallic barrier slowly inched out of the way, Brian found a long, brightly lit hallway on the other side. Decorative chandeliers hung, dotting the center of the ceiling down its length. White lanterns lined both sides of the walls and cast a soft, inviting glow. The oversized hall with all its décor seemed to go on and on.

The station's personnel remained notably absent.

A sinking pit in Brian's stomach grew as he stared down the hall's immeasurable length. "Well, Callie. It looks like your scans are accurate. None of the station's personnel are waiting for us here."

Callie wrung her hands as she gazed down the corridor. "I don't like this place."

Brian inched toward the door's threshold. The hall's soft lighting seemed so welcoming. He went to step inside, but the pit in his stomach knotted and twisted tighter. He hesitated and looked down. Plush white carpeting separated the docking port from the hallway. He gingerly lifted his foot across the threshold. As soon as his boot touched down on the fluffy, cloud-like fibers, an overpowering calm washed over him, and a palpable sense of peace swept all his cares away.

A long-lost memory rolled into Brian's mind.

He closed his eyes as he lost himself in a daydream.

Chapter 8

Warm air cradled Brian, and he relaxed in its embrace. The rush of rolling ocean waves broke on a nearby shore, and sprays of its moisture filled the air. A hint of saltiness mingled with the warm, refreshing breeze.

Opening his eyes, Brian found himself reclined in a chair. He stared up at the underside of a vibrant red umbrella. The decorative fabric, hanging on its outer rim, swayed in a gentle gust of wind. A brilliant sun blazed in the morning sky. The protective shade provided a perfect haven from the day's growing heat. Cool sand pressed between his toes, and an iced drink rested in his hand. The breeze danced and swirled around him, kicking up bits of sand toward the rolling ocean waves that crashed along the shoreline.

I know this place, Brian thought. *This is Mirandian's third moon.*

Another wave crested the peaceful beach.

Birds called to each other somewhere in the distance.

Brian put his drink down on the arm of his chair. He turned and found his wife sitting next to him in the shade, relaxing in a matching seat. She smiled at him, which made her sun-squinted eyes close a little more. The breeze picked up a few of her locks and flipped them teasingly into her face. Wrinkling her nose, she brushed her long curls out of the way. Brian reached to her with his free hand, and their fingers intertwined. Lying back, he nestled in his chair, utterly content. All of his worries seemed to melt away. With nothing but clear, purple skies overhead and his beautiful wife at his side, he relaxed in a virtual paradise.

As the long day wore on, the sun slowly shifted across its route in the sky. Sleepiness made his eyelids heavy. In time, he closed them, ready to succumb to the serenity of the scene. He started drifting off with his arm still bridged to Grace's.

Out of nowhere, a notion of someone lurking around them began nagging at Brian, and an odd sound of something dragging across the sand sent a shot of adrenaline through him. Not quite ready to give up on the serenity of the afternoon, he still clung to slumber's edge. He sensed the other presence lingering on the outskirts of his and Grace's superb beach spot.

Brian continued lounging in his chair with his eyes closed. He just wanted the presence to hurry by, but the entity continued lingering as though it were waiting for something or someone. The minutes ticked away, and his patience began wearing thin. As far as he could tell, the being hadn't moved at all. At the same time, something else began gnawing at him. As he thought back over the entire morning, he couldn't remember seeing a single soul on the beach. He hadn't noticed the lack of other sea-side frolickers until now, but it quickly became his main focus.

Despite himself, a seedling of fear sprouted.

The breeze grew hot. Its lighthearted twirling and skipping morphed into more of a frenzied dance. Beads of sweat pricked Brian's forehead. He tried to clasp his wife's hand tighter, but his grasp only closed on empty air.

Where did Grace go? Brian wondered.

He wanted nothing more than to open his eyes and search for his wife, but he ended up closing them tighter. His attention focused again on the other being on the shore, and he wished the person would just go away. The weighted sound of something dragging across the sand inched toward him.

The pounding of his heart quickened inside his chest.

This is silly. It's probably just Grace, Brian told himself, but he couldn't remember hearing her get up or feeling her let go of his hand.

Brian sensed the entity coming closer.

A sweet smell filled the air.

It doesn't smell like Grace, Brian thought. *And if it is Grace . . . why hasn't she spoken?*

His stomach leaped into his throat.

He ached to know what or who loomed near, but terror gripped him and drowned out any fanciful ideas of looking. The scorching breeze whipped across his skin, feeling more like a fiery furnace. Droplets of sweat collected on his forehead, and one ran down his temple. The entity moved in *so* close—*too* close. Its suffocating weight towered over him.

The sweet smell assaulted his senses.

It's so close. I should be able to feel its breath. Brian panicked. *WHY CAN'T I FEEL ITS BREATH?*

A bird let out an obnoxious call right behind him, and his thoughts froze. He held his breath as the looming presence closed in. The bird called again, but this time, it said a word. His attention split between the entity leaning over him and the annoying bird cawing from behind.

"Brian," the bird called again, but in Callie's voice.

Confusion swallowed him in its disorienting depths.

"Brian," Callie's voice called again.

He felt a tug on his arm.

Daring to sneak a peek, Brian cracked open an eye, expecting to see the horror that loomed over him. Instead, he found himself standing across the threshold of the station's hallway. His front foot rested on the fluffy white carpeting, and his back foot remained on hard metal.

"Are you okay?" Callie stared at Brian, concern etched across her face. She let go of his arm.

Brian turned. The rest of his crew cascaded behind him, still standing in the docking hangar. They exchanged glances with each other.

"You just stopped. Is everything okay?" Sivien stood a pace outside the door, eyeballing the hallway.

"I . . . I think so." A droplet of sweat ran from Brian's temple onto his cheek. He reached up and dabbed the bead. He held out his hand and stared at it.

Callie wiped her forehead. "It was quite a walk getting out here. I'm kind of worn-out too."

Brian slowly nodded. The intense daydream continued fading from his mind.

"There's not a computer console anywhere?" Derek stood at the dock's edge, inspecting the entrance. "With Callie's help, I bet I could have infiltrated the station's mainframe from here and figured out a way to communicate with their personnel. I'd give my circuit boards for a computer interface right about now! We shouldn't have had to board the station unaccompanied."

"Maybe Callie can find one in her scans." Sivien went to take a step but hesitated and glanced at Brian. He lifted his large foot across the threshold and carefully placed it on the carpet. He winced as though he expected something to happen, but nothing seemed to. Tentatively, he took a few more steps into the hall and started looking around.

The rest of the crew trickled through the entrance and fanned out just inside the door. The goliath metal slab started sliding closed behind them as they wandered farther down the hall. Everyone's heads bobbed as they took in the scenery. Flat paint coated the walls in varying shades of white and gray, giving the place a monotone but bright and welcoming feel. Brian peered up at the ceiling. The spacing between each lavish chandelier seemed exact, revealing the designer's meticulous attention to detail. The station's elegant interior looked like it had been ripped straight out of a top-notch vacation brochure.

Brian's attention drifted from the ceiling and walls down to the soft, white carpet under his boots. He noticed circles similar to those they had found in the docking hangar and on the door.

"I wonder what it means," Sivien said, examining the floor too.

Derek's face squinched to one side. "Aye! I expected the future to be more impressive. Maybe we're not *that* far into the future. The rest of this place is just as disappointing as their communications system. It doesn't look very futuristic at all! The only promising tech this place has are those teleports, but the embarrassing lack of computer interfacing . . ." Derek's voice faded into a low grumble.

Zella wandered over to the wall. She stood under one of the lanterns and gazed up at it. The light hung several feet above her, higher than even Sivien's tall frame. She sighed heavily and leaned against the wall. Grabbing the end of her tail, she began purring as she twirled its fur between her fingers. "It's very beautiful, though."

"Yeah, I guess." Derek shot Zella a distasteful look. "But looks don't help functionality. I think there are too many lights and not enough computers. They've got their priorities all messed up if you ask me."

"There's nothing wrong with beautifying, Derek." Zella continued purring and gazing up at the decorative lantern.

Brian touched his goatee. He weighed their next course of action. He wasn't sure if they should proceed, stay here, or return to their ship and wait for assistance.

"What should we do?" Callie asked as though she read his mind.

Brian rubbed the back of his neck. "What can you find on your scans?"

Callie worked Little-G's buttons on her upper arm.

"You know what?" Sivien said. "It's almost worse *not* having anyone here than it is being attacked or fighting our way through hordes of aliens. This silence wears on you. It's so thick it's like wading through raw sewer water. It makes you force your way through with every mucky step."

"Sewer water?" Derek's brows rose. "When have you waded through sewer water?"

"Planet Raghetch." Sivien shrugged, looking a little defensive. "You were there!"

Derek drummed his stubby fingers on his chin. "Oh, yeah. It does ring a bell now that you mention it." His attention drifted back to the surrounding hall.

Callie turned to the green-glowing image hovering next to her sleeved arm. She manipulated the projection and zoomed out, expanding their view of the station. "There appears to be a storage room not too far away. There should be fuel and parts if this station is like other ships."

"You still can't find any personnel?" Brian prodded.

"Not so far," Callie replied. "Why in the cosmos would the station have us land in a deserted section?"

Derek's face lit up. "It *is* abandoned!" he whispered.

"Nay, nay, Derek. It is *not* abandoned," Zella said wispily. She still stared up at the light overhead and twirled the fur at the end of her tail. "They granted us permission to land and everything."

"Maybe . . . " Derek said, glancing across the hall, "maybe it was a ghost who gave us permission. You heard how crappy the transmission was. Look at this place. It's got *some* nice tech. It just doesn't add up."

Callie locked Derek in a stare. "In all of our voyages, when has your ghost theory ever been accurate?"

Derek appeared to be wildly searching his brain for an answer.

Callie resumed the manipulation of her sleeve's projection. It suddenly froze. The glitch left a large break running through the middle of the image. She made a fist and smacked her device, restoring it to its proper function. "I don't know why it keeps doing that."

Derek's eyes widened. "Use finesse, Callie. Please—don't hit him!"

"Sorry. He's just not functioning properly," Callie replied.

"Speaking of not functioning properly, my earpiece is still staticky." Sivien wiggled one of his claws in his ear.

Brian noticed the faint crackle that kept sounding in his receiver as well. "It's probably that interference messing with our devices. Can you find out how far away that storage room is, Callie?"

"Not far." Callie stared at the image.

"I say we take what we need," Derek exclaimed. "Ain't no one here stopping us."

"I agree," Sivien chimed in. "They allowed us on board. They knew our needs. Maybe they expect us to help ourselves."

"I'm not sure how much I like the idea of gallivanting around a ship without an escort, but I also don't like the idea of waiting around, hoping for someone to come." Brian rubbed the back of his neck again. "We don't know how long it will take for a welcoming party to meet us, or if one got dispatched at all. Maybe we *should* continue."

"Plus," Callie added, "if we run into any of the station's crew on our way, we'll just explain what happened. I'm sure they will understand. We got permission to board, after all."

The unanimous agreement from Brian's crew gave him the answer he needed. "We will proceed, then. Callie, show us the way. Just remember, we're only after fuel and parts for our ship. Hopefully, we can find coordinates that tell us where and when we are. We're not here to snoop around. Ghosts or no ghosts." He looked at Derek.

"Ah, flib." Derek snapped his fingers and kicked at the carpet. Squinting, he slowly looked back up. "What about finding food?"

Brian smoothed his goatee. "We still have some provisions on the ship. They should last until we get home. We'll go right back into stasis after we're done with the repairs."

"Oh." Derek's shoulders slumped.

"If we *happen* to find any," Brian sighed, "I guess it wouldn't be too bad of an idea to bring some of it along."

Derek's demeanor brightened. "I can accept that."

Callie started down the hall, leading the way with her sleeve's projection. Sivien pulled Zella away from her perch against the wall. Every time they came to another lantern, Zella's pace slowed, and she stared at it until she passed.

"We will treat this like any other mission," Brian said. "Just because we haven't run into anyone doesn't mean no one is here, and we don't know what to make of this place yet. So, keep your eyes peeled and your guards up."

Brian caught up to Callie at the front of the pack. She finished tapping on Little-G's buttons, and a green laser produced a skeletal outline of the surrounding hall. Every time Callie ran the program, it reminded Brian of x-ray vision. A route started tracking in the miniature three-dimensional model hovering next to her sleeve. The device glitched again and left the image shattered in the air.

Callie balled up her fist. "This stinking thing!" She delivered a mighty blow.

Chapter 9

Derek's eyes popped wide. "Stop it, Callie! Don't hurt him."

The crew's progression down the hall fizzled out while Callie continued inspecting the shattered image hanging in the air. Zella wandered underneath the nearest lantern and stared up at it.

"What is wrong with this stupid thing?" Callie punched her sleeve again. "I can't even map out a route!"

"HEY!" Derek slapped his hands to his cheeks. "If you break that, I have to fix it!"

"Okay, here we go." Sivien sighed.

Callie hit her device again. Derek bit down on his finger and let out a muffled groan. He seemed more concerned about the sleeve than he did about any pain coming from the wedged digit in his mouth.

"Cool it, Derek. I'm not going to break the stupid thing." Callie went back to working with her sleeve. Her efforts to get the image to clear up seemed useless. She stopped prodding it and looked straight at Derek. She winced as if to say, *Sorry, but not really*.

Derek's hands raised into a *stop* gesture. "Don't *you* do it!" He narrowed his eyes.

Callie's delicate hand formed another tight fist. Derek's eyes widened, and his bushy brows rose to the rim of the goggles resting on his forehead.

In one swift move, Callie delivered another blow to the uncooperative device.

Derek turned to Brian. "Can't we take Little-G away from her and give him to someone less abusive?" he whined.

Brian looked at Callie.

She shrugged in defense.

"She's the one who's trained to use him." Brian turned back to Derek. "She's the most proficient with his mind-based interface."

Callie's shoulders slumped. "That might be true, but I can't get him to un-glitch."

"Let me see." Brian sighed and held out his hand.

Callie slid the sleeve off and gave it to him. The shattered, floating image continued hovering next to the device as it exchanged hands. Brian began pulling Little-G up his arm, and it adjusted to fit his size. As he stretched his fingers through the end of the sleeve, he felt the mental link connecting to his mind. Every movement of his gloved hand could lead to a function, depending on his desire. The wealth of its operations waited at his fingertips.

Little-G worked by using three parts: one part thought processes, one part free hand, and one part gloved hand. The three parts together usually equaled one whole headache. With time and training, experts like Callie become inoculated against any adverse side effects. Brian fell a little short in the experience department. He landed somewhere in the realm of a novice.

A mild throb began developing behind his left eye.

Brian sucked in a deep breath, accepting the forming pain. Despite his best efforts, the pulsing misery behind his eye increased. He started moving the fingers of his gloved hand and began working Little-G's interface. When he hit a certain point, he started pushing buttons on the device to restore the sleeve's projection. The green, glowing image floating next to the device suddenly became a pixelated mess. Brian rolled his eyes, and his mind felt like it somersaulted in place. His left eye involuntarily shut halfway, and the throbbing behind it increased. He glanced over at Derek, hoping he wasn't paying much attention.

Derek stared directly at him, and his eyes narrowed.

Brian made a fist.

Derek shook his head and mouthed the word *NO*.

Brian cringed and delivered a blow to Little-G on his bicep. The jab sent an explosion of pain through his entire head but made the image functional again.

"INCREDIBLE!" Derek threw both of his arms in the air and paced around.

"I'm sorry." Brian sighed and gave a gentle tug on the cuff at the top of the sleeve. The device loosened from his arm. The pounding behind his eye began to subside, and he sighed with relief. "But Callie is right. It's not working properly."

Derek stomped off a few feet down the hall.

Brian slid the sleeve off and handed it back to Callie.

"Little-G's not broken, Derek. He's just fine." Callie pulled the sleeve up her arm, and it cinched into place. She pushed a few buttons and manipulated its projection. "I mean . . . he's fine besides the glitching, of course. Look, I've got our route mapped now."

As Derek's fluster fizzled out, Callie took the lead down the hall again. Zella lingered under the lantern but eventually joined Sivien at the rear. Soon, they came upon the first set of doors. The twin barriers sat across the corridor from each other like two titanic towers in an eternal expanse of hallway.

Callie slowed her pace, as did the rest of the crew.

"Is one of these the storage room?" Brian shifted his gaze from one lumbering door to the other.

Callie checked the image hovering next to Little-G. "No, we're not there yet. We have to go through an intersection first."

"Well, if the doors don't bother us," Brian said, "we won't bother them. Just check for signs of life."

Callie pointed her device at the right door, then turned and scanned the one on the left. "I'm not detecting any."

Brian motioned for Callie to continue down the hall. "Then let's keep going." He held a wary eye on the crew members as they passed.

Callie's speed returned to her usual pace, and the crew proceeded. More and more doors dotted the repetitive landscape. None of them opened when the crew passed.

Derek started sniffing the air. "Seriously? You guys can't smell that?"

"You're smelling something again?" Brian looked at Derek.

"Yes. Yes, I am." Derek licked his lips. "I can smell something cooking."

Brian sniffed the air. He tried to pay attention to any scent that might be lingering on it, but he couldn't detect any.

"Maybe it's coming from farther down the hall," Derek said with excitement stirring in his voice. "If we find where it's coming from, can we eat some of whatever it is?"

"There's no smell." Sivien cut off Derek's sniffing inquisition.

Derek looked up at him. "Yes . . . yes, there is. You're just messing with me."

"No, I'm really not," Sivien replied. "There is *no* smell."

"I don't smell anything either, Derek," Zella interrupted.

"Look, we didn't come here to eat," Brian said. "Besides, no one else seems to be able to smell whatever it is you're smelling. Just leave it alone for now."

They came to a cross-sectional split in the hall.

"This is the intersection," Callie said. "We need to go left."

They rounded the corner, and Derek stared at his boots as he shuffled down the new hall.

Brian looked at him. "Maybe we'll find what's making your phantom smell on our way out." He gave Derek a friendly nudge, and blue sparked from their shields.

Derek's expression brightened a little, and he stopped staring at his feet. He sniffed the air again. "Wait, I know that smell. I've smelled it before. But where?" He drummed his finger on his forehead as if the action could jog his memory.

"Let it go," Sivien said. "There's no smell."

"Roasted brekuin meat!" Derek announced. "That's what it is!"

"You know," Callie turned around, walking backward, "I smell chemicals."

"Really?" Sivien asked. "What kind?"

"Sanitization." Callie took in a deep breath. "It might be weird, but I love that smell."

Derek adopted a look of confusion. "No. It's not chemicals at all. It's definitely meat. I'd know the smell of roasted brekuin anywhere!"

"It's smelled like sanitization chemicals since we left our ship." Callie shrugged. "It's bizarre you smell food. The sanitizer is pretty strong in this area."

"It doesn't smell like that, Callie," Derek countered.

"Well, hold up," Sivien said. He flicked his tongue in the air. "I don't smell chemicals *or* meat."

Brian raised both hands, trying to calm his crew. "I don't know what's going on, but I don't smell either. Zella, how about you?"

Zella sniffed the air and shook her head. "Nothing. I haven't detected any scent since we exited our ship, and I have heightened receptors in that department." She pointed at her fine-tipped nose. Her feline attributes stood out as indicators of her authority on the matter. As if to stress the point, one of her pointy ears twitched.

"Can't argue there," Sivien said.

Zella motioned at Callie and Derek. "Your sniffers must be off or something."

Derek grabbed the end of his stubby nose. "Hey!"

Callie scowled.

"I'm not sure if their sniffers are off," Brian said, waving the notion away. "For now, we'll just have to add it to the list of oddities in the station."

Callie slowed her pace again. "This door should be the one, judging by the size of the thing. It is a lot bigger than I imagined." She looked the door up and down as they approached.

"Let's cross our claws and hope it opens." Sivien's statement gained him a few glances from the others. "Or fingers. Whatever."

Callie stopped in the middle of the hall, and the crew crowded around her. Brian broke away from the group and stepped up to the door.

The dark titan didn't budge.

"Of course, the door isn't opening. That would make things too easy." Brian glanced back at his crew, hoping they'd offer suggestions.

"Maybe the doors are voice-activated," Callie said. "The first door opened when Derek said part of the inscription."

Sivien looked up. "There are no inscriptions above this door."

"I can't believe I'm doing this." Brian sighed. He stood straighter and squared his shoulders. "Open."

The door didn't move.

"OPEN." Brian's cheeks flushed with heat as he watched the door remain motionless.

Derek burst out laughing. "I'm sorry. But that's one of the most ridiculous things I've ever seen." He covered his mouth, muzzling his amusement.

Sivien walked past Brian and kicked the door. "OPEN!" He pushed it. The definition of his straining muscles bulged through his uniform's material.

"Maybe Derek is the key. Should we have him try?" Callie asked. "Maybe it will work for only him."

"Wouldn't hurt to try." Brian took a step back.

Derek perked up at the suggestion and strutted over. Sivien cocked his brow and peered down at him. Derek's short stature didn't even breach the height of Sivien's broad waist, but their size difference didn't seem to faze the stocky man. He began shooing Sivien out of the way.

"A little room, please. A little room." Derek cranked his head back, looking up at Sivien from his short height. "Step aside. Step aside."

Sivien glanced at Brian with a look of *I can't believe he's serious* on his face. Brian only shrugged in response. Apparently tired of Derek's prodding, Sivien moved out of the way. Derek quickly took his place. The crew waited for him to work whatever magic he possessed, but he went straight into a low stretch. He brought his hands together in front of himself, interlocking his fingers. He flipped his palms outward and arched them until loud pops cracked from his knuckles.

"Derek, what are you doing?" Sivien folded his arms over his broad chest. "Just open the door already."

Derek waved his hands at Sivien to stop his verbal intrusion. "This is important. I'm getting ready." He hopped and swung his arms in big, rapid circles. Then his movements slowed as he reached the end of his warm-up session. He squared his shoulders and stood tall for his short frame, glaring the door down.

"OPEN," Derek commanded at last.

The door still didn't budge.

"What's the matter with these flib-jibbin' doors?" Derek turned to Brian for an answer.

"All of that, and it still didn't open?" Sivien laughed. "Maybe it didn't like your stretching."

Derek shot Sivien the stink eye.

Without warning, the ominous roadblock started to slide open.

Callie worked with Little-G for a moment. "Maybe the doors are pre-programmed. I'm not completely sure, but maybe that's how the station's personnel allow access: They program them from somewhere deeper inside the station."

"That's an interesting theory," Brian replied.

"Maybe that's why there is no receiving party," Sivien said. "They can program their ship and aren't worried about visitors ransacking anything."

Callie examined the door as it opened to the room beyond. She checked back and forth between the image next to her sleeve and the area beyond the doorway. "According to the Little-G's readings, there are no signs of life in this room, either."

"Come on." Brian walked through the doorway. "Let's see if we can find compatible fuel and the parts we need for our ship."

Chapter 10

Brian inched closer to the opening as the door continued sliding out of the way. He inspected the spacious repository beyond. The chamber looked like a vast metallic library. Each towering aisle lined up in pristine order with the next, and storage containers filled every nook and cranny of their shelves.

"A computer! Finally!" Derek bolted to the right.

"Derek," Brian called after him. "Don't get too far away from the group."

"It's not *that* far away," Derek replied over his shoulder. "I'm going to tear that thing apart! You just wait. I'll have more answers than Callie can shake Little-G at."

The crew gravitated toward the computer in the corner of the room. The massive system branched out from a central unit. Its intricate panels seemed fused with the surrounding walls. The console's main access came all the way up to Brian's chin. With the size of everything else in the station, he considered himself fortunate to see the unit's interface from his height at all. Brian glanced at Derek, knowing his view wouldn't fare as well from his short stature. Brian's attention drifted back to the mainframe. It looked similar to their ship, except for its intricate webbing of circuitry that spread across the attaching walls.

"Massive little network," Sivien said, gawking at the computer. "I wonder how big the beings are that run this place. Everything's so . . . so big."

"That's a great question," Brian said.

Derek got to the computer. He hopped up and hooked one hand around its lower rim. His feet kicked wildly as he pulled himself up. He settled in place with his lower half still dangling over the edge. Then he began plucking away at the controls, looking like an adolescent playing with something he probably shouldn't. He paused and peered down. "Callie, come help me with this thing!"

Callie grabbed the lower rim of the computer easier than Derek, and she climbed to his side. Her slender legs dangled next to his as the colleagues interacted with the interface together.

"What's inside the containers?" Brian rose onto his toes, trying to get a better look. "Is there any fuel?"

"I'm checking," Callie answered over her shoulder.

Sivien stood near Brian, but Zella didn't come as close. She grabbed the end of her tail, twirled its fur, and began humming a mystical tune. The richness of her voice added an intriguing layer to the enchanting melody. Something about the song sounded familiar to Brian, but at the same time, it felt completely foreign.

As Zella continued humming, she hit a sour note. Brian cringed, and thoughts of never getting off the station bombarded him. He pictured Grace's sweet, frozen face behind a stasis pod's dusty glass, waiting for his return—a return that would never come. His eyes misted, and he blinked a few times. He looked at Zella and racked his brain, trying to remember where he had encountered the tune before, but the answer remained aloof.

A sudden realization hit him. In all the years they had spent together as crewmates, he had never heard Zella hum—not even once.

Brian leaned to Sivien. "Has she ever hummed around you before?" He tipped his head in the direction of their feline colleague.

Sivien's confusion grew as he looked at her. "Zella doesn't sing."

Brian continued watching her play with her tail and hum. "Zella, that's a pretty song. What's it called?" he asked her.

Zella stopped humming but kept twirling the end of her tail. Her head slumped to the side, then tipped forward. The movement reminded

81

Brian of a saggy rag doll's head flopping around. One eye peered through her disheveled hair that now draped across most of her face. Her piercing stare went straight through him.

Brian shifted in place. "Are you okay?"

Derek let out a loud whoop at the computer. "We've got it!"

Zella blinked several times and looked over at the commotion. In an instant, her unnerving expression melted away. Brian continued evaluating her, but nothing appeared to be out of the ordinary anymore. He followed her gaze to Derek, just in time to see Callie shoot down an attempted high-five. "What did you find?"

"Only the network to this whole section." Derek raised a fist in victory. He almost fell from his awkward perch and quickly grabbed the surface of the computer. He restabilized his balance with a chuckle.

Brian glanced back at Zella. "Are you okay?" he repeated in a low tone.

"I'm fine." Zella seemed a little surprised by the question. "Why?"

"Just a moment ago, you looked a little . . ." Brian started, but he second-guessed himself with Zella appearing to be normal. "Never mind. It's nothing."

Derek bent at an odd angle and gazed down. "I think we can map our way back home. We found a constellation gold mine. I can get these star charts downloaded to Little-G in just a few clicks. Well . . . with just a little tearing into the computer's hardware, a bit of soldering, *and* just a few clicks on Callie's part—of course. Even if this mammoth collection of circuit boards is a little stubborn, it's nothing we can't handle." He popped his goggles over his eyes, patted the computer, then slid to the floor.

"*And,*" Brian prodded. "What about the rest?"

Derek opened his satchel, grabbed a tool, and started loosening the computer's panel. "Well, Callie might even be able to access the stellar date if she can finagle it just right. We might be able to figure out *when* in the flib we are, not just *where*." He shot Brian a smile.

"I can't seem to track down the stellar date just yet," Callie announced.

"No," Brian replied. "I meant the fuel and parts."

"I'm working on that, too." Callie brought up another image in the computer's hologram. She examined it and pointed to a spot. "This is the room we're in. And . . . even better, it looks like I have access to the system's controls in this section. The master program running the station has already granted it."

"That's wonderful." Zella dropped her tail. She wandered closer to the computer. "Finally, something is going right."

"I also know why this section is so oversized," Callie continued. "This station has many different size zones. This one was built to accommodate visitors much larger than us."

"Why would they have us land here if this section is meant for larger species?" Brian tapped his chin.

"It isn't clear," Callie gazed down at him. "Intimidation tactic?"

"If that's the reason, it sure worked on me," Derek said. "There's something about this place."

"It could be as simple as trying to make Sivien feel more comfortable. It's definitely roomier for him than a lot of places."

"I have enjoyed that." Sivien glanced down the nearest aisle and did a double-take. "Hey! There are loading platforms down there, Callie. Why didn't you say you found some?"

Callie paused and glanced down the aisle, too. Her expression flattened, and she looked at Sivien. "I didn't find them. You just did. They will come in handy for moving the fuel to our ship, though. So, nice find." She returned to her work.

"Oh," Sivien replied.

"'Oh,' is right." Derek's voice started echoing as he climbed inside the computer's console. "One less thing to worry about. Wow, this place is roomy! You're right. It is more comfortable."

Callie motioned to a spot in the hologram. "And look, there are the loading platforms on the computer." She shot Sivien a look.

"My bad, Callie." Sivien raised his hands apologetically. "I'm sorry."

Callie went back to plucking away at the interface. "It really does seem like the computer was programmed from outside this section. Maybe that is why it takes a while before the doors will open. The station has to give permission first, I guess."

A loud crack sounded from inside the computer's base.

"Ah, flib-jib," Derek said.

"Everything okay down there?" Callie asked but didn't look away from her work.

"No worries. No worries," Derek's voice echoed. One of his stocky hands waved outside the console as though he could simply brush away any concern. Sparks flew, and wisps of burnt plastic and seared metal wafted in the air. "Everything's still all under control."

Callie's head poked over the counter. "Well, do be careful."

Derek leaned out of his alcove and lifted his goggles. "Just like how you're careful with Little-G?" He looked at her sleeve.

Callie's mouth fell open as she peered down at him. "Um, more careful than that."

"Right." Derek lowered his goggles and went back to work. Sparks erupted once again from inside the belly of the computer.

"Fair enough, I guess." Callie returned to the display. "And . . . we have success, sort of."

"We can load the fuel and get out of here?" Brian felt a sense of relief. "That's great news. We just need the parts, then."

Callie looked at Brian. "I didn't find either of those. What I meant was that I just stumbled on the master program. I was actually trying to create a communication link with the station again, but this popped up instead."

Brian rubbed the back of his neck. "Oh, not quite what we were hoping for, but okay."

"You should look at this." Callie stared at the hovering display. She propped herself on her elbows and cradled her pale cheeks between her hands. Her feet began to sway as she gently kicked them. "The code is breathtaking."

"How so?" Brian stood on his toes again, trying to get a better look.

"I could swear some of the code's syntax resembles genetic patterns." Callie's voice drifted off as though her attention wandered a million light-years away.

"DNA sequencing?" Brian stepped closer to the computer. "How?"

Callie reached one hand toward the hovering display and cupped a particular spot. She stopped short of touching it and caressed the air instead. "I'm not familiar with this coding language, but some of it seems similar to the ones I know. It's like an algorithm mixed with a biological construct."

"Are you suggesting the system could be alive somehow?" Brian folded his arms across his chest. "As wondrous as Little-G is, even he doesn't have any biosynthetic components. Living matter doesn't fuse well with AIs."

"It does sound preposterous . . ." Callie trailed off. She grabbed the air around the projection with both hands like she meant to enlarge it, but it swiped away before she could complete the motion. A different image quickly replaced it in the air. "Hey! Where did it go? I didn't dismiss it."

"Can you bring it back up?" Brian asked.

"Let me see." Callie's fingers blitzed across the computer, picking up speed as she went. Brian could hardly keep up.

Callie stared at the rapidly changing images as though she were star-dazed. "I must say, the interface is quite dazzling. The architects who built this place must have been brilliant." Her voice trailed off again.

"Is it really that good?" Brian knew that her high standards well exceeded his own.

Callie didn't reply. Her hands dashed across the interface. Her legs stopped swaying, and her shoulders slumped. She leaned forward as her blitzing fingers increased speed even more.

"Callie?" Brian couldn't keep up with the blur of images that flashed in the projection. "CALLIE."

She leaned forward so far that her head entered the holographic field.

"HEY!" Brian smacked her foot. Blue light sparked from her shield.

Callie blinked and looked down at Brian. "What?"

Brian stared up at her. "You were leaning forward into the field, and I—"

"But I found something," Callie cut him off.

"The stellar date?" Derek's voice echoed.

"No. I forgot about that. The computer is extremely engaging." Callie's eyes sparkled, and she turned back to the display. "I found another storage room a few floors up. Well, a few floors and two elevator lifts, basically the same thing."

"Oh, no one cares about that," Derek said. "We need to get the fuel loaded and find the parts I need."

"What happened to the code?" Brian asked.

Callie shrugged. "I don't know. I didn't find it."

"Okay, look. Forget the code," Brian said. "Just locate the fuel so we can load it and get out of here."

"I side with Brian on this one," Derek said. "We should stay on task."

Sivien laughed. "Intentionally wandering into off-limit areas doesn't sound like you at all."

Derek's face popped out from the console. "It sure doesn't." He gave a wink and dove back in.

"I had to search the computer anyway," Callie huffed. "I originally intended to gain access to the programming for the loaders."

"Never mind. I take it back," came Derek's booming voice again. "I side with Callie on this one. The loaders are a must-have."

"There it is," Sivien said.

"Then," Callie continued, "I tried communicating with the station again. I thought it might be helpful. We could at least send correspondence that we're taking supplies back to our ship. It's a courtesy."

"Were you able to establish a link?" Brian asked.

"No," Callie replied. "Not yet."

Derek climbed out of the computer. "She's all ready. Time to download those star charts. At the very least, we can map a route home. Hand him here." He motioned for Little-G.

Callie stopped interacting with the mainframe. She slipped off her mechanized sleeve and passed it to him.

The device tightened around Derek's arm as he pulled it on. As soon as Little-G cinched into place, he doubled over. Both his hands shot up, cradling his head. He spent the next couple of minutes fighting to steady himself. "Little-G's mental interface is just as fun as I remember," he groaned through forced breathing.

Callie smirked.

Derek's hand trembled as he pushed some of the buttons on the sleeve. A compartment opened at the wrist, and he pulled out two long wires. He slowly climbed back into the recesses of the computer, and more sparks flew. "Got it, Callie. Ready to download," his voice quivered.

"I haven't got it back up on the computer yet," Callie said, getting back to work.

"Whenever you're ready. No rush," Derek replied with a slight chuckle that feigned nonchalance. He peeped out from the computer's innards, then gently raised his goggles to his forehead, looking multiple shades of green.

Brian cringed a little. "You need to get that thing off."

"Aye. I will after we're done." Derek's breaths came in heavy puffs. "Get them downloaded already, Callie."

"Giving instructions to the network, now." Callie scrambled. "And, done! It's downloaded. You can take him off now."

Derek disappeared into the computer.

More sparks flew.

"Now, which aisle has the fuel? It must be here somewhere." Suddenly, Callie's smooth interaction with the mainframe turned choppy, and her hands quickened. "You've got to be kidding me!"

Brian searched the projections for what could have struck such a strong chord with her. "What is it?"

Derek emerged from the computer again.

"All of these containers appear to be empty. There is no fuel in them!" Callie said through pursed lips.

Chapter 11

Callie balled her fists, and they quivered in the air. "The da—" She shot a look down at Derek.

He lifted his goggles.

"The flib-jibbin' things!" Callie corrected.

"Nice catch!" Derek winked and pointed shaky finger-guns at her. His skin turned paler green by the second.

Callie rolled her eyes and resumed her work with the computer's interface. "All these containers appear to be empty. There is no fuel here!"

Derek's mouth dropped open.

"What did you just say?" Sivien's eyes widened. "You must be joking. Surely there's fuel in some."

"Can we open a few of them?" Brian rubbed his neck. "I'd prefer a visual inspection just to make sure. Without fuel, we're stuck on this station."

"Of course." Callie choppily pounded on the computer.

An eruption of short-lived hisses sounded from some of the container's breaking seals. Brian nodded at Sivien and Zella, grabbing their attention. He tipped his head toward an aisle, indicating for them to go check.

"Can I take this thing off?" Derek squeaked.

Brian peered down at him. "Yes, you look terrible."

"Thank you." Derek tugged on the device's cuff, and it loosened from his arm. "You don't think there are critters in those crates, do you?"

"Critters would have shown up in the scans." Brian watched Sivien and Zella leave to inspect some of the containers. "Callie, any signs of life yet?"

"No," Callie replied. "Still nothing."

As Sivien and Zella approached one of the aisles, Zella sprung onto one of the bottom shelf's containers and spidered up its sleek-looking side. Sivien stepped up to it too. Already tall enough to reach its lid, he pushed it open. They both peered inside. Zella arched away, looking back at Brian. One of her hands swung free and touched her transmitter.

"It's empty!" came Zella's voice in Brian's staticky earpiece.

Sivien lowered the lid and shrugged. Zella scaled up the next shelf onto a new container, and Sivien wandered farther down the aisle. Clinging to seemingly nothing, Zella attempted to lift her container's lid. Brian wasn't sure if she could get the thing up, but she managed to surprise him. She peeked inside, then dropped the heavy-looking slab.

A loud boom echoed through the room.

"This one's empty, too." Zella's voice sounded in Brian's ear again. She scurried onto the lid and slunk through the narrow space between the shelves.

On the ground, Sivien peered into another container. He touched his transmitter. "Empty."

"This one, too," Zella said. Another loud boom reverberated through the room as she dropped the lid. "Do you want us to keep going?"

Sivien dropped his lid, too.

Brian activated his comm. "We still have to find fuel. Check a few more containers. Maybe spread out a little bit more."

Zella clambered higher, and Sivien walked farther down the aisle.

"They're all probably empty," Callie said. "The computer says they are."

"Look at this place." Brian motioned to the aisles. "How can a storage room this vast be empty?"

"Maybe Derek's ghost theory isn't so far-fetched," Callie said.

A teasing smile formed on Derek's face.

"Don't encourage him," Brian smirked, "or he'll never quit."

"Hey, I resemble that remark." Derek's voice still held a slight quiver.

Brian took a step away from the computer. Wondering what to do next, he tipped his head and rolled it from side to side. He waited for word back from Sivien and Zella on their advanced search, even though he could guess the results.

"This one's empty," Zella's voice chirped in Brian's ear. Another boom filled the room.

"These are all empty," Sivien's voice came soon after.

Suddenly, something Callie had said earlier jumped into Brian's mind. "Wait! Didn't you say there was another storage room?" He looked up at her.

"Um . . ." Callie froze. She looked down at him. Then her expression brightened, and she pounced on the computer. "Yes . . . Yes, there was another storage room. The one that's not in this section?"

"Yes, that one. Can you locate it again?" Brian moved closer. "Maybe this is just where they store the empties."

"I'll try." Callie pored over the display.

"Now we're talking!" Derek sat back against the console. A hint of wooziness still lingered on him.

Brian activated his comm. "Come back. We might have an alternate plan."

Zella quickly descended and touched down next to Sivien.

"I sure hope there's fuel in that other storage room." Brian glanced around the room. "I don't want to go on a wild anserini chase for nothing, especially not here."

Sivien and Zella made it back to the head of the aisle. Zella's perky ears lay flat against her bouncy, short locks. She had scooped up her tail and was twiddling the fur on its end.

"Um . . ." Callie's fingers flew across the console. "It *does* look like there's fuel in the other storage room. Lots of fuel, actually."

"That's the best news I've heard all day!" Derek's coloring continued to return. "We're going to need as much as possible to get back home. I say we take more than we think we need."

"We found fuel?" Sivien asked, without the aid of his comm, as he and Zella continued to approach.

"We think so," Brian replied. "The other storage room that Callie found earlier isn't *too* far from here."

Zella's ears perked up, poking through her hair again. "Oh, yeah. That other storage room." She dropped the end of her tail and hurried toward the computer.

"Any chance you found a communications network so we could talk to the station's personnel?" Brian asked Callie. "At the very least, we could let them know we didn't find any fuel in this section and that we're headed to the other one."

Callie frowned. "No, and I've done several advanced searches, too."

"It's okay. We'll make do," Brian said.

"I did find blueprints to the new section, though. I can download them onto Little-G, so we can route where we're going." Callie peered down at Derek. "It would be easier to find our way with blueprints than by scanning everything."

Brian cringed, and his gaze fell on Derek as well.

"What? No. I just took Little-G off," Derek whined. "You've *got* to be kidding me."

"I'm sorry, Derek," Brian said, "but it would probably help us get out of here faster."

"Flib-jib." Derek placed his goggles over his eyes and extended an open hand toward Callie. She removed her sleeve and delivered it to his waiting grasp. He slid the device back on and swooned as it tightened down. His movements slowed, and he climbed back into the computer. Sparks flew.

"Ready," Derek's voice quivered.

"Downloading." Callie's hand zipped across the computer. "It should be ready to eject now."

"Oh, thank heavens!" Derek said. A few more sparks flew, and he began climbing back out. He looked paler than ever.

"Wow, Derek. You look like crap," Sivien said. "You should get more practice with that thing."

"That's hard to do with master-specialist hogging it all the time." Derek snorted and slid Little-G back off. He offered the sleeve to Callie. She grabbed the device, but Derek held on. "Be careful with him. No more hitting him, okay?"

"I'll do my best." Callie didn't even glance down.

Derek didn't relinquish his hold, and Callie looked at him.

They locked stares.

"I promise," Callie finally said.

Derek let go, and Callie slid the mechanized sleeve back on.

"Don't do Little-G wrong." Derek raised a weak finger-gun at her and winked as he cocked his thumb.

"Um . . ." Callie turned back to the display she manipulated. "We, um, have to go up two separate elevator lifts, but we can find the other storage room with minimal effort. It's more of a straight shot, so we won't have to take a lot of turns."

"How about the loading platforms? Do they have those there, too?" Brian searched the projected hologram. "There are some here. If we need them, we can take them up with us. I don't want to have to double back."

"It doesn't look like we need to take them up with us," Callie said. "The readouts say there are platforms there as well—pickers, too."

Derek slowly stood on his wobbly legs.

"You okay to keep going, or do you need a minute?" Brian asked.

"I'm good to keep going," Derek replied. "I'll start feeling better soon enough."

"Time to move out, then," Brian announced.

As the crew headed toward the door, Brian eyed the oversized obstacle, wondering if it would open this time. The massive titan started sliding out of the way as they approached. A slight spring returned to Brian's step as they sidestepped another problem.

"It's nice to see the door not giving us any issues on the way out," Sivien said as they entered the hallway.

Callie examined Little-G's projection and moved to the lead.

"It is a nice change." Brian smiled and glanced back at the door.

Derek started sniffing the air. "Seriously, you guys don't smell that? It's *so* strong! It's coming from down the hall somewhere." He sped up and breezed past Callie.

"Meat again?" Callie asked.

"Aye!" Derek closed his eyes and drew in a deep inhale. "It's meat. Someone has to be cooking! Mmm."

"Maybe your jerky has gone to your head," Callie snarked.

Derek turned and walked backward. "If it has, I don't mind." As he took in another drag of the phantom scent, his eyes fluttered shut. He turned around and walked normally again, wandering down the hall from one side to the other with his nose leading the way.

Callie caught Brian's attention. With a slight huff, she cocked her brow and tipped her head at Derek.

"Stay behind Callie," Brian called after him.

Derek slowed, but only a little. Callie hustled to retake the lead. Brian motioned for Sivien and Zella to pick up the pace. Sivien did, but Zella lagged behind, twirling her tail. She stared, starry-eyed, at the hanging lanterns on the walls as she passed beneath them.

Sivien took note of her dawdling. "Zella, you're going to have to go faster than that to keep up with Derek," he teased.

Zella shot him a heated glare and hissed.

"Whoa," Sivien chuckled nervously. "I was just playing."

"Well, it's not funny." Zella shoved past him. She tried to secure the end of her tail on its hook, but she missed. It fell and dragged behind her on the floor, but she didn't even notice. She blasted Sivien with another scowl.

Brian considered pointing out Zella's tail, but given her sudden moodiness, he decided against it. He didn't want to set her off even more. He moved to Sivien's side. *"Have you noticed Zella's been acting a little strange?"* he asked with his hands.

"Yes!" Sivien signed back. *"That didn't look like her usual pretend annoyance either. It looked more real. More like she was really angry with me. Zella's never been* really *angry with me before—well, not that angry anyway."*

Brian continued observing Zella. She kept pace behind Callie and stared at another lantern they passed under. The end of her tail still dragged behind her on the fluffy carpet.

Chapter 12

Callie checked the glowing image hovering next to her arm. "At least there aren't very many turns we need to make, so it would be pretty hard to get lost."

"Getting there safely is all that matters," Brian replied.

Callie nodded.

Brian gazed at the monotone hall. It seemed like a never-ending repetitive loop, and his mind wandered to past planets and lodging spots they had visited. Most of them abounded in rich cultural contrast, bursting with different species and exotic things that stimulated the senses. He remembered a foe or two that kept his crew on their toes, but here, in this place, nothing changed or was challenging. He looked up at a chandelier as he walked underneath it. Not a single crystal seemed missing or out of place. Nothing deviated from the repetitiveness.

In time, more dark doors started dotting both sides of the hall. All of them towered over the small crew. Brian examined one and veered close enough that it should have opened. It didn't budge, but he began feeling the weight of someone's gaze again. He kept a wary eye on the door as he finished passing. Sivien bumped Brian's arm on his other side. Its accompanying blue spark jerked him from his concentration on the door. "What?"

Sivien smiled and tipped his head, motioning at something down the hall. Brian followed his gaze to Zella. She batted at a lock of her hair and watched it bounce. Sivien crouched and began tiptoeing toward her. Brian reached out to stop him, but Sivien's stealth belied his size, and he quickly slipped out of range. Brian cringed, thinking of Zella's current mood. She continued swatting at the lock of hair. Sivien snuck closer but remained unnoticed—a feat that rarely happened. He crept up to her tail, which dragged behind her on the floor.

Brian slowed his pace.

Sivien lifted his large boot, then planted it on the end of her tail, pinning it to the ground. He gazed up at her with a wide grin. She continued walking while the rest of her tail fell from its hook. She didn't even seem to notice. Sivien looked at Brian in total confusion.

Brian shrugged. Zella should have reacted immediately to the weight of Sivien's boot. She suddenly halted, grabbed her tail, and yanked without even looking back, but the tug didn't set her free.

Zella looked down at her hip. Her brows pinched together as she turned to investigate. She zeroed in on Sivien standing on the end of her tail. Her head cocked at an unnatural angle, and she regarded him venomously. He squirmed in place.

"SIVIEN!" Zella's high-pitched shriek cut through the hall.

Brian almost couldn't decipher what she had said.

The shrill disturbance caught Callie's and Derek's attention. They paused and turned around. Zella's upper lip curled back, and she bore all of her pearly whites. Her chin quivered with rage. A low growl sounded from deep inside. It got louder, and she crouched into a pounce-ready stance. Her razor-sharp claws sprang from her nail beds. Sivien stopped fidgeting, and he froze in place. His foot remained planted on her tail.

"GET OFF!" Zella roared and let out a hiss.

Sivien stood there, petrified.

Brian gawked at the scene unfolding before him. Zella looked like she meant business. Sensing the rapid escalation, he rushed to Sivien's aid. "Zella," he said in a soft but firm tone. He raised his hands defensively, trying to calm her down.

A wild spark of fury in Zella's eyes made her look like she wanted nothing more than to rip Sivien into a shredded pile of green scales.

Brian put a sharp elbow to Sivien's ribs. A spark of blue flashed from his shield, deflecting some of the force. "He is getting off your tail right now—right?"

Sivien came back to life enough to uproot his boot. "Right," he stammered.

"See, all better." Brian still held his hands up in a non-threatening gesture.

Zella's expression softened, and she blinked a few times. Her gaze dropped to the floor. Her stance eased, and the tension in her body melted away. She began gathering her tail to rewind it, humming the same mystifying tune from earlier. She reseated the collection of loops back to her side. Then, twirling her tail's end with one of her retractable claws, she stared into space.

"Zella?" Brian asked.

She didn't respond.

"ZELLA?" Brian repeated.

Her eyes fluttered, and she stared up at Brian.

"I didn't mean to make you so upset." Sivien swallowed hard. "I was just playing. I won't step on your tail again."

"When did you step on my tail?" Zella glanced around, looking confused.

Derek burst out laughing. "Ah, Zella. That's pretty good. You really had us going! 'When did you step on my tail?' Such a great joke!" His chuckles continued bubbling out.

Brian watched Zella's response to Derek's amusement. Her brows furrowed even more.

"Yeah." Sivien squirmed in place and chuckled nervously. "I stepped on your tail because I was goofing off. You know, like how Callie told us not to? I didn't mean to hurt you, but I might have overdone it."

Zella squinted as if the action could jog her memory. She let out a laugh, but it sounded just as apprehensive as Sivien's. "Yeah . . . just goofing off."

"I promise, no more pranks." A warm smile spread across Sivien's black lips. "At least, not until we get back to our ship."

Zella shot him a mischievous smile back, and her ear twitched. She dropped the end of her tail and slowly stood up. Callie started down the hall again with a slight eye roll, and Derek tried stifling his residual mirth.

Sivien maneuvered to Brian's side. "I'm not exactly sure what just happened," he whispered.

"I'm not either." Brian glanced at Zella. She had returned to batting the same lock of hair. He reached up and gave Sivien the best brotherly clap on his shoulder that he could through his shield. "Just give her some space, okay?"

Sivien nodded.

As they approached another four-way intersection, Callie turned instead of going straight. "This is the way."

Like an ever-thickening forest of black, metallic slabs, the doors multiplied on both sides of the hall. They lined up in perfect unison, like the repetitive lanterns and the hanging chandeliers.

"Are we sure this is the right way?" Derek asked. "It's starting to look like a repeat of the same hall."

"Yes, Derek," Callie replied huffily.

Brian stole a glance at the green-glowing image hovering next to Callie's sleeve. With their exact path highlighted through the maze of corridors, a sense of relief washed over him. Even though his memory proved pretty accurate most of the time, he knew he would have difficulty telling these hallways apart.

The projection glitched again. Callie balled up her fist and hit her device, clearing up the cracks in the image. Brian shot a glance at Derek, wondering if he saw. Derek wandered down the hall obliviously, sniffing the phantom scent in the air. Even though *he* didn't notice, Brian did. The thought of Little-G breaking didn't sit well with him, not with everything looking so annoyingly the same. He knew they could easily get lost in this place.

Brian slid up beside Callie. "Please, try not to hit Little-G so much," he whispered.

Callie half-turned toward him. "It's not like I'm making it glitch on purpose," she whispered back.

"What's on purpose?" Sivien asked.

Derek stopped sniffing and looked over.

"Nothing." Brian waved the attention away. "It's nothing."

They came to another intersection, and Callie's pace slowed. She took a left and studied the floating image for a moment. "We're almost there." She picked up her speed.

The crew hastened down the hall.

In no time, her steps slackened again. "I . . . I think it's this one." She approached the door in question.

Brian sized up the door. "Let's hope it opens." He weaved through his crew to go first.

"It should," Callie said. "It looked like we had access when I searched the computer in the storage room."

Brian stepped up to the door. To his relief, it didn't give him any problems and slid open on cue. A faint, sweet smell rolled out. He inspected the unfurnished space inside. Two lanterns hung on the side walls, and a smaller version of the chandeliers dotted the ceiling.

"Too bad the décor matches the hall." Derek smirked.

"It seems about the right size to be an elevator lift, though." Brian continued his inspection.

"Why is everything so unimaginatively white?" Callie asked.

Sivien shrugged. "You got me."

"At least it smells nice," Brian said, catching some odd glances at the remark.

"Smell?" Sivien cocked a brow.

"See, Sivien!" Derek smiled up at him. "Brian can smell something cooking, too."

"That's not what I meant," Brian said.

"Welp. I'm sad to be leaving behind whatever food that is, but Callie did a great job getting us here." Blue sparks erupted as Derek patted her on her back. "You know what, Callie? I don't care what anyone else says about you. You're all right."

Callie narrowed her eyes as Derek strolled by.

"I'm sure that came out wrong." Brian stepped past Callie and entered the lift, too.

Brian scooted to the far end, and the others shuffled inside. The hallway slowly disappeared behind the door as it slid shut. He waited for the lift to activate, but he didn't feel the usual churn in his stomach from moving between levels.

Derek peered around. "Hey! There's no computer interface in here." He moved his goggles to his eyes and continued looking around.

"Wait. What?" Callie searched the walls too.

Brian looked at her. "Is the lift programmed to take us to the floor we need?"

Derek adopted a thoughtful look with his finger poised in the air. "It's got to be. You saw its pre-programming on the computer, didn't you?"

A blush spread across Callie's pale cheeks. "I don't know. I didn't think to check that."

Sivien moved to the door and started pawing at it. "We're not stuck in here, are we? You know I'm claustrophobic."

Brian weaved his way to Sivien's side and felt around the door with him, but it didn't budge.

Zella migrated to the room's far side and stared up at the lantern. She absently twirled her tail.

Brian took a step back. "The door isn't responding. I guess we could try the voice-activation thing again. Callie, what level do we need?" He tipped his head back and rubbed his neck, trying to release the growing tension.

"Oh, um." Callie floundered over the image hovering next to Little-G. "It's the ninety—"

The lift activated.

"—third floor," Callie finished. "That was weird. I think it started moving before I finished speaking."

Brian thought about the timing of when the butterflies took flight in his stomach. He could swear she was right. "I think I felt it, too. What did everyone else feel?"

Sivien stopped pawing at the door, and Zella continued staring at the lantern. Derek squinted one eye and gazed up, drumming his stubby fingers on his lower lip.

"I think it started before Callie said the level." Sivien scratched his head with a claw.

Brian looked at Callie. "Scan the lift. See if you can find any of the micro-technologies."

Callie scanned the room. "It appears so, yes."

"Zella was right?" Derek balked. "We could have used those teleports easily enough then?"

Sivien shook his head. "We walked that whole hangar, and we didn't have to? I got a bruise for nothing?" He gazed over at Zella.

A crooked smile formed across Zella's face, but she still didn't look away from the lantern.

"Callie is the most proficient with Little-G's mental aspect," Brian reminded him. "If this place really does run off some sort of mental command, she might have been the only one who didn't get fried on the teleports. Things might not be as clear-cut as they seem."

More tipsy butterflies swarmed in Brian's stomach. He knew the lift must be slowing. The fluttering lessened then dissipated altogether. The door slid open, and the same monotone walls that matched the lower level greeted him.

Brian stepped into the new hall, and his crew trickled out behind him. Only the lanterns on the walls interrupted the repetitive, dull landscape.

"Well, we're about halfway there." Callie inspected her sleeve's projection.

"OH!" Zella gasped. "Look at that."

Everyone followed her line of vision to the ceiling above.

Callie's mouth fell open as she stared up. "I've never seen anything like *that* before."

"I've never seen anything like it before, either," Brian whispered.

Chapter 13

No chandeliers hung overhead in these halls. Instead, a seamless wallpaper replaced the fancy décor. Aged, beige paper stretched across the ceiling's width and ran down the entire length of the corridor. The ancient-looking stuff reminded Brian of old parchment paper, a shadow form of literacy from the past. He rubbed his fingers together and swore he could almost feel the dry paper's texture. With the chandeliers missing, he wondered how the hall remained so well lighted.

Brian's curiosity over the lighting quickly faded as he continued studying the ceiling. A curious spectacle on its dated surface captured his complete attention. Someone had taken the painstaking effort of drawing every fine detail of the hall on the antique paper. The artist, or perhaps artists, used what looked like pitch-black ink to create the masterpiece. Thick, bold lines contrasted against thin, faint ones. The exquisite technique provided shading and gave a three-dimensional pop to the rendering of the hall overhead.

As he stared up at the wonder, new lines materialized on the paper's surface. The wispy strands spread like black stains soaking through the paper. He followed one as it formed across a small section and met with another. Several new runoffs sparked to life.

"What in the cosmos?" Sivien said under his breath.

Brian stood with his colleagues, gawking up at the mesmerizing ceiling. Within seconds, the new lines formed the images of every single one of the crew members. The drawn duplicates held the exact positioning and posturing of their counterparts standing in the real hall. The richness and perfect detail that the new drawings captured almost put the live originals to shame. Brian gazed at his duplicate. His flawless ink-twin's stare pierced him to his very center.

The ink copy looked *so* lifelike—perhaps a little *too* lifelike.

Derek scratched his head and pulled his goggles down over his eyes. "I don't get it. This hunk-of-junk station has no communication capability, at least not from what we've found, but then it has something like this." He spread his arms wide into the air, gesturing at the ceiling.

"What in existence *is* this?" Brian continued gawking up. To his astonishment, his ink drawing's mouth kept perfect timing with his own mouth as he spoke. He raised his arms slowly to test more of his drawing's responses. It held in sync with his every move.

"Did you see that?" Callie squealed. She backed up to the wall. Her ink image in the ceiling did the same. "Mine's moving too!"

Brian raised a hand to calm her. "I think it works something like a mirror." He went back to his inspection of the ceiling.

"Yeah, like a weird, paper-drawn mirror—without the mirror." Sivien waved his arms back and forth. He watched his ink drawing do the same.

Zella stared at the ceiling. She picked up her tail and started twirling its end. Her gaze seemed to take her a million galaxies away. "Well, I like it. It's as beautiful as the lights," she said breathily.

Derek scratched his head. "It's definitely interesting, isn't it?"

Callie relaxed and eased away from the wall. "I . . . I guess. It was just unsettling at first. It's . . . it's kind of neat if you think about what it must have taken to make it. I wonder what kind of program this is."

"Yeah, it's got to be some sort of holographic program." Brian continued studying his ink drawing. The fine detail created superb shading that made it seem more like a work of art than a mere computer process.

"I've never encountered a program like this before," Callie said. "And that's saying something."

The eyes of Brian's ink-double grabbed his attention. He had never seen such an exquisite likeness of his own dark orbs before. *They're so perfect, so captivating.* The static in his earpiece crackled a little louder.

The more he gazed into the ink eyes, the more fascinating they became. He soon found that he could venture further into their dark, pooling depths. *I wonder if they can look at me the same way I can look at them.* The unsettling thought stirred some alarm, but the alluring beauty held him spellbound. The surrounding hall faded from his thoughts.

Peacefulness settled on Brian. The all-consuming calm freed him from his cares, but somewhere deep inside, he felt a sense of warning. He brushed aside his pesky internal alarm and dove deeper into the syrupy ink pools of his drawn eyes. In the outskirts of his awareness, the surrounding hall faded entirely from his mind. His ceiling twin seemed like the only thing in existence.

Then his ink-drawn eyes blinked.

The realization dawned on Brian that he, himself, had not blinked.

The caution that Brian had tried stifling a moment before exploded with new life. As his internal sirens spewed all sorts of warnings at him, he tried looking away from the captivating drawn orbs, but his gaze remained fixed. He tried to back up, but his boots felt like they had fused with the carpet. The urge to call out to his crew members fizzled somewhere between the thought and the action. He couldn't seem to get a hold of himself. He just stood there, staring at his flawless, ink-drawn self. The comforting place of solace he had enjoyed mere seconds ago beckoned to him. A confusing battle between his instincts blasting him to escape and the pocket of alluring contentment yearning for his return paralyzed him even more.

What's going on? Brian's mind raced. He grasped at reasonable theories, but he couldn't think of any.

His quickened heartbeat drummed in his ears and drowned out the static crackling in his receiver. The ceiling started moving toward him, or did he move toward it? He couldn't tell. The hall's entire mass felt like it had begun pressing in on him. He sucked in heavy breaths under the crushing weight of the ceiling. *This can't be real!*

As he watched his drawn double come within an arm's length, he took a deep, focused breath and pushed the growing terror from his mind. He forced himself to be calm. Collecting every fiber of willpower, he concentrated on tearing his engrossment away from the enchanting canopy overhead. A daunting crusade for self-control raged. His pulse pounded inside his head. Every beat of his heart brought new, hammering waves that chipped away at his resolve.

He forced himself to blink once—then again.

Using his last bit of willpower, Brian heaved his entire body in a downward thrust. His shoulders drooped, and his head slumped to his chest. He gazed at his feet and blinked a few more times. The pounding in his head started subsiding as he looked away from the ink-drawn eyes. He wiggled his toes, ecstatic to see his shiny black boots planted on the fluffy, white flooring.

He remembered the ceiling pressing down on him. A claustrophobic feeling seized him. He instantly crouched, and his stiffened leg muscles complained. He tipped his head to look up, and his tight neck added its protest. To his surprise, he found that the ceiling hadn't come any closer. His ink-drawn twin still lingered high above on the vaulted ceiling. The duplicate still kept perfect timing with his movement, but the rendering seemed less captivating than it had a moment before. *Did I just imagine all of that?*

Brian's gaze went to his crew, fanned down the hall. They all stood perfectly still, staring up at the ceiling. He moved to Callie's side but didn't attract anyone's attention. Callie continued gawking up. She didn't blink or regard him whatsoever. Her eyes stayed fixed on the ceiling.

"Stop looking at the ceiling," Brian said.

"What?" Callie whispered.

"Stop looking at the ceiling," Brian repeated.

"What's the matter?" Callie blinked and looked down to regard him. "Don't you like the ceiling? I thought you did. You know, I think you're right. It must be a holographic program of some sort. It's breathtaking . . . It's like me, but better somehow."

"No, I don't like it." Brian glanced at the others. They still stared up at their ink-drawn selves. "All of you need to stop looking at the ceiling."

Everyone's gazes fell, and they gaped at him.

"What's the matter with it?" Zella's snappy tone returned. Her line of vision drifted back up. "I think it's magnificent."

"Something's not right with it," Brian said. "I don't trust it. My drawing blinked."

"So?" Zella huffed without looking back down. "They move when we do. We've already established that."

"It blinked, but I didn't." Brian tried driving the point home.

Derek stared at him with a cocked brow. "Maybe you're mistaken."

"I don't know." Callie began fidgeting with her sleeve's buttons. "Maybe there could be something off with the ceiling."

Derek drummed his fingers together. "I agree that the ceiling is weird, but it's also pretty neat. So far, my drawing has done only the same things I have. We have to get a copy of the program before we leave. Then we can install it on our ship. Another point for the station—cool software!" Derek grinned and motioned from himself to Callie as if creating an alliance.

She folded her arms and turned away from him.

"Yeah," Sivien added. "Maybe it's just some weird software they make nowadays."

"Well, my drawing hasn't done anything odd." Zella played with the end of her tail. She still stared up at the ceiling. "I'd love to have this installed on our ship, too, Derek."

"Look." Brian tried rubbing residual stiffness from his neck. "I don't want this program on our ship's mainframe. It feels off. A moment ago, all of you were all staring at the ceiling like you'd lost your senses. And I could swear something weird happened while I was—"

"Well, I like it!" Zella snapped. She glared at Brian. Her stern expression quickly melted away as she looked back up. She turned to expose more of her curves. "I've never looked so good! I don't even mind that it's just a drawing. I look superb."

Sivien eyeballed Brian. "Maybe it was just a trick of your imagination. The drawings haven't done anything other than what we have, at least not that anyone else has noticed."

Brian looked at Callie, hoping for some backup.

"I'm sorry." Callie shrugged. "I haven't seen any of them do anything besides what we have, either. I might not like this place, but so far, nothing's wrong."

Brian knew his argument lacked a substantial base. Callie happened to be the only one who even somewhat agreed with him. She always held more caution, but even she couldn't back him up.

"You know," Derek said, chuckling awkwardly, "it's unsettling that we haven't run into any of the station's crew members, and this place is so isolating. It's understandable if your imagination ran off with you. I'm surprised mine hasn't done that yet."

"I guess it could have been my imagination." Brian sighed, wanting nothing more than to change the subject. "Callie, just take us to the next elevator."

Callie looked at her sleeve's projection. "We need to turn left at the third intersection. The elevator is just a little way from there." She took the lead once again.

"Let's at least not let the ceiling be a distraction," Brian said, using his most authoritative tone.

An uncomfortable silence fell on the crew as they progressed through the hall. Brian shot untrusting glances at the odd spectacle looming overhead. He tried to ignore the captivating visual display but caught himself occasionally staring anyway. The others stole glances at it, too—everyone except for Zella. She rarely looked away. As they passed through the first intersection, the ink images continued keeping in sync.

Brian's ongoing inspection of the ceiling didn't uncover anything else that seemed out of place. *Maybe it was just my imagination.* However, the residual tiredness in his legs and stiffness in his neck claimed otherwise.

As time wore on, Brian's stomach began growling, pulling some of his attention away from the rendered drawings on the ceiling. The sweet hint of edible delights lingering in the air made him hungry.

"You know," Derek said, interrupting the silence. "I can smell cooking on this floor, too. It's not meat, though. It smells sweet . . . sweet like some sort of dessert."

Zella's ears perked at the comment. "Ooh, like what?" She purred, and eagerness flashed in her eyes.

"Don't talk about food, Derek," Sivien grabbed his stomach. "I'm already hungry."

"Hear me out." Derek spread his arms out wide and wiggled his fingers as though he conjured magic.

"Here we go." Sivien sighed.

Derek paused for dramatic emphasis. "The fusion of apples, brown sugar, and cinnamon all mixed together to make—legendary apple pie!" He snapped his fingers and took a half-bow.

"Oh, good grief!" Callie rolled her eyes.

Derek began tailing her. "Have you ever had apple pie, Callie? I've had it once. Homemade, too. It's *way* better from scratch than the synthesized crap you can get from the replicators! It's to die for." He stared off into space dreamily.

Zella moved closer to Derek. "I've never had apple pie. What's it like?" Her ears stood on end.

"WHAT?" Derek's brows jumped. "Well, you're missing out, then."

Callie slowed her pace. "I've had apple pie before. It wasn't that great. It was dry and tasteless. It was more like eating mouthfuls of desert sand."

Hurt washed over Derek's face. "Was the one you tried made from scratch?"

"I don't know. Maybe," Callie replied. "I didn't think to ask."

"It couldn't have been made from scratch." Derek turned back to Zella. "You have to try it from scratch. The crust! The buttery, flaky crust! Maybe I can find a recipe after we get back to base and make it for you."

Zella's eyes sparkled, and she nodded eagerly.

With another eye roll, Callie sighed and quickened her pace.

As Derek continued his glee-filled rant about apple pie to Zella, Brian thought about the dessert for a moment. He remembered eating a piece or two in his lifetime, but never one from scratch. It seemed like a rather mediocre dish, in his opinion. The sweet scent lingering in the air shifted his thoughts to a more exquisite dessert. A delicacy that his mother made on rare and festive occasions.

Cinnamon rolls.

The memory of warm, fresh-baked cinnamon-swirled pastries drifted in. Brian thought back to his first encounter with them. He vividly remembered the dining area in the quarters where he grew up. His mother knew how to use the food replicator's actual cook setting. It took a few failed attempts, but he would forever remember his mother's beaming smile as she set a small plate down in front of him. The single cinnamon roll sat, waiting just for him. Steam escaped its fluffy crust as Brian's mother drizzled a minuscule amount of icing on top. She looked up from her task long enough to flash him a loving wink. The heat radiating from the bread made the sugary goo melt down its sides.

Brian's mouth watered. He closed his eyes and breathed in the sweet scent in the hall. His stomach growled again. Derek still chatted Zella's ear off about apple pie, and Brian tried to ignore his hunger pains. The static in his earpiece increased, and the lanterns flickered faintly.

Derek's apple pie rant abruptly ended. The crew looked at the lanterns on the walls.

The lights flickered again.

Brian's footfalls slowed even more.

The lights cut out altogether.

Chapter 14

Brian stood still in the darkened hall. The green glow from the holographic projection hovering next to Callie's sleeve cast long shadows across his colleagues. The rest of the crew slowed to a stop.

"Callie?" Brian asked for a report.

She worked with her device. More green-tinged shadows swayed and danced across the crew and the walls. "It looks like some sort of power shift. It should be over soon."

"A power shift?" Sivien scoffed. "What exactly is that?"

"I don't know," Callie replied. "All I know is that it's a blackout. It appears that energy is being reverted to this section from somewhere else. Hopefully, it will only take a few minutes."

"I suddenly wish we'd worn our breathing suits." Sivien chuckled nervously. "If the life-support system fails, we're all dead."

"Oh, that's a downer." Derek shuddered. "That's not reassuring at all. As if watching Little-G glowing in the dark didn't give me the creeps enough already, the idea of dying in here sure does. Don't get me wrong— I'm not afraid of death, per se, but I am afraid of outliving everyone else. I'd get awfully lonely. It sounds like a terrible way to go!"

Sivien cocked a brow. The action cast even more shadows across his scaly face. "You sure you'd be the last one alive?" He gave a wink.

"I was," Derek tapped his finger on his bottom lip, "until you said that just now."

Callie shifted her weight. "Unless the life support fails, we'll be fine. This station has the lighting and the environmental controls on two different systems."

"Which means the odds of us dying here are slimmer," Brian added.

Derek cleared his throat. "The odds are fewer, but not zero."

"Well, we'll just have to continue being outliers." Sivien's widening grin multiplied the shadows on his face.

Derek cringed. "I'm sorry, but Little-G's lighting sure makes your smile *way* creepy in the dark." He shuddered.

Sivien's grin faded.

"Callie," Brian said, "what about the lifts? Will they still work?"

"Um . . . I believe so." Callie interacted with her sleeve. "It looks like the elevators are on a separate system from the lighting as well."

"Let's keep moving, then." Brian motioned toward the unventured corridor.

Instead of following orders, Callie wrung her hands and glanced around.

Brian slowly tipped his head toward her, waiting for her to get going, but she didn't budge. He raised a brow, and she sheepishly turned away. Wanting to get this ordeal over and done with, he broke down. "What is it?"

Callie fidgeted with her sleeve, and her eyes darted back and forth across the darkness. The green-tinted shadows continued casting their eerie hue. She leaned in. "Can we wait until the lights come back on?" she whispered.

"What?" The idea of Callie being afraid of the dark blindsided Brian. They accessed the deepest recesses of space for a living. "Um, no. We need to keep moving."

She shrank.

With all eyes on them, Brian waited for Callie to show the way. She hung her head and set off into the darkness. Sivien gave Zella a nudge. With a blue spark from her shield and minimal fuss, they continued through the maze of corridors. A green glow bounced off the encroaching gloom. Callie double-checked her scans now and again.

Thoughts of the ink-drawn duplicates looming on the ceiling weighed on Brian's mind. The idea of them lingering in the shadows high above made his skin crawl. He imagined them gazing down on his crew from their lofty perches. The more he thought about it, the more he could swear he felt the heaviness of their stares. A cold sweat pricked his skin as the memory of staring into his ink-twin's eyes replayed in his mind. He tugged at his collar. The ceiling felt like it pressed down on him again as he remembered the vast expanse of the syrupy, black pools. Goosebumps lifted the hairs on the back of his neck.

The ever-present static in the background of his earpiece increased, and the shadows creeping around Callie's sleeve made it seem like the darkness was crawling. Hushed whispers snuck through the crackling in his earpiece, and he cued in on the faint disturbances. The chattering suddenly bled into his other ear as though it didn't come from the receiver at all. He searched the hall and his crew in the murky darkness, but he couldn't find the origins of the chattering.

The faint whisperings grew.

Brian's steps slowed. "Can any of you hear that?"

The chattering stopped.

Callie, Sivien, and Derek shot glances at each other. Zella didn't seem to notice that Brian had asked a question at all. She just kept twirling the end of her tail.

"Hear what?" Derek asked.

"Um . . . whispering." Brian's cheeks flushed hot. "I can hear someone whispering."

His comrades shared confused glances.

Sivien moved to Brian's side. "No one's been whispering," he said in a hushed tone.

Brian stared up at him. "Are you sure?"

"I'm pretty sure," Sivien said with a nervous chuckle. "I think we would have noticed."

Brian wiped his clammy forehead. Sivien gave him a brotherly clap on the shoulder that flicked faint sparks of blue. Callie continued leading the way. As time slipped by, Brian's attention wandered back to the ceiling overhead. The uncomfortable feeling of being watched resurfaced. Within seconds, the hushed chattering filled the green-tinged gloom of the hall again. He searched his crew and the darkness again, but he still couldn't find the source.

The whispers suddenly increased and started coming from everywhere. Brian tugged at his collar. The entire hall felt like it was caving in on him. His breaths quickened as he suffocated under its weight. He glanced back up at Sivien. "Seriously, you can't hear that?"

Sivien peered down. The dingy green shadows pitching across his face made Brian regret his inquiry.

"I'm sorry." Sivien's forked tongue slipped through his lips. "I still don't hear anything."

The chattering continued to lace the hall, and individual voices became more distinct. Brian's heart beat quicker. No matter how hard he listened, he couldn't make out any particular words. He tugged at his collar again and sank into a slight crouch, wanting to get out from underneath the ceiling somehow. He shut his eyes, wishing the lights would reroute quicker. He just wanted everything to hurry up. In a last effort to keep the incoherent disturbances out, he covered his ears, but the whispers continued prodding at him from all sides.

"Brian!" Callie snapped him from his thoughts.

The inescapable whispers instantly vanished again.

"Where are you going?" Callie pressed.

Brian paused and lowered his hands from his ears. Glancing around the darkened hall, he realized he had passed Callie. "No . . . nowhere." The conviction of the statement wavered with his voice. He rubbed the back of his neck, trying to shake off his nerves as he stood there, waiting for his crew to catch up.

Even in the dim lighting, Brian could make out the concern etched on Callie's features as she stepped past him to retake the lead. She fidgeted with the buttons on her sleeve even more.

"And here I thought you knew the way for a minute." Derek smiled as he passed Brian too. "That definitely *would* have been odd."

"Yeah, I don't know the way, Derek." Brian rejoined the party at its rear. Thoughts of the ceiling kept creeping back in. Faint whispers fused with the white static in Brian's earpiece. His thoughts circled back to them, no matter how hard he tried to push them from his mind.

The lights suddenly flickered back on.

The hidden whispers faded from Brian's earpiece entirely, but the static remained. He breathed a sigh of relief.

"Did Callie call it, or what?" Derek asked. "I'm so glad those ugly lanterns are back on!"

Zella scowled at him, and Callie gave a slight nod.

Brian glanced up to check the ceiling, not quite sure what to expect. His imagination seemed to keep running away with him. The antique paper remained as it had been earlier—a creamy, beige backdrop with an ink-drawn work of art detailed on its surface. Despite himself, Brian kept stealing glances up at it. The crew's drawings still mirrored every move they made, from what he could tell. His comrades gazed up every once in a while, too. Zella's growing enthrallment with her drawn duplicate made him increasingly uneasy.

Callie slowed and approached a door. "This should be the elevator."

The titanic metallic slab slid open.

Callie observed the quaint room as she entered. Brian and Derek followed close behind. Sivien went to step inside, but he hesitated and glanced back at Zella. She didn't make any sort of move toward the lift. She just stood there in the hall, staring up at the ceiling. Her fingers frantically twirled the fur on the end of her tail.

"Zella, are you coming?" Sivien gestured for her to enter the lift.

She took a few shuffling steps toward the entrance but stopped.

"Zella?" Sivien prodded again with all the softness of an overgrown lizard.

"I DON'T WANT TO LEAVE HER!" Zella threw her arms into the air and reached for the ceiling. "She's so beautiful! I can't leave her. I *won't* leave her!"

Derek's brows jumped. "What the flib-jib?"

Brian stared at Zella in disbelief. He shifted his gaze to Sivien. *"What's the matter with her?"* he signed.

Sivien's hands flew into action. *"I don't know. She almost ripped my head off about the tail thing, and now this. This isn't normal."*

Zella kept reaching toward the ceiling, lifting up on her toes.

"I don't know what's gotten into her," Sivien added.

Brian peered up at the ceiling in the lift, and his ink duplicate stared down at him. He formulated a quick plan but hated himself for it. "Zella, we're not leaving her behind. She can come with us."

Zella's arms dropped a little, and she looked at Brian. "Really?"

"Really." Brian gestured for her to check the ceiling in the lift.

As Zella stepped closer to the threshold, she cast a heated glare at Sivien's outstretched hand. He raised both hands defensively and backed up into the lift. She played with the end of her tail and resumed her love-lust stare at the ceiling. With everyone in the elevator, the door slid closed.

Shaking his head, Sivien shrugged at Brian.

Not quite sure what to do himself, Brian shrugged back and turned to Callie. "I guess we need the level we're headed to."

Callie opened her mouth to answer, but the instant fluttering in Brian's stomach told him they had begun moving between levels without her saying a word.

Callie glanced up at the ceiling. "I really don't like this place." She fidgeted with her sleeve.

"We're almost done. We'll be headed back to our ship soon," Brian said. "Something *is* off with this station. We should probably do our best to get what we need and get out of here."

Zella started humming softly. The tune drifted through the lift like a gentle, forlorn breeze.

Brian turned to her. "Don't look at the ceiling anymore," he firmly instructed.

Zella's gaze dropped to Brian. She cocked her head at an unnatural angle and scowled. "Are you *ordering* me to stop looking at the ceiling, *Captain?*" She extended a retractable claw and continued twirling her tail's end.

Brian stood straighter and squared his shoulders. "Yes, Zella. It's an order."

A flash of rage streaked across Zella's feline features. Her eyes narrowed. "Okay. Whatever you say, *Captain.*" Her icy tone matched her stare.

"Thank you." Brian tried softening his order.

Zella gave a leering smile.

Derek raised his finger as though he wanted to add something, but Brian shot him a *not right now* look. Derek lowered his hand without saying a word. The churn in Brian's stomach predicted the end of the brief elevator ride. The crew stood in utter silence as the fluttering faded and the door slid open. They shuffled into the new hall. Brian checked the ceiling, hoping to see chandeliers again. To his dismay, the ink doppelgängers and the drawn hallway were still there.

"Why does everything have to look annoyingly the same?" Callie asked.

"New question," Derek interjected. "Did we actually move anywhere?"

"That's actually a good question," Sivien piped in.

Callie turned to her sleeve for answers, and the projected images glitched again. "AH! For the love." She glanced at Derek.

Derek winced and turned away.

Callie smacked the device, and the image unjammed. "And . . . yes. It's the right floor." She set a brisk pace.

"Aye, the quicker we go, the quicker we can get out of here." Derek started huffing from exertion as he matched her speed. "Smart move, girl!"

Callie waved Derek's comment away and guided the crew straight through a four-way. In time, they approached another. She veered to the right of the hall. As she rounded the corner, she let out an ear-piercing shriek and scurried back. She shuffled against the wall, and her eyes darted wildly, searching the intersection's ceiling. She raised her sleeve, aiming Little-G's weaponry at an unseen adversary.

"What happened?" Brian hurried to Callie's side.

She tried backing up even more but only raised onto her toes as though she were trying to meld with the very wall. Her breaths came in short, shallow puffs, and the color drained from her face. Her fingers hovered over her sleeve's arsenal, ready to discharge. She stared wide-eyed at the ceiling.

"What is it?" Brian searched the intersection's ceiling. He unholstered his own weapon.

Chapter 15

The rest of the crew took up a strategic position in the hall. Brian edged past Callie, putting himself between her and the new corridor. He readied his gun and slowly peeked around the corner. He found nothing but an empty hall.

"I . . . I thought I saw something." Callie continued backing against the wall. She pointed her sleeve up at the intersection and fiddled with some of its buttons. "On the ceiling!"

Brian inspected the empty hallway. He found only the beige wallpaper with the ink-drawn replication on its surface. "I can't find anything out of place. What exactly did you see?"

"Are you sure it wasn't just your own drawing?" Derek asked.

"No!" Callie scowled at him. "It was something else. It was something big moving farther down the hall."

"Hello?" Brian called out. The rest of the crew held their positions as Brian continued investigating the new hall's ceiling. He spent several minutes examining it, but he found nothing there and nothing out of place. "I just don't see anything there."

Callie eased away from the wall. "You don't see anything? Something was there. I saw it. I looked down at Little-G to check our location. When I looked up again, it was there. It darted across the ceiling. Seriously, you don't see anything?" She leaned around the corner and peeked at the new hall from behind Brian.

"Did you see anything in the real hall?" Brian began lowering his weapon.

"No." Callie wrung her hands. "Just on the ceiling."

"Was it just movement, or did you see a shape or person?" Brian pressed. "Anything you could identify?"

"I guess it could have been about the size of a humanoid." Callie's gaze dropped to the floor. "I don't know. I caught only a glimpse of it."

"Maybe it was just her imagination, too." Derek grinned.

"Maybe it was, maybe it wasn't." Brian shot Derek another *that's not helping* look, and confusion replaced Derek's smile. "I *do* think this place has an effect on people, though."

Brian gazed at Zella. She stared in the crew's general direction but didn't focus on anyone or anything. Derek looked at her too. His brows furrowed as though he had just found out about a problem. Sivien's lowered his gaze to the floor.

"I'm not ready to discount whether Callie saw anything, but we do need to stay focused." Brian moved farther into the new corridor and reholstered his weapon. "Let's get to the storage room. Then we can get the fuel back to our ship. I'm growing tired of this bizarre station."

Callie shuffled around the corner, tailing Brian. The rest of the crew trickled after.

"You believe me, don't you?" Callie kept her eyes glued to the ceiling.

Brian slowed. "Try not to worry about it. We're so close to getting out of here. Soon it will all be a ridiculous memory."

Callie moved ahead, retaking the lead, but stopped in her tracks. "I . . . I can't go first. I just can't do it." She backed up against the wall.

Sivien wrinkled his nose. "What?"

Callie shuffled in place against the wall. "I . . . I don't want to go first. I *can't* go first. Can't someone else do it? I can still give directions. I just don't want to go first. It's really only a few more doors from here." She motioned down the hall.

Zella perked up, and her ears stood on end. "I can do it."

"NO," Brian said with more force than he meant.

Zella's expression soured.

"I mean . . ." Brian softened his tone. "I need Sivien to go first."

"Why him?" Zella shot Sivien a death glare. "He's not the fastest, and he has no stealth. He's only big and strong."

"Oh, ouch." Derek grimaced. "That's got to bruise the ol' pride hole."

Genuine hurt settled on Sivien's scaled features.

Brian considered Zella's recent behavior and calculated a persuasive angle. "That's true."

Sivien's mouth fell open. "Hey, even though I'm not human, I still have feelings."

Slightly raising his hand to hush his friend, Brian continued, "I need you in back, just in case anything happens from behind. We need greatness at the helm of our exit strategy, and, Zella, you're the best we've got." Considering her recent, odd behavior, he didn't feel too bad for the slight manipulation tactic he had just pulled.

Zella held her head high and shuffled to the back with no more fuss. The flattery seemed to work.

Sivien meandered to the front. "Where to?" he mumbled.

"Six doors down, on the right." Callie slowly peeled herself from the wall.

Sivien took the lead.

"It's okay," Derek chimed in. A few sparks flew from Callie's shield as he gave her an awkward pat on the shoulder. "Sivien's the biggest and strongest. He can take out any imaginary things that show up in the ceiling from here on out. Don't you even worry about it!"

Callie glared at him.

They passed a few doors, and Brian searched the ceiling for anything out of place, but nothing grabbed his attention. Their ink drawings continued to keep perfect timing with their every move as they progressed down the otherwise bland corridor. Callie stared at her sleeve's projection.

"Slow down." Callie manipulated the image. "We're getting close."

The crew approached one door in particular that stood out from the others, and their pace slowed even more. It looked about the same size as the door of the first storage room.

Sivien came to a stop a few yards away and eyed the ebony barrier. "Is this the one? I think it's the one. Unless I counted wrong." He waited for Callie's confirmation.

Callie slunk up behind him, using him as a shield against whatever might lie beyond the door. She double-checked the three-dimensional image hovering next to her arm. "I believe so. Our red dots are standing in front of the storage room's door. This has got to be the one." She rose onto her tiptoes and peeked around Sivien's bulk a little more.

Brian glanced across his crew, sensing no one wanted to be first through the door; even he didn't want to go first. The station possessed a knack for inspiring uncomfortable feelings. He trudged forward. As he stepped up to the oversized barrier, it started sliding open on cue. The scene beyond the door stole his momentum. His mouth fell open as he crossed the threshold. His heavy boots made contact with hard, metal flooring once again, and he stared at the room. The crew's pace slowed as they trickled out around him.

Everyone came to a stop.

"What the flib happened in here?" Derek balked.

"Isn't that the question of the last twenty-four-hour time increment?" Callie shadowed Sivien.

"The questions of the day are sure piling up." Brian glanced across the storage room. For the most part, it matched the first one they encountered, but the size of this room put the other to shame. Many containers were scattered and overturned on their sides, making the place look like a disorganized nightmare.

"Wow, this place is trashed." Sivien gazed at the room. "I sure hope we can find some fuel in here."

Brian sighed heavily. "I sure hope so, too."

"What do you think happened?" Derek scratched his head and lowered his goggles to his eyes.

Brian squinted as he assessed the place. "Scavengers, possibly."

"How could scavengers gain access this far into the station?" Sivien asked.

"I don't know." Brian smoothed his goatee. "That's a great question."

"I'm still not picking up any other signs of life on my scans." Callie inspected her sleeve's projection. "Obviously, someone has been here, though. From the look of things, maybe we should be glad they left."

Derek pointed to the far right corner of the room. "The computer is in the same place."

Brian looked. Even the computer took up more space on the walls than the last one had. His gaze shot to the ceiling. He found antique paper in this room too, but the room's vaulted height went impressively higher. Each of their ink duplicates hovered around the drawn entrance, just like his crew members were positioned in the actual room. He breathed a little easier at having more distance between them and their ink images. He went back to observing the rest of the scene, and his fraction of ease quickly faded.

Derek drummed his fingers on his lips. He squinted one eye and wrinkled his nose. "I wonder if there's any food in here. I could use a replenishment of my supplies." He rubbed his hands together as a grin formed.

"Food? Have you lost your mind?" Sivien looked at him.

"Aye." Derek winked and shrugged. "It's not like we have a ton of supplies on board our ship."

Sivien cocked a brow and glanced around. He lifted a claw to his scaly chin, looking like he suddenly pondered scavenging for food too.

"Stay on task," Brian insisted. "Callie, Derek. Check the computer. See if you can find the fuel and the parts we need. If there's an entry log you can access, try to find out what in the cosmos happened here."

Derek headed toward the computer, but Callie looked back at the door and watched it finish closing behind them.

"Everything will be okay. Let's hurry so we can get out of here." Brian nodded toward Derek, encouraging Callie to follow.

Callie hung her head and stood there for a moment. With a sigh, she turned and followed Derek's lead. Brian wandered toward the nearest aisle and took in more of the chaos. He searched for clues left behind by the room's previous occupants that would explain why the place had been left in such disarray. Sivien and Zella tailed him, surveying the conditions as well.

Zeroing in on the nearest top-sided container, Brian slowed, then stopped. He crouched in front of the lidless, metallic box and peered inside, but the shadowy innards didn't disclose any of the room's secrets. He waved a hand across the opening, barely breaching the interior. "Its lights don't work, and it's empty." His voice bounced off the bare metal. He stood and slowly circled the container but couldn't find any explanation for its peculiar resting place. Sivien stepped next to Brian, drawing him from his thoughts.

"You really think it's scavengers?" Sivien folded his arms across his massive chest.

"Maybe." Brian glanced around the room. "It's hard to tell."

"I think I've found something." Callie's voice chirped in Brian's receiver.

Brian signaled to Sivien and Zella, and they followed him. They weaved their way through the scattered containers that dotted the receiving area around the door. At the computer, Callie's legs dangled over the edge as she interacted with its mainframe. Derek had climbed all the way up and slumped over a portion of the console nearby. His chin rested on one hand, and he held a piece of jerky in the other. The smacking of his lips made his head bob up and down.

"What did you find?" Brian asked.

"Well, I've found bits and pieces of information," Callie said. "I think adding them all together could tell us some things. I can't promise the accuracy of the synthesized data, though."

Derek perked up. "Do tell, Callie. I love a great ghost story." He tore off another bite, and the sound of his loud chewing filled the air.

"There are *NO* ghosts, Derek!" Zella suddenly blew a cork. She covered her ears. "*AND*, stop chewing with your mouth open. It's *DISGUSTING!*"

Derek's jaw dropped. A big glob of chewed jerky fell to the front of his mouth as he stared at her, wide-eyed.

Zella brought a hand away from her ear and listened. "Thank you, you revolting glutton!" She lowered her other hand.

Everyone stared at her.

"Dang, Zella." Sivien cringed. "That's overly harsh."

"That's totally uncalled for," Brian added.

"It's *his* own fault." Zella glared at Derek. "Always so consumed with food. He's disgusting!"

Brian stared at her. "That's *completely* out of line."

Derek swallowed hard and put the uneaten portion of jerky back into his satchel. "I'll just save the rest for later. It's okay. I didn't know I was bothering anyone."

Brian thought back on all the years they had spent together as a crew. This was the first time Zella had ever become agitated with Derek's eating habits. Usually, she shared in his food shenanigans, probably due to her feline biology more than anything else.

Zella smiled smugly as she continued glaring at Derek. She looked rather pleased with herself for making him put his snack away. Sivien and Callie exchanged glances with each other, and Brian felt the growing pressure of his command. Zella's conduct kept getting more out of hand.

With a sigh, Brian cleared his throat. "Zella, consider yourself verbally reprimanded."

"WHAT?" Zella placed both hands on the curves of her hips.

"You need to treat Derek with more consideration and respect. That kind of outburst at another crew member won't be tolerated." Brian waited for Zella's reaction. His training led him to respond based on how a situation played out. *If* things escalated, *then* he would up his game to take care of it.

Zella narrowed her eyes, locking her stare on Brian. She folded her arms. "Fine." Her cold tone spat ice daggers at him, but she didn't further an argument.

Brian looked up at Callie. "Finish your report." He cast a watchful gaze back at Zella. She pinned her ears and furiously twirled the fur of her tail with a claw. He peered back up at Callie.

"Um . . ." Callie's eyes darted from Zella to Brian. She wrung her hands and turned back to the computer. "Obviously, someone else accessed the storage room before us."

"How long ago?" Brian asked. "Did we just miss them?"

Callie pressed a few more buttons. "I can't tell. I still can't find the stellar date. The computer might have dazzling programs, but it seems like it only gives me information that it wants to, not the information I ask for."

"Everything on this station is odd." Brian rubbed the back of his neck. "Tell me what you *did* find."

"It seems as though a different crew was in the middle of loading supplies, and then they just stopped," Callie replied. "That's all I could find. They just stopped."

Sivien glanced across the room. "That's what all this mess is?"

"Any surveillance footage?" Brian pressed.

Callie glanced up at the room's ceiling. "I couldn't find any in the computer logs, and judging by the ceiling, surveillance isn't a feature the engineers included in the station's designs."

Derek gasped. "*What!* No surveillance?"

Brian raised a hand to quiet him. "What about fuel? Is there any still here?"

"That's where things start looking up," Callie said. "It appears there is still fuel in many of the containers left on the shelves."

"Fuel?" Sivien's face brightened, and he clapped his claws together. "YES!"

"YES!" Derek joined Sivien with more whoops.

"It will probably take a little time to round up the platforms," Callie continued over the dissipating cheers. "We will need to clear a pathway so we can load them, but we should be able to find enough fuel to get us far away from this station."

"Where are the pickers?" Brian asked. "We'll need at least one to get the containers loaded onto the platforms."

Callie searched the three-dimensional image hovering over the computer. She pointed to the far left of the room. "Um, the closest one is down that aisle, and it's surrounded by fuel."

"That's convenient," Brian said. "What about parts?"

"I haven't found them yet," Callie answered.

"Well, you two stay here and keep working with the computer. Try to find something that Derek can dissect into parts for our ship." Brian turned to Zella and Sivien. "We'll head down the aisle and start getting the fuel loaded."

Callie ran a finger along the computer's edge. She glanced down at Brian sheepishly, then quickly looked away.

Brian moved closer. "Look, Derek's going to be with you the entire time. You won't be alone."

Callie looked over at Derek. He smiled at her, and her head drooped.

"You'll be okay." Brian patted one of her dangling feet, making it spark and sway. "I promise."

"I'll take good care of you." Derek's smile widened. "Don't you even worry about it."

Brian glanced at Zella. She still twirled her tail. At some point, she began humming to herself again. He sighed. "We'll start by clearing the aisle with the picker. You and Derek can send platforms over to us so we can load them with fuel."

Callie nodded.

"Aye." Derek half-saluted. "We've got this."

Chapter 16

Brian started toward the aisle that Callie had indicated.

Sivien joined him but turned around and walked backward. "Come on, Zella."

Brian's pace slowed, and he glanced back as well.

Zella scowled and dropped her tail but hurried to tag along.

They crossed the receiving area and neared the head of the aisle. Brian gazed up at giant statues standing like mammoth-sized guardians at the end of each row. It looked like their purpose was to ward off unwelcome guests, as though they were the defenders of this vast treasury. Passing one of the massive, metallic feet, Brian and his colleagues rounded the corner of an aisle. In the distance, a large machine rested its lifting arm on one of the higher shelves. The picker's body tipped at an odd angle, leaving one of the rear tires raised in the air. The large vehicle took up a good portion of the aisle.

"The station has been so empty." Sivien looked around. "I wondered why they left in such a hurry."

"Whatever the reason was," Brian replied, "leaving in a hurry is never a good sign."

"I'll race you to the picker," Zella interrupted. Her sharp teeth peeked over her bottom lip as a sly smile spread across her furry face.

Sivien's face scrunched to one side in sheer confusion. "What?"

Brian stared at Zella, dumbfounded.

"I'll give you a head start." She sank into a pounce-ready stance, shifting her weight from one foot to the other.

Sivien's pace slowed, and he stood a little taller. He cocked his eyebrow and gazed down at her. "You'd still lose."

"A race might *not* be the best idea right now," Brian chimed in.

Sivien eyeballed Zella.

"We should probably stay within close proximity to each other." Brian glanced around at the aisle's state of disrepair. "We don't know —"

Sivien burst into a full sprint down the aisle. "First one to the picker wins!"

"Hey!" Brian yelled after him, but it didn't do any good. He rubbed the back of his neck.

Zella sank deeper into her squat and sat on the back of her heels. She picked at her nails. With a sigh, Brian started jogging. He knew racing might not be the smartest move, but he also didn't want to get left behind. He picked up his speed. Soon, Sivien had made it a quarter of the way to the picker, and Brian wondered how far Zella would let them go before she joined the fray. Pushing himself a little harder, he stole a glance back at her. She still sat in the same place, extending and retracting her claws while she nonchalantly opened and closed her hand. Knowing the damage her shredders could cause made him shudder. He tried to think of something else.

Before too long, Sivien approached the halfway point, gaining a good lead ahead of the others. Brian shifted into an all-out sprint to close the growing gap. It took him a while longer, but he began nearing the midway mark himself. A sudden blur of fur whizzed past him, knocking some momentum out of his stride. He tried salvaging his speed, but watching Zella zip toward Sivien stole his concentration. Her sprightliness still gave her a fighting chance to take first place. Instead of catching up, Brian worked on not being left too far behind.

Sivien and Zella dashed through the toppled containers spewed along the aisle. Her quick, sleek movements contrasted with his bulky bumble around the debris, helping her gain more ground. A smile found its way to Brian's lips as he watched his two crew members interacting the way they usually did, but a bitter rumble in his stomach made him grab his side. The burn that accompanied the growl made him feel queasy. He slowed his speed and watched Sivien and Zella pull farther ahead.

As the race continued, Brian's hunger pains calmed, and his smile returned. With Zella interacting like normal, it made things seem right, but in the back of his mind, he wondered how long it would last. He believed the key to permanently restoring Zella to her senses lay in getting her back to their ship.

Sivien came within range of the picker. Just when Zella looked like she might lose after all, she suddenly leaped forward and landed on all fours. All of her limbs began working in unison, creating an unconventional gallop. The unusual stance shot Zella toward Sivien like a bolt of lightning.

Brian's efforts to catch up fizzled out as he watched Zella streak down the aisle. She vaulted onto Sivien's shoulder and launched off him, breaking his momentum. Somersaulting in midair, she landed on the front of a container on the second shelf up. She zipped across its surface so fast that she defied the station's artificial gravity. The metallic boxes became like another floor to her.

Sivien, who had somewhat recovered his momentum, bolted toward the picker at a dead sprint. He came within a few yards of the machine. Meanwhile, Zella sprang from the containers and landed on the picker's tilted top. A high-pitched squeal erupted as she slid to a full stop. She moved to the machine's edge and peeked over its side.

Sivien jogged up and tagged the picker's large wheel.

Zella started laughing.

Sivien folded his arms over his massive, heaving chest. "And where . . . did you learn . . . how to do that?"

Zella's chest rose and fell with equal speed. "From myself . . . and just now." She swung herself through the cockpit's glassless window and powered the machine up.

Sivien reluctantly meandered behind the picker and began spotting her. Gears ground as Zella shimmied the machine's lifting arm out from its snagged spot on the shelf. All four wheels touched down again.

Brian finally got to the picker himself. His breathing slowed while he began cooling down. He moved to the opposite side of Sivien and helped spot Zella. "Looks like you guys are figuring things out just fine," he called to Sivien over the hum of the picker's engine.

Sivien gave Brian a clawed thumbs-up. "It looks like whoever used the picker before got it stuck trying to lift too much at once. They were really in a hurry."

"I can't say I blame them." Brian glanced at the papered canopy high overhead.

Brian began inspecting the state of the picker a little more closely. At least the previous users hadn't left it damaged, and it seemed hefty enough to get the task done. Some bits of light streamed through the cockpit's top, catching his eye. He leaned over to get a better look and found several long tears in the metallic roof. Gauging by the angle of their trajectory and the loud squeal when Zella landed, he had a distinct impression that she had made them. She didn't just slide to a stop—she clawed her way to a stop.

Brian winced.

"Good news." Callie's voice came through Brian's staticky earpiece. "Whoever was here before left some loaded platforms behind. Not many, but some. They were in the back of the storage room, so I've programmed them to go to you. Let me know when you have the aisle cleared so I can bring them the rest of the way to the front."

Brian activated his comm. "I will. Thank you, Callie." He continued helping spot for Zella.

They worked together, moving the displaced containers spewed across the aisle. Once they stacked the containers a few high, they would start a new pile. The work went faster than Brian anticipated. The mess turned into several neat rows in almost no time. Soon, the loaded platforms Callie had mentioned arrived as well. As Zella finished her task, she maneuvered the picker behind the last stack of containers she had created.

Brian activated his transmitter. "Callie?"

"Yes, Brian," Callie chirped in his ear.

"Can you unseal the containers on the platforms?" he asked. "I want to make sure they have fuel inside before we bring them with us."

"Yes," came Callie's reply.

Brian moseyed toward the platforms with Sivien. Each of the hovering machines would fit only one container. As he and Sivien approached, hisses erupted from the lids as their seals broke. He stepped up to the nearest one. The platform pulsed bursts of hot air onto his shins as it worked hard to float in the air.

"I found only four loaded containers that weren't capsized or in some kind of disrepair." Callie's voice broke through the static again. "I've discovered more empty platforms that are prepped for loading, though. I've sent them to you from a different section in the storage room. Derek is creating a link between all of them so I can control them through Little-G. I should be able to program them to the elevator lifts and down to our ship with the new network."

"Aye! These here platforms will soon do our bidding. Mwahaha." Derek interrupted the transmission using a mad scientist's voice. Derek's fake, evil laugh subsided in Brian's earpiece.

"That's fantastic news." Brian pushed the container's lid open a crack. The lights inside turned on. A wispy fog wafted around two large fuel cells. He lowered the top back down with care and looked at Sivien with a smile. "Well, there's fuel in this one!"

Sivien leaned toward the next container in the line. He lifted its lid and peered inside. "There's fuel in this one, too!" He flashed a bright smile that matched Brian's. He lowered the lid with a satisfactory nod and headed off to inspect another one.

"Once Derek finishes creating the network," Callie continued, "he and I are going to retrieve parts."

"You found parts?" Brian asked.

"Yes," Callie replied. "We found some parts that will work. If everything goes to plan, we should get back here at about the same time as you."

"Okay," Brian said, "sounds like a perfect plan."

"Well, it *is* one of mine," came Callie's voice.

Sivien lowered the lid of the next container. "This one has fuel as well." He scurried to the last one and peeked inside. He gave Brian a thumbs-up and eased the covering back down.

Brian pressed his transmitter again. "Hey, more good news. The containers on the platforms are full, so you can reseal them."

"That *is* good news!" Callie replied over the sound of the containers resealing. "I've calculated how many containers will fit in our holding bay. It can handle anywhere from eight to eleven. That's enough to be well prepared, even if we run into more *happy* little computer malfunctions. I've found enough loading platforms to do the job and have sent them to your section. They should be there any minute."

Brian glanced down the aisle in the direction where they had come in. A long, straight line of platforms glided toward them. "I can see them now. We should be done soon."

"See you when you get back up here," Callie's voice chimed again. "Over and out."

"Over and out." Brian looked up at the picker. Zella reclined in its cockpit, batting at a piece of hair. The unloaded platforms Callie had sent them came to a rest as they hit the end of their programming.

"Zella," Brian called to her, but she didn't respond. He activated his transmitter. "Zella."

She continued staring off into space.

Brian looked at Sivien.

"You got me," Sivien said with a shrug.

Brian waved his arms and climbed the first step to the picker's cab. He cupped his hands around his mouth. "ZELLA!"

Zella startled and looked down at him. An instant scowl formed on her face.

"Time to load," Brian said. "We need a few more containers."

Zella rolled her eyes, and she pounced on the cockpit's user panels with a slight huffiness in her movements. The machine's gears ground and protested under her care, which only increased her agitation.

"Don't break your new toy." Sivien moved to spot her again.

Her icy gaze fell on him.

"I'm only teasing." Sivien raised his hands in defense.

The picker groaned as more gears caught. Zella turned her murderous stare from Sivien to engage with the machine.

Sivien's shoulders drooped, and he moved back to his side to continue spotting.

Brian shook his head and moved to his own spot. Loading the containers went quickly, or maybe it just seemed that way. He occasionally checked the ceiling while they worked. Their ink selves still matched their every move. The duplicates loaded containers onto platforms in the illustrated storage room high above. It was nice to have them so far away.

Soon they placed the last metallic box on its respective transit.

"That's the last one." Sivien looked happy to be done.

"Time to head back up to the front," Brian said.

Zella maneuvered the picker to the side of the aisle. She shut the machine down, and it let out a loud, piston-releasing sigh. She climbed out the cab's window instead of exiting through its door. Leaping from the side of the bulky engine, she tucked into a sprightly front flip and landed on her feet.

The team started back down the long aisle toward the front of the storage room.

"How about another race?" Zella grinned at Sivien.

Sivien's expression instantly soured. "I don't think so."

Zella giggled and placed both hands over her heart, implying Sivien's reply had hurt.

At that moment, everything felt right in Brian's world.

As they journeyed, the faint static crackling in Brian's receiver increased, and he could swear he once again detected the quiet whispers embedded in the white noise. The chattering flooded over to his other ear, and the disturbances seemed like they came from everywhere. He searched his surroundings and found something stirring in the shadows behind one of the containers. He zeroed in on the area, and everything became a blur as he snuck closer to investigate.

A sudden burst of pain cracked across Brian's temple, and waves of misery pulsed through his entire skull. Cradling his head, he stopped in his tracks. The whispers vanished under the waves of pounding agony. Stumbling back, he peeked through his fingers to see what had hit him.

To Brian's surprise, he found himself standing beside one of the statue's feet at the end of the aisle. He rubbed his head and gazed up at the unfriendly-looking guardian—the culprit of his injury. "How did we get *here?*"

"What did you say?" Zella twiddled the end of her tail.

"How did we get back to the front of the storage room already?" Brian rubbed his temple and scowled at the colossal statue's foot.

"We walked." Sivien stood a few feet away from Zella. He stared at Brian. "We've been here for a while."

Brian stopped rubbing his head. "Seriously?"

Sivien glanced around sheepishly. "Yes."

Brian turned and peered down the aisle. Stacks of containers rested on both sides down to the loaded platforms. The machinery hovered in the middle of the row, waiting for more programming. The long trip back to the front of the storage room felt more like a blur than anything else—a short blur he couldn't remember.

Chapter 17

"Brian." Callie's voice chirped in his ear, igniting fresh waves of pain. "We found the parts that Derek needed down other aisles. We're collecting the last one right now. We shouldn't be too much longer."

Another bitter rumble clawed at the insides of Brian's stomach as the pounding in his head subsided. With a sigh, he touched his transmitter. "We're done loading fuel, and we're waiting for you up front."

"What are we going to do in the meantime?" Sivien asked.

"How about we take a little break?" Brian slid his pack from his shoulders.

"Really?" Sivien perked up.

Brian continued rubbing his head and looked around for a place to rest. "I don't know how long it will take for Callie and Derek to get back, but we could probably eat while we wait." He lowered his pack to the floor next to the statue's foot and sat down. He flipped the pack's leather flap open.

"A break would be nice. Right, Zella?" Sivien smiled at her.

Zella glared at him, and her ears flattened. "Yeah, I guess." She dropped her tail. Eyeballing the surrounding area, she sauntered over to one of the toppled containers. The opening revealed an empty, dark interior. She gave it a quick inspection and scaled its side. Plopping down, she dangled her feet over the opening's ledge.

Brian leaned against the statue at his back. He rested his head on its chilled surface as the pounding in his temple continued to abate. His gaze fell to the empty container Zella claimed as her own. The grim implications the abandoned capsule hinted at made him wish Callie and Derek would hurry. He didn't want whatever had happened to the room's previous occupants to happen to him and his crew.

Zella slipped off her pack and started rummaging through it. Sivien slung his own pack up next to her. She stopped picking through her supplies and glared at the leather-bound intruder, then down at Sivien. He went to swing himself up, but her piercing stare stopped him in his tracks. She slowly placed her hand on his pack and started inching it to the container's edge.

"Don't push it off, Zella." Sivien shook his head.

Zella paused and stared at him blankly. Then her eyes narrowed. In one swift move, she swiped Sivien's pack over the edge. Sivien grabbed at it as it fell, but the bag slipped through his grasp. It landed hard on the floor, spilling its contents everywhere. Zella held her icy gaze over Sivien while he knelt and started collecting his things.

"Sivien, you can sit next to me." Brian patted the floor.

"You won't push my stuff off anything, will you?" Sivien glared up at Zella.

Zella's ear twitched as she looked smugly down at him.

"No." Brian peered around. "I'm already on the floor. There's nothing to knock it off of."

Zella lazily opened a ration by peeling the silver packaging away. A yellow, crumbly-looking brick sat on the inside. She stretched out and lay down. One of her legs dangled from the container, swinging back and forth.

Sivien shot another glare up at Zella. "I guess there's not a whole lot of room up there, anyway." He gathered his pack into a heaping armful and moved to Brian. He tossed his things down and flopped beside them on the floor.

Brian gave Sivien a reassuring smile. Sivien forced a smile of his own as he tended to his mess on the floor. Brian turned to his pack and began rummaging through it. Pulling a ration out, he looked it over and peeled away the wrapper. As soon as the crumbly, yellow block touched the air, a thick aroma blasted him. He started coughing, and his eyes watered. A hint of honey accompanied the strong smell. The soft sweetness did its best to mellow out the ration's fumes, but it also failed miserably at the job.

Sivien laughed at Brian. Opening one of his rations, he started coughing as well. "Um . . . are we sure this stuff is still edible?"

Brian looked up at Zella, who had already begun eating, and he shrugged. "I guess so."

"Fair enough. Cheers!" Sivien hoisted his ration into the air. He tipped it toward Brian. "Here's to hoping this doesn't kill us, give us food poisoning, or turn us into a new alien species because it's been infested with some sort of larva."

"I guess I can toast to that." Brian touched the corner of his strong-smelling ration to Sivien's.

Sizable crumbs fell to the floor.

Brian brought his so-called food back from the toast, but he hesitated to eat any. He cringed and watched Sivien take a bite of the crumbly, spongelike brick.

"You know." Sivien chewed for a moment, then swallowed hard. He reached for his canteen. "It doesn't taste *too* bad. It's just impossible to choke down."

Brian could think of a million other things he would rather eat. The smell from his ration kicked up unpleasant memories of other meals he would have preferred to pass on, too, but the hunger clawing at his insides pressured him to proceed. He broke off a piece and brought the unsavory morsel close to his mouth. Trying not to think about it, he held his breath and popped in the bit of dry sponge.

The initial burst of pungent flavor brought tears to Brian's eyes. It melted into a pasty mush with the consistency of grainy dental paste. He gathered the gritty sludge ball to the back of his throat and tried to swallow. Sivien's words rang true: The ration didn't want to go down.

Sivien leaned over with a pained look stamped across his face. "Mine's awful. How about yours?"

"The same," Brian admitted through puckered lips.

"Do you want to trade?" Sivien smiled.

"They're exactly the same." Brian chuckled and tried stomaching another bite. Its sand-like texture gritted between his teeth. At least the disgusting meal doused some of his hunger's burning flames. He leaned back against the metal foot and watched his green-scaled friend choke down another bite.

The soft sound of Zella's hum drifted over.

Sivien closed his eyes for a moment. Then he looked up at her. "What song is that? I could swear I've heard it before."

Zella paused for a moment. "Um . . . I don't know. It's the song playing on the station's speakers."

Brian and Sivien exchanged glances.

"Zella," Sivien said, looking around, "there are no speakers."

"What?" Zella sat up a little. "What do you mean, there are no speakers?"

"Nothing, Zella." Sivien immediately raised a hand. "I didn't mean anything. It's just a pretty song. That's all."

Zella stared at Sivien for a moment. "Yeah, it is a pretty song," she said at last. She stretched and lay back down. She continued humming and began kicking her dangling leg again.

Sivien started playing with one of his pack's straps. "It does make me feel kind of sad, though."

"It made me sad at first, too." Zella hummed. "But it doesn't anymore. Now, it makes me feel excited to be alive."

Zella hit a chord that tugged on Brian's heartstrings. He quickly got swept away in a whirlwind of emotion welling up inside of him. His eyes misted, and he sat in disbelief of such a powerful note.

"It's such a pretty song. It speaks to my soul." Zella continued humming. She started gazing at the faraway ceiling the way an astronomer would observe distant galaxies.

"Zella, don't look at the ceiling," Brian reminded her.

Zella's song cut out. She fixed Brian with a glare. "Yes, *Captain*." She propped herself up on an elbow and twiddled the end of her tail.

Sivien moved his hands to the side of his pack, out of Zella's view, and began motioning to Brian. *"She looks really pissed at you."*

Brian side-glanced at Sivien, lost for words.

Sivien suddenly started looking around. He tipped his head and flicked his black, forked tongue out of his mouth and into the air. He turned his head the other way and flicked his tongue again. "Can you feel that?"

"Feel what?" Brian asked.

"Okay, I'm going with no." Sivien's tongue wagged through the air again. "Can you smell it, then?"

Faint vibrations began trembling through the metal at Brian's back. A soft hum from an engine started filling the air. "That might be one of the platforms. It's probably Callie and Derek. At least, I sure hope that's Callie and Derek." His assumption proved to be spot-on as their voices began sounding over the faint rumble.

"I still wish I could have found extra food." Derek's voice became more audible. "Not a single morsel in the lot of them."

"Please tell me you didn't spend time searching for food after I told you to focus on finding the parts," Callie said.

"No. You know I wouldn't blatantly disobey your orders," Derek replied. They rounded the corner of one of the other aisles. "But I might have checked for rations in the containers that I *did* open."

"And how many was that?" Callie made eye contact with Brian. She course-corrected and headed toward him, with Derek in tow.

Derek mumbled an answer.

"You've wasted time, Derek. And look," Callie motioned to the rest of the crew, "everyone has been waiting for us to get back."

The platform that followed them stopped at the end of the aisle. It hovered in place, waiting for more instructions.

Brian sighed. "You got a little off task, huh?" He ran a hand through his short hair.

"You said we could take any food we found," Derek countered. Then he stared off into space. "You know what would have been an even better find?"

"A sudden portal through time and space that would take us back home?" Sivien smirked.

"Even better than that." Derek winked.

"Oh," Callie sighed, "this ought to be good."

A bright smile formed on Derek's round facial features. "Finding some homemade apple pie. Apple pie made with real apples—tart apples." He licked his lips.

"Pie again? Really?" Callie glanced over at Zella.

Derek looked at Zella as well and lowered his voice. "Did you know that tart apples make the best pies? The tartness of the apples contrasts against the sweetness of the sugar and—"

"Give it a rest, Derek," Callie said.

"It's okay." Brian stuffed his ration back in his pack and stood. He stretched his stiff legs. "We can talk about apple pie later. Right now, we need to get going."

"What? But everyone's eating!" Derek whined. "Me and Callie haven't taken a break yet."

"You can eat once the platforms are moving down the hall to our ship," Brian said. "We can ride them back, and you can snack as long as you like."

Derek frowned. "I guess. The most important thing is that I *do* get to eat." He shrugged.

Sivien gave him a wry smile. "You're going to love your rations, Derek. They're only a *little* dry and get caught in your throat just a *little* bit. Nothing a swig of rehydrated water won't fix." He sucked down a gulp from his canteen.

"Rehydrated water?" Derek asked with a smirk.

Sivien lifted his canteen in the air and wiped his mouth. "Yep, you just add water to your empty flask, and voila." He laughed and stuffed his drink into his pack.

Brian smiled despite himself.

"That's got to be one of the worst jokes I've ever heard." Callie placed her hand on her hip but suppressed a smile.

"Adding water to dehydrated water is just putting water in your flask." Derek chuckled.

Sivien beamed.

Brian turned to Callie. "Can you program the platforms to the door of the storage room so that we can get started back to our ship?"

"That won't be a problem." Callie began working with her sleeve.

Brian slung his pack over his shoulder, and Sivien climbed to his feet as well.

"Derek and I have already created an operating network between Little-G and the platforms," Callie said. "I think we just need someone to stand in the doorway to keep it open long enough for all the platforms to move through. It should be smooth sailing after that. Riding them down the hall would be nice. It will save our weary feet from the walk."

Derek looked down at his boots. "That's the best news I've heard all day! It'll be nice to have a break from walking. Won't it, my little piggly-wigs." He rocked back and forth from heel to toe.

"Piggly-wigs?" Sivien scoffed.

Derek shrugged and stopped rocking. "What do you call your toes?"

Sivien laughed. "I don't."

"Has Little-G picked up any sort of correspondence with the station yet?" Brian continued.

"No. Not even once," Callie replied.

"I'm just double-checking," Brian said. "It would still be nice to have face-to-face contact before we left. Well, *any* contact, for that matter."

"I haven't picked up any other signs of life the entire time we've been on this station," Callie replied. "We can have Zella send a transmission expressing our gratitude on our way out."

"In that case," Brian said, "we're ready when you are."

Callie finished interacting with her sleeve. "I've just programmed the platforms to line up at the door." She smiled.

"Then it's time to head out," Brian announced.

Chapter 18

Brian looked down the aisle of the loaded platforms. One by one, the machines started gliding toward the front of the storage room as they followed Callie's new programming. Derek peeked around the statue's foot and rose onto his toes. He bobbed there for a moment, then relocated to a better vantage spot.

Callie headed to the room's entrance.

"Derek, come on." Brian interrupted his stocky friend's gawking at the oncoming platforms. He motioned with his head, indicating to Derek that he needed to rejoin the group.

Derek stared at Brian for a moment. Then his eyebrows rose. "Oh, right." He quickly began following.

Zella still lounged on her perch on the abandoned container, humming to herself.

"We're headed out," Brian called to her.

Zella glared at him but started packing up her things.

Brian caught up with Callie and stole a glance back at Zella. "I think it would be best if we split into two groups. Two of us on the first container and three on the last."

"Two groups?" Callie asked. "I think we should stick together."

"Well, we need to keep eyes on both ends of our supply chain instead of just one," Brian replied. "In case we run into anything—or anyone, for that matter. We'll have a representative of our crew on either end."

"I guess having two groups seems logical. What's the configuration?" Callie asked. "Can I go with Sivien?"

"Derek will escort the platforms with me in the front," Brian said, "while you, Sivien, and Zella secure the rear. We can stop at the other storage room on our way out and grab a picker. That will make loading things onto the ship easier. While we're getting the fuel aboard, Derek will make the repairs we need with the parts we just found. Then we'll disembark. It's as simple as that."

"But I want to sit in the back," Derek spoke up from behind. "Why do I have to sit in front?"

Brian glanced back at Zella. He drummed his fingers on his chin. "A captain has a Gallus gallus domesticus, a Canis lupus, one unit of Zea mays, a deceitful associate, and one holding bay. The captain has to cross a galaxy—"

Derek raised his hands to his ears. "Okay. Okay! You know I don't like riddles." He stopped walking and turned to watch the advancing platforms.

"Everything finally seems to be working out," Brian told Callie.

They came within range of the door. It opened without hesitation. Brian stood across the threshold, and Callie joined him.

Brian inspected the opening. "Even the doors are finally cooperating."

"It is a nice change of pace," Callie said, twiddling a finger around one of her braids. "Things are finally looking up."

Together, they watched the progression of the platforms crossing the receiving area. Derek stood a little way off, eyeballing some containers down a nearby aisle. Sivien and Zella migrated toward the door. Sivien seemed to be keeping a smart distance away from her.

"Yes. Things are finally looking up," Brian replied.

Callie began interacting with Little-G and stepped into the hall. "Brian?" Her voice sounded from the corridor.

"Hmm?" Brian continued watching the platforms progress toward the door. The last one passed between the towering guardians at the end of the aisles.

"The ceiling," Callie said, her tone laced with concern.

"Just try not to look at it too much," Brian replied.

"Um . . ." Callie said. "It's changing."

Brian turned.

Callie pointed at a spot on the ceiling in the hall, not too far from where she stood: a flat, silver disk covered the antique paper. Brian moved closer to examine the phenomena. The blotch on the ceiling looked like liquid mercury that had pooled on the paper's surface. While he stared at it, he could swear it increased in size. If it had enlarged, the amount was so minute that he couldn't quite tell for sure.

"Is that thing getting bigger," Callie asked, "or is it just my imagination?"

Brian continued observing the pool of mercury-like substance on the ceiling, still unsure. He stood very still and used his ink-drawn twin as a marker to gauge whether the circle increased in size. He watched and waited. The metallic matter slowly spread and touched the top of his drawing's head.

"It's definitely getting bigger," Brian said.

Callie looked down the hall in the direction they had come. "Looks like there's more than just one."

"I don't know what this stuff is," Brian checked the other way, "but it's everywhere."

Callie scanned the ceiling with her sleeve. "Its components are not found in our database."

Several spots of the mercury-like matter dotted the antique paper's surface. Some were small—the size of coins—while others swelled much bigger. The patches spread like bacteria growing in a petri dish. One of them got so large that it exceeded the circumference of a cleaning bot.

Brian looked back up at the first spot he and Callie noticed. As he watched it spread, he inadvertently took a step forward. The ink from his drawing started to bleed into the metallic substance. The pitch-black liquid billowed into the smooth-looking silver, and the mixture shone for a split second as the ink absorbed into the mercury's depths. Suddenly, the whole patch began reflecting the hall below. Brian found himself staring up at a perfect replication of the corridor in which he stood. Within the hall's reflection also stood his mirrored image. He started up at it, and it stared right back. He moved his hand back and forth, and his reflection kept perfect timing.

"It's a mirror," Brian said. The mouth of his reflection moved in sync with his while he spoke. "Why is it a mirror?"

"The ceiling is turning into a mirror?" Callie asked. She crept to Brian's side.

Both of their reflections stood in the spreading mirror's surface.

"What do you think this stuff is?" Callie asked. Her reflection matched her every movement, too.

Brian was lost for words as he glanced at the ceiling. The newly formed mirror quickly spread, overrunning all of the antique paper. As the growing, reflective spots touched each other, they fused like magnetized water droplets and doubled in size. Brian rubbed his fingers together. He couldn't help but wonder how the spreading substance would feel. He imagined the ripples his touch would create on the mirror's smooth, glass-like surface might be the same as if he were to throw pebbles in a serene pond. His fascination grew into a deep-seated desire to explore the depths of the mirrors' lagoons.

"Wow." Callie's monotone voice broke the silence. She sounded light-years away. "Zella's right. It *is* beautiful."

Callie's soft voice broke Brian's concentration. "What?" he whispered.

She didn't respond.

Brian tore his eyes away from the growing spectacle overhead and looked at Callie. Her gaze remained locked tightly on her reflection. Brian waved his hand in front of her face, trying to break her fixation on the ceiling, but she didn't seem to notice. She didn't even blink.

"Callie," Brian said.

She still didn't respond.

"CALLIE!" Brian snapped his fingers in front of her face.

He grabbed her arm, and sparks erupted from the friction of their shields as he turned her body toward him. Her head didn't move an inch, and her wide, unblinking eyes continued to stare vacantly up at the ceiling. Brian gently cupped her face with his hand, and sparks of tiny, blue static electricity flickered as their shields repelled each other. He forced her head to turn, but her eyes clung to the mirror, refusing to relinquish their gaze.

"CALLIE!" Brian said again.

Callie's eyes rolled and then realigned. She blinked a few times and looked at Brian. She glanced down at his hand, cupping her face. "What are you doing?" She went to brush his hand away, but he released his hold before she could.

"You were staring at the ceiling," Brian said. "I couldn't get you to stop. What was I supposed to do?"

"I was looking at it, just like you were," Callie replied defensively.

"Then how did you get turned toward me?" Brian tipped his head, accentuating his point. He waited for an answer.

"I . . . I don't know," Callie stammered.

"There's something extremely off with this place. I don't know what it is, and I'm done finding out. Let's round everyone up and get out of here." Brian motioned for Callie to go back with him to the storage room to get the others.

Callie didn't budge. "I've got a sick feeling. Something isn't right. I feel like we're not going to make it out of here." She glanced up at the patches of mirror that engulfed the ceiling.

"Don't say that." Brian extended his hand to her. "We got ourselves in. We can get ourselves back out."

"No. No, we won't. We won't be able to get out," Callie whispered and glanced back up at the ceiling. "Something is going to happen . . ."

Brian took Callie by the wrist. He pulled her away so she wouldn't become engrossed with the mirror again. He caught a glimpse down the hall as they re-entered the storage room. The patches of mirror continued merging into one giant mass that consumed most of the antique paper. At least the substance stayed on the ceiling. None of it ran down onto the walls.

A sense of urgency spurred Brian on. He knew he needed to get his crew back to their ship. The platforms sat hovering in a long line just a few yards away from the door, waiting for further programming. Sivien leaned against one of them next to Zella, who vacantly hummed and twirled the end of her tail.

Brian looked around but couldn't find Derek. "Fall in! We're leaving—now!"

Sivien stood up straight. He seemed a little surprised by Brian's abrupt tone. Zella stopped humming but didn't stop twirling her tail.

"Has anyone seen where Derek went?" Brian asked.

Sivien shook his head, and Zella didn't respond.

Brian touched his comm. "Derek? We're headed out. Where are you?" He didn't reply.

"Derek, give us your position." Brian tried again.

Still, no response came.

"Callie, can you check for Derek's life sign?" Brian sighed and rubbed the back of his neck. "This is a fine time to lose someone."

As Callie started interacting with Little-G, a deep boom sounded.

Derek's smiling face popped out from behind an aisle guardian.

"I'm here." Derek waved. He finished shimmying out from behind the metallic giant and kicked the adjacent container. Then he took off toward the crew.

"Food?" Callie asked.

Derek adopted a sheepish look.

"Did you find any?" Sivien perked up.

"Maybe." Derek ho-hummed for a second then frowned. "No."

"Don't worry about food," Brian said. "We won't need it anyway. Once we get back to our ship, we'll go into stasis after we set a course. We have enough supplies to last until we get home. There will be plenty to eat then."

"If we can even *find* home," Derek said, staring at the floor.

"We'll find out more from the coordinates we downloaded to Little-G. We just need to get back to our ship." Brian stood taller to make an announcement. "Callie, get these platforms moving."

Callie leaned closer to Brian. "It's happening in here, too," she whispered.

Brian glanced up. "Try not to worry about it," he said in a low tone.

"Try not to worry about what?" Sivien asked.

"Okay." Brian sighed. "There's one more thing. I'm sure it's nothing, but the ceiling in the hall is turning into a mirror instead of that paper hologram we found when we came in."

Callie wrung her hands. "And apparently, it's happening in here, too." She looked up at the ceiling.

Sivien gaped at the ceiling. "Oh, that's really cool—I mean weird and bad." He shot a glance at Brian.

Zella dropped the end of her tail. "It's not weird and bad. It's breathtaking." She raised her arms in the air.

"Your orders are to not look at the ceiling." Brian held his gaze on Zella. "I believe it has some sort of hypnotic hold over you when you do."

Derek's eyes widened, and his mouth fell open. "Haunt—"

"At this point, Derek," Brian said, cutting him off, "I don't know if it's haunted or not. All that matters is getting back to our ship. So, find something or someone else to focus your attention on, as long as it's not the ceiling. Whatever you do, don't look up! Got it?"

"Don't look up." Derek saluted dramatically. "Yes, Sir!"

"Zella?" Brian said.

"Yes, I heard you." Zella folded her arms across her chest. "I got it."

Sivien gave Derek a light shove toward the loaded platforms. Blue light sparked from Derek's shield.

"Well, what are we waiting for?" Sivien copied the same mad scientist voice Derek had used earlier. "Let's get these here platforms moving!"

Using the momentum from Sivien's nudge, Derek spirited up the side of the first container with surprising agility for his stocky build.

Brian climbed up and sat next to him. "We're ready." He looked down at Callie and nodded.

Chapter 19

Callie's fingers skipped across Little-G. Brian and Derek swayed as their fuel-filled ride started moving through the open doorway. The instant the platform entered the hall, the presence of the mirror loomed overhead. Brian looked up. The height of the metallic steed forced him and Derek closer to the ceiling. He gazed down the hall but couldn't find any remaining portions of the antique paper left. The mirror had covered it entirely. He reminded himself that the ceiling might have a strange pull, but nothing more.

"We'll wait here and hop onto the caboose while it passes," Callie's voice chirped in Brian's ear.

Brian turned and gave her a thumbs-up.

Derek slid his pack off his shoulders. "What's the food taste like?" He crossed his legs and dropped his supplies on his lap.

Brian thought for a moment, trying to put the taste and texture of the rations into words. "I'll go with a honey-kissed . . . sponge-grit-cake."

Derek stared at him blankly. "Hmm, that sounds fantastic!" He slid his pack out of his lap and started digging in the satchel on his hip instead. His probing search didn't produce any results.

"All out of jerky?" Brian asked.

Derek's shoulders slumped. "I really wish I could have found some food in at least one of those containers."

"There will be plenty of food when we get back home," Brian said. "Good food."

Derek stopped digging in his satchel and stared down at the container. He ran his finger along its edge. "Yeah, good food."

A light breeze fluttered through Brian's hair, and he settled in for the long haul of the trip. Soon, soreness spread across his backside. He shifted on the hard metal, trying to lessen the discomfort. Not finding much reprieve, he turned around to check on their progress.

The platforms glided through the doorway and turned down the hall one at a time. They looked like a line of mechanized insects headed back to their nest with their collected goods. He was glad his crew was almost out of the bizarre station. He looked up once again. His uncanny reflection peered back at him. It, too, rode on top of a container in the mirror world above. Contrary to how Brian felt, his perfect duplicate looked just a skip away from smiling.

Brian glanced at Derek's reflection, sitting right next to his own. His gaze dropped to his real colleague sitting beside him. The light breeze caught Derek's hair as well, making the frizzy mess sway under its gentle touch. His goggles rested across his forehead, and he sat with his eyes closed. He sucked in the air with deep, steady breaths.

A faint, sweet scent still lingered in the hall, and Brian assumed it was the cause of Derek's deep inhales. Brian's thoughts drifted to cherished memories of cinnamon-swirled pastries. He closed his eyes and took in a long drag of the ambrosial scent swimming in the air.

The lanterns on the walls flickered, snatching his attention back.

"Flib-jib, not again." Derek peered around the hall. "I don't like it when the lights go out. It gives me the heebie-jeebies."

Brian touched his comm. "Callie?"

"Yes?" Callie's voice sounded in his ear.

"Is the network rerouting energy again?" Brian asked.

The lights flickered again.

"Yes, it looks like it." Callie's voice carried concern in its tone. "It's probably another blackout."

The lights flickered and went out altogether. The palpable darkness consumed the entire hall. Brian brought his hand in front of his face, but he couldn't see a thing.

"Yep," Derek said. "There's the heebie-jeebies I was talking about."

Brian wished he sat in his captain's chair on his bridge instead of on the cold, hard, fuel-filled container. He shifted again and touched his transmitter. "How long do you guess they will be out?" The constant background static in his receiver increased.

"It's hard . . . say," Callie's answer was broken up by the white noise. "It might . . . a little . . . last time."

Brian buried his head in his hands and rubbed his face. Tipping his head back, he dragged his fingers through his hair until they settled on his neck and shoulders. He started working his tense muscles.

Suddenly, the brightness from the lights slammed his senses. He squinted and touched his transmitter. "Callie, I thought you said it would take a while."

The container Brian and Derek rode on came to an abrupt halt, jolting them forward. Brian's eyes slowly adjusted to the light as he looked around. Peering over the front side of his steel steed, he found the elevator lift's door.

It slid open.

The platform seemed to have come to the end of its programming.

Brian sat up straight and did some quick calculations. The distance they needed to go and the time they had spent traveling didn't add up. His hand shot to his transmitter. "Callie?" He turned around. He could see the last container hovering in the middle of the hall in the distance. Zella lounged while Sivien searched their platform.

"Callie isn't here," Sivien's voice responded in Brian's earpiece. The static had diminished.

Brian touched his transmitter again. "Callie, where are you? I don't have a visual on your location."

Still no response.

Brian turned around even more. Pins and needles exploded through his legs. At some point, his lower body had fallen asleep.

"What should we do?" Sivien's voice came again.

"We have to find her," Brian replied. "She couldn't have gone far. Is she in any of the gaps around your platform?"

"Not that I can see," Sivien said, looking over his platform's edge.

"Well, we'll search all of them if we have to." Brian tipped his head to Derek and motioned for him to examine the other side of their container.

Derek turned to check. "Agh, my legs fell asleep." He dragged himself to the edge and peered over the lip.

Brian stretched his stiff legs more and leaned over, inspecting the long space between the platforms and the wall. More pins and needles swept through his lower body as the circulation returned to his extremities. "I don't see her. Nothing seems out of place, either." He looked back at Derek.

"She's not down my side either." Derek shook his head.

"Where did she go?" Sivien's voice chirped in Brian's ear.

Brian gazed down at the last container. Sivien leaned past Zella, checking her side. She didn't move an inch to make it easier for him to get around her. She just stayed in her lounging position.

"I don't see her anywhere," Sivien's voice came again.

"How did you lose her?" Brian asked. "Wasn't she sitting right next to you?"

"Yes, she was. I don't know how we lost her." Sivien scratched his head. "When the lights went out, it was impossible to see anything."

"We need to find her. We'll have to do an area sweep." Brian looked at Zella. He didn't think she would be much help while her inattentiveness and periodic indignation persisted. He touched his transmitter again. "Zella, stay there while Sivien checks around the platforms on your end. Keep a visual on the top of the containers for us."

"Fine," Zella replied in a snappy tone.

Ignoring her peevishness, Brian eased himself down the side of his container near the open elevator door. His legs cramped the moment his feet touched the floor. He leaned against the hovering platform and steadied himself.

Derek also hopped down and stretched out his legs. "Oh, ouch. I think I sat a little too long in the same position." He let out a slight chuckle.

Brian glanced at the platform. He knew he needed to check its underside, but his imagination ran wild with all the different creatures that liked to cling to the underbelly of things. He cautiously bent over and inspected. Finding nothing unusual, he went straight to the alleyway on his side of the container and gazed down the long path between it and the wall. He paused and looked at Derek, who had moved to his respective side. He gave a nod, and Derek nodded back.

Brian started down the alleyway on his side. He thoroughly inspected the gap as he went. In the distance, he saw Sivien round one of the platform's corners at the end of the line. Even with the container taking up the middle of the hallway, there was still enough room for Sivien to fit his bulky body in the leftover space. His searching tactic seemed to be circling each container to clear it.

"It's like she just vanished," Sivien said through the comm.

The comment reminded Brian of the lights going out. "I'm not convinced she did. Anyone else notice a loss of time?" The silence that followed was a clear indicator to him of his crew's uncertainty. He came to the end of his container.

Derek rounded the corner on the opposite side at the same time. He looked at Brian. "No. I didn't notice a loss of time."

"Try to remember." Brian bent over to check the next platform's underbelly. "You just said you sat too long in one position, right?"

Derek paused.

Brian looked up and stared at him.

"I guess I did," Derek said. "My legs still hurt."

They resumed their search and headed down their respective sides of the next container.

"Yeah," came Sivien's voice. "We climbed onto the last container when it was leaving the storage room. Then the lights started flickering like they did on our way in. After that, they went out. The next thing I knew, we were stopped, the lights were back on, and Callie was gone. It's like we skipped a part, or I can't remember or something."

Brian glanced up at the mirror on the ceiling. His reflection stared back at him. The feeling that *it* might know what happened to Callie weighed on him uncomfortably.

"Why can't we remember?" Derek asked.

"I don't know," Brian said. "It could mean everything, or perhaps nothing at all."

"She's not here." Zella interrupted the conversation through the comm. "Can we stop looking for her already?"

Brian stopped in his tracks. "Um . . . no, Zella. She's got to be somewhere. Why don't you and Sivien hold your position while Derek and I come to you." He resumed his search.

"Fine!" Zella replied.

Brian and Derek continued working their way past each platform. The thoroughness of their investigation took longer than Brian wanted, but as they got closer to the end of the line, he felt confident that they hadn't missed anything. They met up with Sivien behind the last container at the end of their search. No one found any signs of Callie.

Derek drummed his fingers on his bottom lip. "Maybe she just hit her head or something. Could she be somewhere down the hall, passed out?"

Sivien's mouth dropped open, and his eyes widened. He stuck a claw into his ear and wiggled it around. "Did I hear that right? What could she have possibly hit her head on? Nothing's hanging down. Unless you're suggesting that she fell and hit her head on the floor."

Derek nervously fidgeted in place. "You never know. She could have fallen off the container and hit her head when it went dark."

Sivien's face scrunched to one side. "Well, I'm not buying that."

"We don't know if she hit her head," Brian said. "And we won't know unless we find her."

"Can't I just stay here?" Zella peeked over the edge of the end container she still occupied. "I can keep an eye on our stuff."

"No. We need to stay together." Brian looked up at Zella. "The last thing we need is another missing crew member."

Zella scowled at Brian and started climbing down from her perch. Sivien offered her a helping hand, but Zella slapped it away. "I can do it myself."

Sivien recoiled from what looked more like hurt feelings than any physical pain.

"Zella," Brian cautioned her. "Watch your attitude."

With another heated glare directed at Brian, Zella sprang from her perch on the side of the container. Completing a full somersault, she landed on her feet. Her eyes narrowed as she looked up at Sivien. "Sorry." She began twirling the fur on the end of her tail with one claw, not looking sorry at all.

Derek sighed. "If Callie has Little-G, how are we going to find our way back to the storage room without her?"

"Easy." Brian tapped his temple. "From memory. It was a pretty straightforward route, not too many twists or turns."

"Right," Derek replied. "And what if someone else goes missing in the meantime? What then?"

"No one else is going to go missing because we're going to find her and get back to our ship together." Brian set the crew's pace down the hall, but Zella lagged behind. "It's not like we haven't had to retrace our steps before."

"Yeah, but we haven't had missing time before," Sivien countered.

"What we don't have is missing space." Brian turned slightly and motioned toward the hovering platforms. "They stopped in front of the elevator lift at the end of their programming. We can easily find our way back to the storage room from here. We know the way."

"I sure hope we find her soon," Derek said. "I can't seem to shake these heebie-jeebies. It's like the ceiling has extra eyes."

"Well, I want you to keep *your* eyes peeled." Brian examined the hall as they went. "Let me know if you find anything—anything at all. She's got to be somewhere, and we're not leaving without her."

Chapter 20

With tentative strides, Brian continued searching the hall as they made their way back to the second storage room. No clues as to Callie's whereabouts stood out to him. The absence of any signs of a struggle on the walls or floor made him feel confident that they would find her in one piece. He couldn't believe she had just wandered off. He stole a glance up at the mirror on the ceiling.

As Brian continued down the hall with his remaining crew, the reflected world above continued pulling his attention. He tried his best not to look at the mirror, but he found himself glancing up anyway. He noticed the others peeking up at it, too, and knew he wasn't the only one losing battles with concentration. To his dismay, Zella seemed almost entirely enthralled with the reflected hall.

They approached another set of doors, and the urge to look up consumed Brian and gnawed on his resolve. Suddenly, a high-pitch tone squealed over the crackling static in his receiver. His hand jumped to his ear, and one eye squinted partway shut from the deafening sound. He wrenched the device from its placement.

The door on his right began sliding open. Brian froze, and the others stopped in their tracks. He slowly looked at the new room.

"None of these doors opened the first time we came through," Derek whispered at Brian's side.

"No. No, they didn't." Brian stared at the new opening and took a couple of steps toward it.

The room was well lit. The carpet ended at the door, making the dark metal flooring stand out. The entire place was filled with oversized tables and chairs. Brian glanced up to see that the mirror covered the room's ceiling, too.

Sivien moved toward the threshold and peered inside. "LOOK!" He bound into the room.

"Sivien!" Brian called after him.

"Little G!" Sivien shouted over his shoulder.

Brian and Derek rushed to the doorway, but both hesitated to go beyond. Zella eventually sauntered over. Sivien dashed farther into the room. An object resembling Callie's sleeve lay on the floor in an opening between some tables and chairs.

Sivien maneuvered through the network of oversized obstacles for a few seconds before simply pushing them out of his way. He made something of a zig-zag line to the device on the floor, seeming to care very little about the disorder he created in the room. He shoved aside the last table that barred his path to the sleeve. Bending down, he scooped it up and looked it over. "It's definitely Callie's."

Brian cupped his hands around his mouth. "CALLIE?" he called into the room.

No reply came.

Glancing around, Brian made out a large, oval-shaped dining bar in the middle of the room. Its counter matched the dark metal found on the floor, the tabletops, the chairs, and elsewhere in the station. Several food replicators were sprinkled throughout the room. Everything appeared oversized, like the rest of the station.

Derek wandered toward the first row of tables. He suddenly stopped and turned to Brian. "What room is this?" His blue eyes got big and sparkled with excitement.

Sivien looked around. "It's a cafeteria."

"I knew I could smell something cooking." Derek's face brightened even more, and he bound into the room. He darted back and forth like he wasn't sure which way to go first. "FOOD AT LAST!"

Zella sighed and cozied up against the wall just inside the door, keeping it open. She started picking at her nails. Brian took a few strides to stop Derek's floundering dash, but his desire quickly fizzled out as Derek jetted off to a food replicator.

"We'll never get him back now." Zella stared vacantly at her nails. "Might as well let him go."

Derek made impressive time to the machine and climbed it. His thick fingers jumped across its interface with haste, giving it orders. "I don't know what kind of food this is, and I don't care!"

The food replicator blared unpleasant chimes at him but didn't produce a meal.

"What the FLIB!" Derek slammed his hands down on the stubborn machine.

The unpleasant chimes rang out again.

Derek balled his fists up and started raining blows onto the interface. A red light began flashing, joining in with the chimes. He slid from his perch. "GIVE ME FOOD!" He pummeled the side of the replicator. His hands started leaving bloodied fist stamps on its shiny, metallic surface.

"Derek!" Brian gaped in disbelief and started crossing the room. "What are you doing?"

Derek began pushing and pulling on the replicator, trying to capsize it, which only ended up making him convulse in place. The rock-solid tank he battled didn't even budge. "GAAAH!" he yelled and slumped to his knees on the floor. He buried his head in his bloodied hands and began sobbing.

Brian stopped in his tracks. He looked at Sivien, completely baffled.

Sivien shook his head and shrugged. His eyes fell on Little-G in his hand. "Derek, can you see if you can find Callie?" He pitched the device across the room to where Derek sat.

The sleeve landed on the metal floor and slid to a stop at Derek's knee. His hands lowered slightly.

"I'm sorry the replicator didn't give you any food," Sivien said. "If we find Callie, we can get off this station, and you can make Zella that app-pile-fly."

Derek lowered his hands a little further from his face. "It's apple pie," he huffed. He noticed the blood on his fingers and began inspecting them.

"Can you find Callie's location from her life signs?" Brian asked.

Derek's demeanor soured as he looked down at Little-G lying next to him on the floor. "I'm not as good with Little-G as you are. Why did Sivien throw him to me?"

Sivien glanced at Brian, then back at Derek. "Well, it wasn't working for Callie very well. If he's broken, you're the one who can fix it."

Derek grumbled as he picked up the sleeve and went to put it on.

"You're going to clean your hands off first, right?" Sivien asked. "You're bleeding."

Derek paused and looked down at his hands again. "Yeah, what happened, anyway?"

Sivien's mouth dropped open.

Brian stared at Derek. "Well, just a moment ago, you were going ape crazy on the food replicator."

"Oh, I was? I don't remember that." Derek glanced up at the machine. He looked back down at Little-G and began pulling the device up over his mangled hand.

"That's a bio . . . hazard . . ." Sivien trailed off as Derek slid the sleeve further up his arm.

Brian cringed.

"Okay." Sivien threw his arms up. "So, we're tossing all the safety protocols into the dead of space now. I got it."

"A little blood won't hurt its programming." Derek swooned and spewed a few complaints under his breath as Little-G tightened. His hands flew to his head. Steadying himself, he let go with one hand and then the other. "Seems like he's working just fine to me."

"Yeah, but with blood gumming up its interface now, for how long?" Sivien looked highly annoyed.

Derek began plucking away at the sleeve's buttons. "I can fix it if I need to," he mumbled as his speed increased. He worked the device for a few minutes. His brows furrowed, and droplets of sweat glistened his forehead. He managed to get the green, three-dimensional image back up and running. He stopped prodding at Little-G and inspected the holographic projection.

Derek's gaze jumped to Brian. "There are only four life signs here: you, me, Sivien, and Zella." He cupped the side of his head again with one hand.

"And it's working properly?" Brian asked.

Derek let go of his head and pushed a few more buttons. "It seems to be working properly enough. Callie isn't here, according to the scans."

Brian stared at Derek.

"That can't be right," Sivien said. "The readouts are wrong. She's got to be here somewhere!"

"Let me see." Brian stepped toward Derek and gestured for the device.

Derek loosened the sleeve, slipped it off his arm, and tossed it. Brian went to snatch it out of the air, but his grip slipped on smudged blood, and Little-G fell to the floor. He picked it up with a slight eye roll and slid the soiled thing on. A light throb started pounding behind his left eye. Pushing past the growing waves of pain, he began searching the device for answers.

"She's got to be here somewhere," Sivien said. "Where else could she have gone?"

Brian concentrated on the task at hand instead of responding to Sivien.

"I didn't think there was anywhere for her *to* have gone." Derek still knelt on the floor by the food replicator, staring down at his mangled hands.

Brian searched the programming for something Derek might have missed. The throbbing waves behind his eye pounded harder and engulfed his entire head as he engaged with the sleeve's network. At the end of his search, he got the same results as Derek. He repeated his investigation, and it brought him to the same conclusion. He tried again and again. Time after time, try after try, his inquiries found only the four life signs of him and his other three crew members standing in the cafeteria.

Rhythmic agony pummeled the inside of Brian's skull. He brought a hand up to stabilize his senses. The miserable waves continued hammering away, keeping time with his beating heart.

Suddenly, Little-G's programming froze. Ensuing shock waves began pulsing everywhere, even through his teeth. Before he knew it, he had balled up one fist and delivered a mighty blow to his sleeved bicep. An explosion of exquisite misery seized his mind, and his jaw clenched. He sank to his knees, losing control to full-body spasms.

"No!" Derek reached out a hand from across the room. "Please tell me you didn't just do what I think you did."

The three-dimensional image hovering next to Brian's arm froze, and he clawed at the device, trying to get it off. The sleeve wouldn't release, so he forcibly peeled Little-G off his arm. As the device's mental network tore from his mind, the ceaseless pain engulfing his senses began to disconnect as well. He breathed easier but looked over at Derek apologetically. "I . . . I think I did." Little-G slipped from his hands and fell to the floor. The image still hovering near it was a pixelated mess.

"Brian?" Sivien asked.

"Why did you do that?" Derek stared at him fiercely.

"I didn't mean to break it." Brian hunched over the device, holding his head. "I don't know what came over me."

"BRIAN?" Urgency laced Sivien's tone.

Brian turned. The motion ignited residual misery, and he swooned as his mind spun. "I said I don't know what came over me. I'm sorry." His voice reverberated in his head as he spoke.

"Brian, LOOK!" Sivien said.

Forcing his mind to focus, Brian saw Sivien staring at the ceiling, transfixed. He followed Sivien's line of vision to a particular spot in the mirror. Through his disorientation, he noticed something moving on the reflective surface.

A well-groomed alien crossed the room in the ceiling. The being's flowy white hair outlined its chiseled face and vibrant, blue skin. Some of its white locks waved across its forehead and ended near the back of its elongated neck. It wore what appeared to be another crew's uniform. The navy-blue material looked comfortable and had impressively straight seams. The blue man's demeanor flaunted an air of haughtiness.

The blue-skinned being sat down on a stool at the dining bar in the ceiling. As if on mute, it began mouthing noiseless words to someone on the other side of the counter. The alien acted as if it were ordering a meal, but everything it said remained absolutely silent.

"You guys see it too, right?" Derek asked.

"I think so." Brian couldn't peel his eyes away from the ceiling.

Chapter 21

As Brian continued staring up at the blue-skinned man in the mirror, a golden drink suddenly appeared on the counter in front of the being. The glass seemed to come out of nowhere. Ice cubes floated in the frothy beverage. The alien stirred the refreshment with a decorative, clear rod and nodded as though thanking an unseen party.

The alien picked up the golden beverage and brought the carbonated drink to his lips. As he took a long, savory swig, Brian felt the chilled liquid wet his own parched lips as it gushed down his dry throat and quenched his thirst. The blue-skinned being took a few more gulps and beamed as he toasted his glass in the air. He placed it back down on the counter. Taking the clear rod, he swirled the golden, bubbly liquid again.

Derek smacked his lips. "I can almost taste it."

A swift movement caught Brian's attention, and he ducked. Another alien appeared in the ceiling. The uniform it wore matched the navy blue of the man sitting at the bar. The new creature flaunted feminine grace as it weaved through the tables in the mirror world above. No hair grew on the top of her head. Instead, heaps of pale skin curled in on themselves. The flesh of her high cheekbones swirled like twisted calluses. Even with the unsavory mounds of spiraling flesh, her appearance remained quite fair, and she carried an air of gentle strength.

Several tentacles extended out of the ends of the female alien's sleeves, and thicker ones protruded from her uniform's bottom. The octopus-like limbs circled and twisted around each other. The lower limbs pushed and pulled her across the floor, giving her the appearance of gliding effortlessly over the mirror's room. She drifted through to the tables on the ceiling that Sivien had moved. She stumbled on a misplaced chair. Down below, in the real cafeteria, the same chair moved simultaneously. The alien stood, straightened herself, and continued on her way.

At the bar in the ceiling, the blue-skinned man turned and took note of the tentacled female. A broad smile spread across his face. Still void of any sound, he beckoned her over. She responded with a warm grin of her own and changed course through the tables. As she breezed past Sivien's reflection, she paused. Tipping her head, she waved a tentacle at him. Sivien's mirror image stood there, looking just as dumbfounded as the real Sivien below. The female alien brushed off his non-response to her seemingly friendly gesture and continued past him.

When she reached the bar, she stood at the blue-skinned being's side and greeted him without a sound. He motioned for her to take the seat next to him. She accepted the invitation by gliding into the spot. While she got settled, the blue alien leaned closer, inaudibly chattering away. She tipped her head back in silent laughter.

Derek and Zella erupted in laughter as well, catching Brian off guard. He glanced at Derek, then at Zella. "Can you hear them?"

"Of course not," Derek said through his chuckles.

Zella giggled at Derek's answer. A wry smile spread across her lips. Still leaning against the wall near the open door, she scooped up her tail and started twirling its end. The responses did little to persuade Brian that they didn't hear the couple at the bar.

Derek closed his eyes and sucked in a deep breath as though he were drinking in the air. "I can sure smell it, though! I told you someone was cooking. I wonder if I can get that waiter to cook something for me, too?" He opened his eyes, and they glazed over. He continued staring up at the seated couple.

"Derek." Brian looked up at the mirror. The blue-skinned alien and his tentacled friend sat at the otherwise empty bar. "There is no waiter."

"Of course there is!" Derek looked down from the mirror, scolding Brian. His anger instantly melted from his features as his gaze drifted back up to the ceiling. "He's right there: the one who brought the drink to that blue man. I don't know what species he is, but he seems like a nice enough fellow."

Brian turned to Sivien as though he could settle the dispute. "Did you see someone bring the drink?"

Sivien continued gawking at the ceiling and shook his head. "No."

"Derek, the drink just appeared there," Brian countered.

Derek laughed again. "Things don't just appear out of nowhere."

Another giggle erupted from Zella.

"Oh, here it comes." Derek stared starry-eyed at the ceiling, drawing Brian's attention back up to the reflected world in the mirror. "I wonder what kind of food that is."

Brian searched the bar on the ceiling around the blue-skinned alien, but he didn't see anything or anyone else. Suddenly, a plate filled with a steaming entrée instantly appeared, just like the golden drink had barely a moment ago. The being tipped his head as though he thanked the unseen party again, and the tentacled female sitting next to him began ogling the dish.

The aroma of slow-cooked meat overtook the faint, sweet smell lingering in the air. Brian breathed in the new aroma. Tantalizing thoughts of how the alien's food would taste drifted into his mind. He couldn't tear his eyes from the captivating scene. Colorful, steaming vegetables were piled on one side of the plate, while a large cut of meat took up the other. A thick, simmering sauce pooled around them both.

Brian's mouth watered, and his stomach growled.

He remembered the last disgusting meal he had eaten in the storage room. He could still feel the muck sticking to the back of his throat. He swallowed hard and almost gagged. An intense desire to replace the repulsive recollection began flooding his mind. He closed his eyes and breathed in another drag of the tantalizing aroma permeating the air. The memory of the ration wedged in the back of his throat faded as he fantasized about eating the mouthwatering dish in the mirror. He could swear he felt the crispness of the grilled vegetables sinking between his teeth.

Brian's eyes fluttered shut as a bouquet of flavors saturated all of his senses.

His appetite raged.

"Aye!" Derek blurted. "I have to have it!"

Brian's eyes popped open.

Derek floundered toward the empty bar in their room, tripping over tables and chairs as he went. He tumbled to the floor, but he never relinquished his gaze on the ceiling. "It smells so good!" He clambered back to his feet and kept going.

The feast in the mirror drew Brian's attention away from Derek, who bumbled farther into the room. Brian's gaze wandered back to the blue-skinned alien just in time to see him pick up his utensil from the counter. The being slid the silverware into the side of the meat, and steam erupted from the food.

Brian's hunger clawed at his insides.

The blue-skinned alien took a portion of the meat and swirled it around in the simmering sauce. He then brought the dripping morsel up to his lips and blew. Wispy strands of steam floated away on the current of his breath. He slid the delicacy in, and a burst of flavor filled Brian's mouth. The alien continued eating his savory meal. Brian stood there dumbfounded, watching the man consume the meal as though he were devouring the robust entrée himself. More bewilderment set in as he tried to reconcile with the fact that the food in the mirror didn't exist.

The tentacled alien flagged the unseen party behind the bar. She carried on a brief, silent conversation with the invisible being and gestured toward the blue-skinned alien's dish. Brian began wishing Derek had gotten the food replicator to work.

"Derek," Brian mumbled as tipsy thoughts of his friend re-entered his mind.

He remembered Derek bumbling toward the bar a moment ago. A dump of adrenaline surged through his body, and he tore himself away from the engaging scene overhead. Brian searched the room for his crewmate and found him standing underneath the couple in the ceiling, staring straight up at them. Blinking several times, Brian tried to shake off a daze and began maneuvering his way through the tables in pursuit of his red-haired friend.

"Derek," Brian yelled, trying to break his comrade's concentration on the mirror. "Get back here."

A new sensation shifted through the room, stopping Brian in his tracks. He couldn't quite pinpoint what created the odd sense of vertigo he was suddenly experiencing, but he felt it to his very core. The sheer fabric of reality seemed to have been disrupted around him. An invisible force started pressing in on him from all sides. He tried to continue his trek across the room, but the unseen force held him firmly in place.

Small ripples developed on the mirror's surface as the vertigo increased. The disturbances moved toward an epicenter over Derek's head and melded together as one, swelling and stretching to form a large droplet of liquid mirror. The images in its reflective surface warped and elongated as the disturbance grew.

A pit in Brian's stomach urged him to hurry to his friend. With the invisible force pressing in on him, the premonition did little to get his legs moving again. He watched in horror as the bucket-sized droplet of liquid mirror increased in size. He tried calling out to Derek, but his rising terror choked out any audible sound.

Derek didn't seem to notice the changes happening directly above his head. He kept gazing at the elongating images of the couple as the droplet continued to swell. A cold sweat broke across Brian's skin, and his heart skipped a beat. He wanted to break free, but dread continued draining the strength from his limbs.

Soon, the large droplet dangled only a few feet above Derek. Tingling energy sparked through the air. The smell of the blue-skinned alien's meal oversaturated Brian's senses, and a wave of nausea hit him. His mouth began filling with slippery saliva—a warning to make haste to the nearest waste receptacle.

The hanging droplet started changing shape. Many colors churned on its surface. Certain hues took over, and a three-dimensional likeness of Derek began forming at its end. The more the droplet stretched down, the more it looked like Derek. The end of the dangling mirror became a perfect replica of Derek's torso. Below its waist, it remained in a liquid state, stretched and fused with the rest of the ceiling.

The new ceiling-Derek hung there, upside down—a mirrored image of the real Derek.

Derek's gaze fell from the spectacle that formed above him, and he stared at Brian. The hollowness in his eyes etched itself into Brian's mind.

A peaceful smile spread across Derek's lips. "I think I can smell apple pie!" he whispered. His ceiling duplicate dipped down and made contact with the tips of his hair. The clone began losing its shape and coloring as it poured over his head.

"DEREK!" Brian shrieked, pressing his hands hard against his cheeks. He had lifted them to his face at some point, but he couldn't remember when.

Derek continued peacefully smiling and stared vacantly off into space as the droplet began burying him under its bulk.

Zella giggled.

Derek's gaze went up to the ceiling, or at least would have. The liquid mirror covered his face as he tipped his head upward, smothering him under its mass. Patches of his shield started lighting up in glitches. The mirror continued to gather on his shoulders, running down his torso. He didn't even squirm as the mirror coated his whole upper body. His shield flickered out altogether.

An inner battle raged within Brian to respond. With every fiber of his being, he wanted to pull Derek out of the dangling droplet of the mirror. He focused all of his energy on moving his feet. One boot slid a step toward his colleague. He bore down even harder and managed to make a little headway. The thick air around him made him feel as though he were trudging through invisible sludge, but each heavy footfall came a little easier than the last, and he began making progress. He formed a plan to pull Derek out of the reflective muck.

"SIVIEN," Brian called through gritted teeth. "Help me get Derek."

The large lizard-man didn't seem to move a muscle as he continued staring at the spectacle of the ceiling consuming their friend. Brian closed half the distance to Derek as the mirror swallowed the stocky man to his thighs. The downward flowing ripples on the ceiling slowed, then stopped. At the same time, an odd pulse made all of Brian's senses flop.

Time stood still.

The bizarre sensation pulsed again, and the ripples started back up in reverse. The droplet began to move back up and into the ceiling. Derek remained encased within the liquid mirror's folds. His limp feet lifted off the floor and dangled in the air as he rose.

"NO!" Brian pushed harder through the thick atmosphere.

The ceiling swallowed Derek down to his knees and hoisted him even higher.

Coming within range, Brian zeroed in on what remained of Derek's dangling feet. He jumped, and the mysterious force made the black boots slip right between his grasp. He landed and fell into a crouch, ready for a second try. He leaped back into the air and seized the front of Derek's left boot. The foot bent under the added load.

"SIVIEN!" Brian hung on.

Chapter 22

Still hanging from Derek's foot, Brian managed to steal a glance over his shoulder. His spirits sank. Sivien stood in the same spot as before. He stared up at Brian.

"Sivien!" Brian thrashed his feet around, trying to get more of his attention. "HEY! Wake up!"

Sivien blinked a few times.

"Help me!" Brian yelled.

Sivien lifted a hand to his temple and shook his head. He started bumbling through the tables as though he had just awakened from a daze.

Brian tried anchoring Derek down with his weight to buy more time, but he felt his grip slipping. He didn't know how much longer he could hold on. A thought came to him of shifting his hold to Derek's ankle. Without a moment to lose, he lined himself up and propelled his whole body into the air. The action gave him enough hang time to readjust his hands, but the thick force kept him from gaining a firm grasp. He slipped off Derek's boot and fell several feet to the floor. He landed off-balance, which stole precious seconds for a rebound. He quickly looked up to gauge the distance for another try.

To Brian's horror, the ceiling sucked Derek's feet up beyond his reach. He slowly stood and watched Derek's boots disappear into the reflective pool blanketing the ceiling. As the droplet finished smoothing out, the ripples dissipated altogether. The ceiling looked as if nothing had ever happened.

Sivien finished floundering to Brian's side. His eyes remained glued to the ceiling.

Brian remained motionless, staring up at the mirror alongside Sivien. A measure of sense slapped him back into reality. He stood just a little taller than the oversized tabletops, and he was starting to feel very exposed. Dropping back down into a crouch, he got as far away from the ceiling as possible. He searched his surroundings to take cover and tugged on Sivien's pant leg. "Get down! Get down!" he yell-whispered.

Sivien gazed down at Brian with a look of confusion. In a flash, his eyes got big as the light of recognition flipped on. He dropped to the floor next to Brian. "What in the name of holy macrocosm just happened?" Sivien managed to squeak out. His green scales took on a paler hue.

"I have no idea." Brian crawled under the nearest table. "But I feel like we need to stay down."

Sivien tried to scoot under the table next to Brian. The oversized furnishing still left a good portion of his bulky backside exposed. Brian poked his head out from underneath his newfound shelter and scanned the ceiling again. The mirror's surface seemed just as smooth and sleek-looking as it ever had. The alien couple still sat at the bar, and the female now enjoyed a drink and steaming entrée of her own. They made silent, casual-looking conversation, but Brian wasn't focused on them. He stared at the only being in the reflected surface he cared about—Derek.

Derek's reflection now wore the same uniform as did the couple sitting at the bar. He moved closer to the pair and made some sort of comment. The blue-skinned alien motioned for him to take the seat next to the tentacled female. Derek's reflection obliged and sat down. He appeared to hail the unseen person behind the bar and carried on as though he had ordered something.

Brian looked down from the ceiling and examined the bar in the real room. The seats remained empty but lined up perfectly with the ones in the mirror above. He glanced back up. Derek finished ordering and started a conversation with the couple. The trio broke out into silent laughter.

Zella laughed, too.

Brian turned and looked at her.

She still leaned against the wall near the open door. She hadn't moved an inch from where she stood before Derek got absorbed. Zella stared at her tail and combed the fur on its end with her retractable claws, as though she had somehow missed the whole event.

"Zella!" Brian hissed at her. "Get down! Get under a table. Didn't you see what just happened?"

Zella didn't make a move or even acknowledge Brian. She continued combing her tail's fur.

"ZELLA!" Brian tried to get her attention again.

Zella began humming the same tune from earlier and still didn't look up.

Brian started shimmying under the tables, making his way across the room to the door. Sivien shuffled toward Zella too, but his bulky mass caught on the tables and chairs and dragged them along. Squeals sounded from the furniture's legs as they hitched a short ride on Sivien's backside. Brian cringed and turned. Shooting Sivien a look, he motioned at the ceiling with his head as an indicator to keep the noise down.

Sivien shrugged apologetically, and Brian proceeded. Only slightly less clatter sounded from the giant lizard-man as they continued toward Zella. Brian made it to the edge of the tables. One particular chair piggybacked a ride on Sivien and squealed for an excruciating amount of time. Brian cringed at the long, drawn-out screech.

Zella quit humming and looked up from her tail.

"Zella," Brian whispered harshly and waved his arms.

"What, *Captain*?" Zella asked.

"Zella, get under a table!" Brian ordered.

"I don't want to get under the table," Zella replied.

"It's probably safer than standing out in the open," Sivien chimed in.

Zella folded her arms across her chest. "I don't want to climb underneath the tables. You two look like a pair of idiots, and I'd prefer not to join you."

"This place isn't safe." Brian ventured past the table's edge and motioned for her to come to him. "Didn't you see what just happened to Derek? Get down."

Zella rolled her eyes. "Stop telling me what to do. I'm getting tired of it!"

With a mistrusting glance at the mirror, Brian left the refuge of the table to fetch her. He hunched over, putting as much distance as possible between himself and the unpredictable ceiling. Zella's posture shifted into a defensive stance. Sensing her response would be a little tricky to handle, Brian slowed his approach. He inched closer and watched her scrutinize his every move. The excessive scootching sounds coming from behind him broadcast Sivien's changing location. The racket finally stopped, and he knew his backup had cleared the last row of tables.

Brian eased slightly to the right, an offensive ploy he knew Sivien would detect. Due to past training sessions, he knew Zella would recognize it as well. As if on cue, Sivien came into his peripheral view, hunched over and flanking him on his left. Hot fury began radiating from Zella's seemingly calm, feline features. He knew she must have perceived his budding plan.

"I said NO!" Zella sneered.

"Zella." Sivien inched closer and glanced up at the mirror. "You don't know what you're saying. It's not safe here. We have to take cover and figure out what to do."

Zella glared at Sivien. Her lip curled, and she let out a low growl. She dropped her tail, which returned to its natural placement at her side. She settled into a pounce-ready stance.

Brian spread his hands out in front of himself, trying to appear non-aggressive. "Zella, what are you doing? It's us. Your crewmates." He motioned back and forth from himself to Sivien as he crept closer.

Her gaze shifted back to Brian, and her eyes narrowed as her claws extended.

"The station's getting to your head somehow. You're not thinking properly." Brian glanced up. "Just come with us. We need to take cover."

Zella's ears flattened. She hissed, then pounced. She zipped toward Brian with lightning speed, but he quick-stepped to the side, narrowly missing a knee strike aimed at his chest. Her instant reversal slammed a blow into his back that pitched him forward. Pain exploded through his lungs as he scrambled for balance.

"Zella, stop!" Sivien rushed in.

"That's not very nice." Zella turned on him and batted his hands down with her claws.

Sivien yelped and recoiled.

"Two against one? That isn't fair." Zella's foot snapped up and cracked his head backward.

Sivien groaned and grabbed his face as he retreated a step.

"Well, come on, tough guys." Zella eased back into her stance. "You two just can't help but pick on a defenseless woman."

The burning in Brian's lungs lessened. He could swear she had nailed him with full force through his shield. The memory of her pinching Sivien's underarm earlier leaped into his mind. He remembered that she had figured out how to bend the transmitter's light and bypass it. "Zella, this is madness . . . We're not your enemies," he said between labored breaths.

Zella's attention zeroed in on Brian. Her expression soured even more. "I'm not crazy." Her fur shimmered as she started bending the room's light around her.

Sivien rushed in and caught her by the scruff of the neck, thwarting her transition from visibility. He lifted her into the air with one hand and continued to hold his head with his other. She started kicking and clawing at his arm. "Ouch! Stop that!" He shook her.

She clawed at him all the more.

"That's enough!" Sivien shook her a little harder. "If you're not crazy, then stop acting like it."

Zella went limp and hung there, dangling in defeat.

Sivien glanced up at the ceiling and crouched a little. "What do we do now?"

"Get back under the tables!" Brian crouched too.

Zella let out a crazed cackle. A wild spark flashed in her eyes, and a deranged smile spread across her lips. She swung her legs out straight in front of her and up over her head. Sivien's eyes went wide, and he held her as far away from himself as he could. As she continued her acrobatic ascent up and onto his arm, her fur began shimmering. She started bending the light again and faded from view as she finished curling onto his arm.

Claw marks streaked across Sivien's sleeve.

"AAH!" Sivien started flailing and released whatever hold he had left on her.

Within seconds, deep gashes slashed across his uniform, exposing his ribs. He howled in pain. Another set of slashes ripped across his leg, and his knee buckled. He leaned hard to one side, grabbing his newest wounds. Zella's giggle erupted from somewhere, and her laughter bounced off the walls.

Brian fell into a defensive stance. He searched the area for any sign of Zella's location. A sudden crack to his jaw banished his senses to a swirling abyss of misery. He tried to steady his spinning mind. He blinked several times as the threatening blackout started to fade. "Zella, we're your friends." The sound of his own voice reverberated in his head. Small, white stars shot across his vision like tiny, tipsy meteors, unsure of their orbital trajectory.

Out of nowhere, Sivien slammed face-first onto the floor. His gigantic body landed in a heap. He shook off his daze and managed to climb to his hands and knees. "Zella! That was uncalled—" His voice turned into a high-pitched squeal and cut out altogether. He started clawing at his neck in a frenzy.

Pushing past the last tipsy meteors still swirling in his vision, Brian staggered toward his massive friend. Sivien's claws fumbled about his neck limply, and he slumped to the floor. Zella's giggle sounded again, and she reappeared. Her knee dug into Sivien's back, between his hulking shoulders, and her foot leveraged against his head. Her tail looped around his neck. Her muscles strained as she pulled it tight. A crooked smile fused with her curled upper lip.

Sivien's sloppy tugs at the unconventional noose around his neck slowed to a stop.

"NO, ZELLA!" Brian bolted toward her.

Brian collided with Zella. Blue sparks erupted from their shields, and they both went flying into the hall. Brian tucked into a clumsy roll on the soft carpet but rebounded quickly. Sivien began coughing and gulped in air as he became free from her tail. Zella recovered and sprawled out like a spider on all fours.

Parts of Zella's shield lit up, frozen in a glitch. She locked gazes with Brian and smoothly stood. She peered down at her chest and plucked her transmitter from its placement. "I don't need this, anyway." She crushed it in her furry hand. The glitching shield instantly disappeared.

She dropped her transmitter and kick-launched it down the hall.

Brian stole a glance at the ceiling and hunched over. "Zella, this place isn't safe. We can talk about this after we take cover."

A flash of fury streaked across her features. With a flick of her wrists, her retractable claws lengthened.

Brian stood defensively. "I see talking is still off the table." He dug his back boot into the fluffy carpet.

Sivien staggered to the opening of the door and leaned against it, somewhat recovered from Zella's unconventional chokehold. He looked like he wanted to jump in and help but didn't know quite how.

Zella slunk toward Brian.

"It's the ceiling, Zella," Brian continued. "It's messing with your head."

Zella pinned her ears back.

"We're not . . ." Sivien sucked in more air as he went for the collapsible ax strapped to his chest. Instead of unsheathing it, though, he shook his head, looking like he was second-guessing the idea. "We're not going to hurt you."

Zella's glare shifted to Sivien. Brian held his ground, not sure how to proceed. He hoped they could talk some sense into her before things got even more out of hand.

"Something's wrong with this station, and we . . ." Sivien coughed. "We need to take cover."

Brian crept forward. Zella's ear twitched in his direction, and she shimmered out of sight. A gust of wind disturbed the air around Brian, and a set of razor-sharp claws slid across his cheek. He didn't even feel any drag as they sliced through his flesh. It took a few seconds for his body to recognize the fresh wound. Then searing pain exploded across his face.

His hand went to the injury, and he stifled a cry.

Chapter 23

Warm blood ran down Brian's cheek. He looked at Sivien. "She could be just about anywhere. See if you can taste where she's at." He dabbed the strips of skin hanging on his face with the end of his sleeve. He hated the idea of being little more than a ball of yarn served on a silver platter to an overgrown kitten.

Sivien's tongue flicked in the air. He tilted his head, and his tongue flicked again.

Blind to the whereabouts of his attacker, Brian stood at the ready.

Sivien's eyes got big. "She's behind you."

Brian leaped forward as the force of a blow cut through the air at his back. His hands shot up, defending his head, but he miscalculated Zella's attack, and another strike landed hard in his ribs with a crack. The impact knocked the wind out of him. Agony streaked through his chest. He swung at the spot where he assumed Zella was but connected with only air.

A blow to Brian's shoulder knocked him off balance, and he fell to his knees. The force from the attack almost masked the fact that Zella had gouged another series of slashes in him. When he caught a glimpse of the damage, he could see deep into his muscles. Searing pain coursed through his new wound. He peered around the hall. "Zella, enough!"

Sivien moved closer to Brian. His tongue flicked again, and he slowed. He tipped his head, and his eyes narrowed. Cautiously, he started shuffling around the hall, tasting the air. His eyes suddenly went wide, and he blocked an invisible blow, but his legs flew out from underneath him. He landed hard on his back, and his hands popped up to shield his head. Slashes erupted across his forearms. He howled and kicked out with one leg. A high-pitched shriek sounded, quickly followed by a thud against the wall.

"Zella, are you okay?" Sivien sat up and began patting around on the floor. "I didn't mean to kick you so hard."

Brian climbed to his feet. "Is she injured?" He hobbled to Sivien's side and helped him search.

"I don't know." Sivien continued pawing at the carpet. "I can't find her."

Gashes erupted down Brian's right thigh. He cried out and pressed a hand over the deep slashes. Sivien jumped to his feet and grabbed the area around Brian, but Zella had light-footed out of reach somewhere.

"She's moving so fast. I can't keep up with her!" Gouges suddenly sliced across Sivien's stomach, and he grabbed them with another wail.

Like a kitten toying with its prey, Zella bounced back and forth between Brian and Sivien, leaving a trail of ripped uniforms and flesh in her wake. They hunched into defensive balls. Brian's shield lit up with several glitches forming in its protective field. He bided his time through the onslaught, waiting for an opening he could exploit. With Zella still hidden under the cloak of her invisibility, his hopes of finding one seemed just as dashed to pieces as he was becoming. A sudden blast to the center of his back hurled him through the air. He landed on his hands and knees as the air rushed from his lungs.

Brian's body screamed for air at the bottom of the forced exhale. Falling into his training, he focused on his surroundings and waited for the ability to inhale. As his shrieking lungs calmed, he controlled his gasps for air. He had always wondered how death would take him. He'd never once entertained the idea that it would be at Zella's hand.

Brian braced himself for the end.

Zella's shrill cackle suddenly broke the hall's silence.

Leaping to his feet, Brian zeroed in on the frenzied laugh's origin and took a swing. His well-aimed fist collided with Zella's small, furry jaw, and cut short her hysterical laughter. She reentered the realm of visibility, staggering around the hall.

Brian tackled her to the ground.

Sivien peeked out from his defensive hunch.

"We need to sedate her!" Brian pinned Zella to the floor.

Sivien began fumbling for his pack.

"Get your med-kit!" Brian yelled as Zella began squirming under his weight. "Hurry!"

Sivien grabbed the whole pack and yanked it off his back. Tipping it bottom-up, he shook the bag, and its contents spilled all over. He picked through the mess, searching for the desired items. He found a small container and ripped it open to reveal a gun-like medical device.

Brian felt Zella's strength returning to her as she struggled underneath his hold. "FASTER!"

Sivien slammed a vial into the gun's loading chamber and hustled over. Brian tightened his tactical embrace around Zella, and Sivien brought the medical device up to her furry neck. Suddenly, her whole body heaved, partially breaking Brian's hold. She smashed the back of her head into his face. Misery burst throughout his head as his sinuses crunched. Blinding agony welled up behind his eyes, and bright, warm blood began dripping from his nose. Zella wrestled out from underneath him. Sivien caught one of her arms and made another attempt at sedation. Brian tried to secure her legs, but a sudden kick to his head sent his world back into orbit.

Zella made a deep growl, followed by a hiss. A series of hollow thuds and muffled groans came from Sivien, and he collapsed into a heap. He writhed on the floor. Zella plucked her other foot from Brian's weakened grasp and stood.

Blinking hard, Brian tried to refocus, grabbing at Zella. His small glimmer of hope that he might catch her collapsed in his clumsy attempt. She shifted in place, and Brian knew a kick was headed his way. He leaned back to avoid it, but not far enough. The moment her boot collided with his head, his mind eclipsed from all thought. His surroundings faded into a haze. The weightless sensation of falling cradled him in its eternal embrace until he landed hard on the floor.

Brian strained as he tried to ward off the all-encompassing darkness, but the void of unconsciousness loomed ever nearer. The liberation from his cares seemed so enticing, but his loyalty to his crew—his cherished friends—fueled his utter refusal to give in. His world started to come back into focus, along with a renewed sense of clarity.

He blinked a few times, and his eyes rolled around in his head. A hint of double vision touched everything he saw, but his sight soon merged back into focus. He lay on the floor with his cheek pressing against the soft carpet. The steady pressure stabilized his spinning mind. He found himself sprawled out in the middle of the hall. The blood drizzling from his nose pooled into a crimson stain.

Sivien crawled past in pursuit of Zella. Brian flopped his head to the other side so he could find her. Spinning stars spotted his vision again, but he saw her strutting down the hall. She turned on her heels and faced them. Sivien stopped in his tracks, and his arms shielded his head.

"I'm not going to hide underneath the tables with you two morons. Just look at you." Zella laughed. "You two are pathetic."

Sivien peeked at her through the crack between his arms.

Zella stopped glaring at them and gazed up at her reflection in the mirror. She lifted her arms. "I want to stay here with her. Isn't she beautiful?" She raised onto her toes and stretched toward the ceiling as if she could reach it, but by then, she almost could.

The thickness of the atmosphere suddenly returned, and ripples formed in the mirror. A bucket-sized droplet began swelling over Zella's head. The flowy, reflective substance formed hands and fingers that grew to match Zella's outstretched arms. The developing duplicate reached for Zella, too. The end of the droplet took on the three-dimensional shape of her upper body, but its lower half remained fused with the ceiling below its waist.

Brian forced himself to try to get up. Darkness threatened to overtake him on the outskirts of his vision. "Sivien . . . Zella." He tried to give direction, but his weak voice thundered in his head.

Zella's fingertips brushed against her duplicate's. As soon as they touched, the droplet began running down Zella's hands and arms. It started losing its shape and coloring as it reverted into its liquid state.

"NO! No, no, no . . ." Sivien started repeating as he quickly crawled the rest of the way to Zella. He started tugging on her. He yanked, but she wouldn't pull free. Anguish settled on all of his features, and quiet whimpers escaped his trembling lips. "Truce, Zella. Please, no, no . . . Truce!"

Brian managed to drag himself a few inches across the floor. The pressure inside his head spewed more blood from his nose. His shoulder, leg, and several other minor injuries battled for his attention. Shifting his weight, he pulled himself a little farther along the carpet. The bright red flow from his nose drizzled a steady line as he went. He gazed up at Zella.

The droplet of liquid mirror flowed down her arms, engulfing her shoulders.

Brian's gut wrenched.

The droplet started flowing up Zella's furry neck. She continued smiling as a layer of the stuff coated her bottom lip and spread over her teeth. Brian could still make out her jovial smile as it blanketed the rest of her face and swallowed her entire head.

"No, no, no . . ." Sivien whispered over and over as he continued tugging at her waist. He suddenly wrapped her in a bear hug, and his bulky muscles strained as he heaved backward.

Zella's stiffened body didn't budge.

The liquid mirror flowed down her torso but stopped above Sivien's arms. He stopped moving.

Tiny vibrations disturbed the droplet's surface right next to Sivien's face. The choppiness of the mirror smoothed out, and it began reflecting his image. His shoulders drooped as he stared at himself, and the tension in his muscles seemed to melt away.

"Sivien. Don't look at it." Brian's weak voice barely broke the silence of the hall. He clawed his way across the floor to his friends.

Sivien's eyes slid shut. As he opened them again, they glazed over.

The liquid mirror continued its trek down Zella and blanketed Sivien's arms, too. His shield started glitching.

Brian grabbed the heel of Sivien's large boot. Blue sparks erupted under his hold. "Don't look at it. Don't look at it . . ." he repeated.

Sivien's eyes looked heavy, and he closed them. He turned and bowed his head. "Truce."

Zella's mirror-covered hands emerged from the droplet and cupped Sivien's scaly cheeks. He leaned into her embrace. The droplet quickly engulfed his head and spread down his bulky shoulders. His shield flickered out.

Brian's weak tugs on Sivien's boot slackened even more.

With Sivien still cradling Zella in his mirror-coated arms, her feet lifted into the air, and the droplet began uprooting the pair from the hall. While the reflective substance continued engulfing the rest of their bodies, it lifted them higher.

Brian gave one last tug on Sivien's boot as it pulled away. His lizard friend disappeared in the ceiling's folds along with Zella. The mirror's surface smoothed back out and returned to normal.

Brian stared up at the only trace left of Sivien and Zella—their reflections lingering in the mirror. The duplicates now wore the navy blue uniforms, just like Derek's had in the cafeteria. They conversed awkwardly with each other, but Brian couldn't hear them. Sivien started down the hall, leaving Zella standing alone. She turned and went the other way.

Brian slumped against the floor and drifted from consciousness.

Chapter 24

Submerged in the nothingness of some sort of eternal void, Brian floated from one half-thought to another. Space and time refused to ground him to any sense of reality in this place. The hollow nook of existence provided an escape from all of his misery and sorrow. He willfully surrendered to the contentment it offered and began settling in to make his rest in the nothingness permanent—but something brought him back from the brink.

Some sort of sound.

He focused on it, and it came again.

As though propelled by thought alone, Brian started drifting toward the disturbance. The weightless feeling of floating somewhat re-energized his senses. The sound rushed in again, somewhere beyond the void of his current existence. It held a rhythm. He concentrated on it more. It seemed so familiar, but he couldn't quite put his finger on why. The sound came once more, and his memory sparked.

Waves.

Crashing waves.

Brian mentally patted himself on the back. *Why was that so hard to remember?*

Another distant wave crashed on an unseen shore, and Brian drifted toward the soothing sound that interrupted the void. A warm breeze lifted him and rushed him farther along. He reclined in the wind's gentle current as it swept him away.

Tiny particles of a salty sea misted the air around him.

The darkness of the void faded as the lightened hue of day dawned. Brian found a dense fog billowing around him as the gentle breeze continued carrying him toward the waves. The misty morning brightened, and the atmosphere separated into puffy clouds that parted for him while he traveled. The intangible fluff dispersed until a sanded landscape appeared beneath him.

A beach? . . . The ocean?

Brian continued sailing in the breeze. A shore came into view, and another gust of air picked up from the opposite direction. The crosswinds held him in place, and his bare feet touched down on cool sand. The misty fog and clouds dissipated further, and his surroundings solidified even more.

The heat from the sun bore through the fading fog. Brian squinted in the sudden noonday brilliance. A biting sting formed behind his eyes, and they watered. Adjusting to the sun's brightness, he wiped the moisture away and began taking in his surroundings. He found himself reclining in a chair with an ice-cold drink beside him. A red umbrella was propped open above him, but it provided little shade because of the time of day. The peak of noon must have passed a while ago.

Mirandian's third moon? Brian came to his senses more fully as he looked around. *What am I doing here again?*

He sat up and surveyed the beach. Sand and rolling waves stretched out as far as he could see.

Where is everyone?

An empty chair sat next to him in the sand. A small flicker of recollection hit him. *Grace!*

He searched the empty beach for his wife and climbed out of his chair. Hunching under the long reach of the giant umbrella, he scanned the area but found no sign of her.

"Grace?" Brian listened for a response.

The rhythmic roll of the ocean waves continued its timeless game of dashing onto the beach, then retreating. The decorative fabric hanging on the umbrella's outer edge flapped in the soft breeze. He stepped out from underneath the foldable red canopy. Stretching to his full height, he looked around.

Brian cupped his hands around his mouth. "GRACE?" Echoes of his voice bounced off the perfect, purple sky.

Something told him she wasn't here.

He turned from the shore and headed toward the resort located just off the beachfront. The sand slowed his pace as his feet sank in with every stride. He observed the scenery around his little resting nook and saw nothing but dunes beyond.

He stopped in his tracks.

Where's the resort? A sickening feeling grew in his stomach. He tried to swallow, but a dry lump caught in his throat.

The brilliance of the day suddenly seemed to dampen.

Brian glanced up, expecting to see a puffy cloud obscuring the sun. To his surprise, there wasn't a single blemish dotting the sky. He wondered what had caused the depressing change in the atmosphere. The breeze against his back kicked up wispy whirlwinds of sand. He suddenly felt the weight of someone's watchful eyes. When he glanced across the dunes, he saw nothing. Still, the strange sensation persisted. It seemed to be coming from behind him. Hairs on the back of his neck stood on end, and he slowly turned, hoping to find his wife but bracing for something else.

Brian's chair remained under the massive umbrella, and his drink sat undisturbed on the furniture's arm, but Grace's chair was occupied by a large mound of bulbous blubber. Portions of its beige, clammy-looking flesh bulged through every crevice of the seat. His stomach flopped at the sight of the thing.

Uh, what is that? Brian thought as he stared.

A hint of something sweet kissed the air, and a gust of hot wind whipped across the beach. The temperature increased by at least ten degrees. Sweat pricked Brian's forehead, and he longed for the shade under the umbrella. With the new strange mound sitting in his companion's seat, any eagerness to approach the shelter to escape the sun quickly diminished. Something inside urged him to flee, to escape to the dunes at his back, but his growing curiosity overpowered the impulse.

Brian stared at the inconsequential-looking mass of blubber. The top portion of the mound started sagging over the back of the chair, and he wondered whether the thing was strong enough to endure the heat of the day. A slight sense of pity pulled on his heartstrings for the creature's imminent demise.

Brian chuckled to himself over his absurd feelings. "I don't even know if you're alive. Can you even feel pain?" he asked the thing. Sweat collected on his brow.

The beige blubber continued bending over the back of the chair until it sagged to the sand. The sturdy seat couldn't handle the blob's offset weight, and it tipped over. The rest of the mass fell out of the chair, dumping its bulk onto the ground. The bulbous pile looked more like a hefty mound of gristle than anything else, but it wasn't melting from the heat of the day like Brian had thought.

The temperature increased even more, and droplets of sweat dripped from Brian's face.

Another gust of scorching wind picked up.

The scent in the breeze thickened, and the bold sweetness tied Brian's stomach in knots. He started backing up. He turned to flee to the dunes, but his feet sank deeper into the sand. The sound of heavy dragging across the ground accompanied the mountainous blubber as it suddenly cleared a significant distance toward him. He battled to gain footing. His heart hammered inside of his chest. An unseen but tangible weight pressed on him from the very air. He stumbled to the ground as the invisible force bombarded all of his senses. His stomach turned somersaults as he continued watching the mound sludge closer. The bulbous creature closed the gap between them in what felt like an eternity but was, perhaps, mere seconds. He couldn't tell anymore—time felt like such a blur.

The mound stopped advancing when it was about a foot or two away. It cast its shadow over him as its towering mass blotted out the sun. Brian could tell that the ever-thickening scent in the air was wafting from the thing. He gazed up at the beastly blob. The shade it provided did little to alleviate the scorching heat of the day as the air grew even hotter. Droplets of sweat ran down the middle of his back.

The bulbous beast started forming a horizontal separation along the width of its belly. The split deepened and widened, and a dark hole began opening on its inside. Brian's curiosity slightly dampened his panic. In the boiling heat of the blob's shade, he found himself becoming enthralled with the creature, unsure what to make of it all. The invisible force in the air slowly relinquished its hold.

The hole in the blubbery skin became rounded on the top half and flattened on the bottom. It began looking more like a giant's mouth, frowning its disapproval at him. More of the sweet smell blasted Brian. It saturated the air like a repugnant breath. Despite Brian's disgust, his imagination ran wild with the possibilities of what he might find inside. Before he knew it, he was leaning forward to get a better look.

Brian worked his feet free from the sand and slowly crawled toward the belly of the beast. Suddenly, the top lip of the opening rose higher overhead, and the bottom lip burrowed below the surface of the sand. A rumble shook the ground beneath Brian and made cracks split through the soil's dry surface around him.

The quaking subsided.

Brian gazed into the gaping mouth that was now missing its bottom lip in the sand. The penetrating darkness of the deep pit within the inner beast was visible past the open maw. The overpoweringly sweet smell in the air turned his stomach, and he was hesitant to get too close to the thing. Still, he felt compelled to explore the new cave-like hole it had made in the ground. He dug his back heel into the loose soil and carefully edged closer to the opening. Some of the wispy strands of sand trickled into the depths of the blubber's dark innards.

Peering inside, Brian found that the cave-like interior went on for several yards in all directions—including downward. He did some quick calculations because the size of its interior didn't seem to match the size of its exterior. He leaned back and examined the blob's surface, double-checking his estimations for accuracy. As he reinspected it again, he came to the same conclusion: The blubber mound really did appear to be bigger on the inside than it was on the outside. The absurd notion offended the very fabric of reason, but he couldn't logic away the facts sitting right in front of him.

A flash of movement in the blob's darkened insides stole Brian's attention. He held his breath and focused on the area, waiting for more movement. Seeing nothing, he chuckled at his nerves. *How silly of me. Of course, there's nothing in there.* His merriment faded to a smile.

With his curiosity about the disgusting blob satisfied, he climbed to his feet, ready to search the dunes for the obscure vacation resort he couldn't find earlier. Just as he went to step away, more movement inside the pit caught his eye.

Chapter 25

Brian stood on the beach, peering into the blobby mound's belly. Looking down to the cave-like pit inside, he saw something stirring in a fold on its back wall—right where he thought he saw movement earlier. Dirty, pale-blue fingers wiggled their way out of a crease and revealed a worn, weathered hand. Another hand wormed its way out behind it and caught hold of a clump of the darkened substance that made up the walls. The hands clawed their way into the cavern, and the two arms further emerged from the unholy place of their origin. Something dark and round then began pressing through as well.

Brian stared at the spectacle. The thing emerging between the arms started resembling the shape of a head. As it continued to squeeze out of the crevice it was creating, Brian noticed it had long, stringy black hair. The dirt-filled locks parted in the middle of the creature's pale forehead and opened up around its face like dreary curtains. Its blue-tinged skin hung from its haggard bones. Sunken sockets, where its eyes should have been, hinted at what kind of soulless monster it might be. The corpse-like thing continued squeezing itself out of the fold in the wall. Tattered rags that had once been a uniform clung to its shabby torso. The humanoid corpse flopped onto the dark floor as the thing finished emerging from whence it came.

The heated wind of the beach whipped across Brian as he kept his petrified gaze fixed on the blob's pit-like belly. The tattered corpse clawed across the pit's floor in his general direction. He instantly hoped the thing couldn't climb out and get him somehow.

More movement caught Brian's eye from another spot on the wall. On the far right, another pale-blue arm emerged. A sweeping glance across the pit revealed many creatures' dirty hands and limbs erupting from several places within the sweltering, deep cave. Brian heard something plop on the sand next to his foot. Tearing his attention away from the ghoulish creatures climbing out of the dark cavern walls below, he looked at the ground near his boot.

A bucket-sized glob of clear gel sat on the sand. It sagged as though the blistering heat had started melting it away. Its moisture darkened the ground around it. An identical *plop* sounded next to his other foot. He glanced over and found a similar clear glob melting beside his boot. He gazed up, looking for its source. High above, the goop gathered and hung along the blob's top lip. Another large droplet fell. The pungent, sweet smell wafted from each glob of goo, and the image of a huge, drooling mouth entered Brian's mind.

Leaning away from the opening, he started backing up.

A low rumble began shaking the sand underneath him again. His boots sank in, submerging his feet up to his ankles. He tried lifting them back out, but the ground swallowed his legs up to his calves. His jaw dropped as he watched the sand at the edge of the beast's belly begin to pour into the dark pit that made up its insides. The blubbery mound shook as if it were the cause of the ground's quaking.

The beast's belly opened even more, threatening to take in a giant mouthful of the beach. Brian flailed as he tried to extract his feet from the collapsing sand—but they wouldn't budge. More sand cascaded into the pit, and he saw dozens of pale, blue-skinned creatures crawling around inside. They clambered over each other as they fought to get to the crumbling opening—where Brian was sinking into the sand. Some of them staggered around on their legs, but many of them dragged themselves across the grimy darkness.

Brian was thrust off balance as his weight pitched forward. The sand around his feet was spilling into the pit—and seemed to be taking him with it. His mind raced as he searched for some way to free himself. Suddenly, something large sprang out of the sand right behind him. He turned as much as he could and immediately recognized the thing as the bottom lip of the blubbery mound. It must have been the cause of the quaking ground. The blob was taking a sizable bite out of the beach, and Brian felt like a tasty garnish atop a meal. The beast's bottom lip continued rising out of the sand. As its height increased, it quickly became a wall between him and the dunes beyond.

The growing barrier to Brian's freedom rose to the height of his chest. He hooked his arms onto the ledge while the sand around his legs completely fell away, then pulled himself up as far as he could. There was nothing he could hold onto that would allow him to vault over the lip. He locked his elbows into place and continued his frantic search for leverage. The zombie-like creature's shufflings sounded in the darkness below.

The bottom lip continued to rise, with Brian dangling from it. The same gel-like substance that dripped near his boots earlier began forming everywhere he touched. He started losing his grip in the slick, snot-like muck. He slipped and fell a couple of feet, but he caught hold of another nook with one hand.

Dangling over the dark pit, he stole a glance over his shoulder at the ragged horde below. They crowded each other while still more of them clawed their way out of the walls. He wiped his free hand, now coated with the odorous gel, on his uniform's leg and swung wide. Hoping for a crevice he could wedge his fingers into, he launched his hand through the thickening goop and fished for a more stable hold. His frantic efforts increased as everything became slicker.

Brian's weight-bearing arm finally slipped from its hold, and he fell the rest of the way down. He landed hard but quickly scrambled to his feet. Backing up against the wall, he shuffled as far away from the creatures as he could. His breath came in short, shallow bursts as he pressed against the hot, black substance at his back. The sweltering heat of the pit's air made his lungs burn. The mouth of the beast started closing high over-head, and the light from the brilliant afternoon outside began fading. The ghoulish monsters crowded around Brian in the growing darkness. He pushed even harder against the boiling wall at his back.

Suddenly, a haggard, blue-skinned hand shot out of the wall next to him and started flailing. A decaying head immediately squeezed out of the same hole as the limb. It turned to him, and Brian peered into its soul-less, sunken sockets. The creature continued to emerge from the wall, and Brian stared at it breathlessly. Its jaw opened beyond a natural capacity, and a subhuman, guttural wheeze dumped its putrified breath into the air. The beastly thing reached for him, and Brian tripped over his feet as he tried to scramble away. Another rotted hand burst from the wall on his other side, halting his retreat.

The light from outside continued to fade.

Brian sank to the floor as the sea of rotting flesh pressed in on him.

The mouth of the pit closed with a thundering boom that made the walls and floor tremble. He couldn't see a thing. The sound of his own rapid breaths filled his ears. Brian closed his eyes, wishing himself out of the pit. The creatures quietly shuffled around him in the dark. He felt one of the things latch onto his thigh. He frantically tried shaking it off, but it wouldn't let go. Another grabbed his shoulder. He balled up his fist and swung in its direction, but the attack missed hitting anything substantial.

The monster clinging to his shoulder dug deep into Brian's flesh. He could only imagine the hideous beast sinking its rotten teeth into him. He started throwing punches in every direction, but he never landed a solid blow. A set of claws raked across his cheek. He cried out, but no sound escaped his lips.

The creature that had latched onto his leg bore into the muscle. Brian ground his teeth as he gritted through the pain. Fiery fingers touched his eyes and started pushing in on them. The back of his head smashed against the wall as the decaying digits began pressing through his lids.

A scream curdled in Brian's throat, but only a muffled groan escaped his lips. The rotted fingers pierced his eyes and drilled in farther. He threw wild punches at the filthy monsters, but every swing only sliced through the blistering air. The lava-hot pokers continued drilling deeper and deeper. Brian's flailing slowed as his sanity began breaking.

His head spun, and an odd shift dazed his senses.

Brian suddenly felt himself being pulled from the cavern until the place almost didn't seem real. Even with his eyes clamped shut, he sensed a change in the lighting of the room. The boiling heat and foul stench of the place faded even more, but the torture welling behind his eyes remained the same. His leg still screamed foul unpleasantries at him, and his ribs, cheek, and shoulder joined in the fray. Even so, the nightmare of the monster-filled pit drifted farther away.

Coming more to his senses, Brian became aware that, at some point, he slipped into unconsciousness. A groan escaped his lips, and his head pounded. *Was it all just a dream?* He covered his face with a hand, warding off the excruciating brightness of the surrounding light.

He worked on cracking one eye open. The dazzling brightness of the lanterns that hung on the walls ignited new waves of throbbing misery through his head. He squinted and forced his eye to stay open. Fuzzy spots orbited in his vision as he focused on his surroundings. Half-heartedly glancing around, he realized he was lying facedown on a soft, white carpet in an empty hall. He forced his other eye open and slowly blinked.

Nothing looked familiar. *Where am I?* Brian wondered.

He let out another groan, but he almost couldn't tell that the sound had come from him.

Fuzzy spots still wandered around in his vision, and suffering settled in as an intimate companion instead of just a mere acquaintance. All the pains the monsters had inflicted on him in his nightmare appeared to correspond with injuries he had sustained. The spectacular misery seizing his body left him wishing for sweet relief.

More of his dull groans filled the air.

Pushing past his physical torment, he edged his way onto his side and teetered there. He finished rolling over in a heap, and new throbs of agony crashed through him. His trembling hands moved to cup his pounding temples. Looking up, he noticed the mirrored-covered ceiling high above. He racked his mind, but he couldn't remember how he had gotten here. He couldn't remember anything.

Look at all the blood. Brian stared up at the mirror on the ceiling. *I wonder what happened.*

He blinked a few more times. The grogginess in his mind didn't clear. He examined himself in the mirror. His nose was swollen and bruised.

Ugh, that looks bad enough to be broken. A slight smile peeked at the corners of Brian's lips. *At least it didn't make my nose crooked this time.*

Deep gashes streaked across one cheek and left his skin hanging. The eye directly above the gashes opened only halfway, and he almost didn't recognize himself. The taste of blood trickled down the back of his throat. His force field lit up in patches. He pulled the device from his uniform's breast, and the glitching blue energy field disintegrated altogether. He examined the damaged gadget.

Looking back up at the mirror, he noticed the stains on the carpet around him. *I think all of that is* my *blood.* Reality started kicking in, but a palpable sense of calm began settling over him as he lay there. The throbbing pressure in his head began lessening, and a wave of relief washed over him as he continued staring at himself in the mirror.

Somehow, the shrieking pains of his injuries quieted.

A sudden awareness cut through Brian's daze like a three-point plasma splitter through Talzien metal. *Where's my crew?*

Brian peered down the hall and saw one of his crew's packs a short distance away. Its contents looked like debris scattered around on the floor. A slight memory sparked of Sivien dumping it out, but Brian couldn't remember why. His gaze floated back up to his reflection in the mirror.

Maybe I can just rest here for a little while. It does look like I've been through quite a lot. Brian's cares started melting away again. He barely noticed his reflection's fine details becoming clearer, as if they had somehow moved closer.

His eyes began to burn. *When was the last time I blinked?* He couldn't remember.

The mirror didn't seem so far away anymore.

You know, it's so close I could almost touch it. His hand drifted upward.

He stared at his mirror image, which no longer looked two-dimensional. Right before his eyes, it formed into a genuine life-size replica of himself, reaching its hand toward him. A sense of peace engulfed him while he watched the perfect duplicate dangle closer. Its expression changed from the blank look he had to a wide, menacing grin.

Chapter 26

Terror seized him.

The peaceful, hypnotic hold Brian's duplicate cast over him broke. All at once, his physical torment came rushing back in. The return of his miseries was crippling. His doppelgänger hung just an arm's length away, and its eerie smile hinted at some sinister plan. Brian shuffled his feet against the soft carpet, trying to gain some traction. Arching his back, he dug heels in and pumped his legs. His boots caught, and he scrambled out from under his low-hanging double. Gaining distance, he noticed the thing fused with the ceiling at its waist.

His full memory came flooding back.

Brian's ceiling-twin began reverting into a liquid state and lost its three-dimensional form. The disintegrating double started retracting into the reflective canopy above. Brian grabbed his implosion gun from its holster and opened fire. The shots hit the dangling portion of the mirror, and the blasts discharged bouts of thunderous energy. The droplet's innards churned wildly as its reflective depths billowed with darkened, ink-colored clouds. Within seconds, the berserk tempest calmed, and the ceiling resumed its ascent from whence it came.

Brian's gaze fell to the gun in his hands. He stared at it in disbelief.

It had always worked—on everything.

Brian peered up at the ceiling directly above him, and his ever-present reflection stared back. He aimed and fired again and again. Electrical lightning bolts discharged throughout the mirror, creating a violent upheaval in its liquid surface. He stopped his shooting rampage and slightly lowered his gun, waiting to see the effect. As the tumult began to calm, the ceiling smoothed back out, quickly returning to normal. The reflected hall and Brian's mirror image remained high above—completely unscathed.

He lowered his weapon and lay there, unmoving. His heart drummed, and his physical torments continued their assaults. He took special care not to stare directly at his image for too long. Eons seemed to pass while he waited for another droplet to descend.

Everything in the ceiling seemed to pause along with him.

Why isn't it trying to get me again? Brian wondered. Then a disturbing thought occurred. *Maybe* it *has to have its food tenderized before it can consume it.*

"This can't be real!" Brian whispered out loud to himself. He glanced across the hall, taking in his surroundings. "This has got to be a joke! I'm still on my ship. I'm still in my stasis pod, and I'm dreaming—I'm having a horrific nightmare. Grace will laugh when I tell her about this and how crazy it is."

The absurdity of it all drew a single chuckle from Brian's lips. *This can't be real!* He looked back up at his reflection. More uncontrollable laughter bubbled to the surface. He couldn't hold it in. He started laughing hysterically. His crazed merriment escaped as he lay there on the floor, but it quickly morphed into uncontrollable sobs. Hot tears began rolling down his cheeks. He dropped his gun and buried his pounding head in his hands. The salty droplets stung as they soaked into the gashes on his face. Trying to capture the painful liquid with his sleeve, he wept until the hope of ever waking up from the nightmare fled.

As his tears slowed, Brian's head pounded even more.

He gazed down the hall toward the closed cafeteria door. The contents of Sivien's pack remained scattered across the floor. His attention leaped to the vials spewed around the deserted med-kit. The beating inside his head reminded him of the precious pain reliever stowed in his own med-kit. His ribs ached as he reached for his pack, sandwiched between himself and the floor. With trembling hands, he wrestled it out.

His fingers quivered as he flipped the flap open. He located his med-kit and found one of the vials. Then he fumbled it into the med-gun's loading chamber and locked it into place. He pressed the contraption to his neck and winced as he squeezed the trigger. The soft sound of the device's release accompanied its sharp bite that dug into his skin. Artificial relief instantly flooded his system from the injection site. Brian let out a sigh. As the medicine began taking more of a hold, his shoulders relaxed. Even his trembling hands calmed.

Brian lay there, basking in the delivery from his pain, and a slight chill from his blood-soaked uniform advised him of his first task. "Wound care," he mumbled. Scooping up his gun, he reholstered it. He crawled to the nearest wall and dragged his pack along with him. With great effort, Brian climbed into a sitting position. The medication coursing through his veins began quieting even his severe injuries. He tipped his head back against the wall, resting for a moment. His eyes felt heavy, and his lids fluttered shut. All his pains seem to fade away.

Time felt like a blur.

Soon, renewed waves of agony began prodding Brian back to coherency. He forced his groggy eyes open and found himself sagged against the wall in a semi-upright position with his head cranked to the side. His pack lay on the floor next to him. As he started straightening his stiffened body, pain spewed from his various wounds and a newly formed crick in his neck.

He dislodged the empty vial from his med-gun and inserted a new one. Then he changed the device's setting to a smaller dose—just enough to take the edge off the pain. He leaned back against the wall. With another soft click and a pinching bite, more medication coursed through his veins. Relief started dousing the fiery injuries once again. The relentless pounding in his head died back down to a manageable level. He looked at the med-gun and calculated how many doses remained.

Brian shot a glare at the mirror overhead. Then he turned his attention to the rips in his uniform, starting with the ones on his arm. He pulled one of his ionic hunting blades from its concealed sheath and ran the knife vertically up his sleeve. The material fell free from his arm, dangling at the shoulder seam. He inspected the deep gouges Zella had left. The wounds still seeped blood, and he wondered how much of the precious liquid he had lost.

He cut the dangling sleeve, and it fell free to the floor.

Tossing his blade onto the discarded fabric, Brian turned to his med-kit. He fumbled around inside and pulled out the antiseptic. He doused his hands with the chemical. The liquid's frosty touch rapidly evaporated. He found gauze and saturated it with the solution, then draped the dressings across the gashes in his shoulder. He gasped as the antiseptic's bitter bite sank its icy teeth deep into the wound. The exquisite pain raged, even with the pain reliever coursing through his veins.

The arctic chemical's nip began subsiding.

Brian removed the gauze and hoped he had cleaned the injury well enough. He examined the gashes again. *Yep, they'll need stitches.* He sighed and rolled his eyes.

The needle and thread came out next.

A residual tremble still lingered in his hands, but he steadied his fingers alongside the first gash all the same. He pressed the sharp tip of the needle into his skin. To his relief, he felt nothing. He assumed the pain reliever had kicked in more fully. Stitch after stitch, he sewed the wound closed and set off to mend the next gash. When he finished with his shoulder, he repeated the process on his thigh. In time, he tended to all the injuries except for those on his face.

Brian glanced up at the ceiling mirror and examined the slashes across his cheek where bits of loose skin hung. Zella got him pretty good. His attention focused more fully on his reflection, and he glared at it. Keeping perfect timing, his reflection glared right back. He knew he couldn't use the mirror to accomplish this task. He turned back to his pack, looked for something else that would work, and grabbed the first ration his fingers laid hold on. The memory of his disgusting meal from earlier rolled in. Cringing, he quickly pushed the recollection right back out.

He brought the package up and inspected it. His blurry likeness on its semi-reflective surface provided just enough detail to work with. Brian lifted his chin and tipped his head, getting a better look at the loose skin hanging from the deep slashes. His goatee was caked with dried blood, and fresh seepage leaked from his nose. Moving past the gory scene, he went to work applying antiseptic to his cheek.

Make the stitches small, Brian told himself—even though he was sure the gashes would scar no matter what. He shot glares up at the ceiling while he worked. A flash of anger surged. *This place stole everything from me.*

He sighed and focused on mending himself.

Soon, he pulled the last of the loose skin together with a final stitch. Tying the string off, he inspected his handiwork in the blurry ration's packaging. He didn't do too bad with his moderate medical training and rudimentary tools. Finishing up, he cut the thread and tossed the soiled instruments back into the med-kit.

The last item of business came to mind, and Brian gently touched the swollen bridge of his nose. His fingers drifted to his upper lip. The stubble was sticky and matted with blood. He grabbed more gauze and carefully began packing each nostril, hoping the bleeding would stop soon. Finally satisfied with his work, he put the med-kit away. His attention gravitated to the contents of Sivien's pack spewed across the floor.

He eyed the medications and rations.

Scooping up his pack, Brian strained as he pushed away from the wall and crawled across the floor. The aches and pains continued to gnaw on the outskirts of his senses, chipping away at the soothing effects of the medication. When he reached the scattered mess, he started rounding everything up and silently thanked Sivien for not throwing the stuff around much farther.

As Brian picked through the pile of goods, he placed the most useful items in his pack. His thoughts wandered to Sivien and Zella. The memory of the pair trapped in the mirror's liquid-like folds haunted him. He remembered his crew members' doppelgängers lingering on the ceiling's surface after getting absorbed. Glancing up, he saw only the reflection of the barren hall above. His mangled image was its sole occupant.

Brian's thoughts shifted to Derek's reflection sitting with the two other crew members at the bar. Turning, he looked at the closed cafeteria door and remembered the uniform Derek's duplicate had been wearing: the same uniform Sivien's and Zella's reflections had been wearing. *Maybe . . . just maybe, my crew could still be alive somehow.* The thought started sinking in.

His mind grabbed hold of the idea and refused to let it go.

Maybe Derek's still in the cafeteria.

He slung his pack onto his uninjured shoulder, leaving the rest of the goods in a pile. He crawled toward the door but wasn't totally surprised when the thing didn't slide open on his approach. For a moment, he stared at the large massive slab denying him entry. Then he reached out and half-heartedly pushed on it. It didn't budge. Climbing to his knees, he placed both hands on the door and pressed on it with all of his might.

It still denied him access.

"OH, COME ON!" Brian balled his fists and slammed them against the door. "LET ME IN."

He started hammering away. "YOU THINK THIS IS FUNNY?" He stopped his assault on the door and glared up at the ceiling. He braced himself against the cold barrier and climbed to his feet. Pushing past the immediate head rush, he unleashed his fury. His onslaught didn't even leave the slightest dent in the metal, and his fists started stamping bloodstains with every blow.

The towering slab seemed oblivious to Brian's presence.

"WHY WON'T YOU OPEN?" Brian wailed.

He slammed his fists against the uncooperative door and glared up at the ceiling. His battered reflection glared right back. His shoulders slumped, and he slid to his knees, leaving bloody fist streaks down the dark metal as he went. He crumpled into a heap at the door's foot and hung his head in defeat. He leaned forward and placed his forehead against the unmovable foe. The chill of the metal soothed his overheated skin.

Brian didn't care to move or shift into a more comfortable position. In time, his anger defused slightly, and exhaustion overtook him. He felt himself slipping in and out of consciousness. The last dose of medication soon started wearing off, and the relentless gnaw of his injuries increased, invading his senses once more. Getting a hold of himself, he reluctantly shifted in place, and his ribs shot dull pain through his chest. He carefully turned around and rested against the door. He peered down at his bloodied hands. They had begun swelling from his frenzied assault on the door. Chunks of skin were missing from his knuckles, and he had a possible broken finger or two. He stretched out one leg and then the other. Pins and needles instantly spread throughout his lower limbs.

Brian slowly slid his pack to the floor with his swollen, stiff hands. The med-gun rested at the very top, just inside the flap. Double-checking the dosage, he put the device up to his neck and forced his puffy finger to squeeze the trigger. It released. He exhaled as more medication raced through him. Stuffing the device back into his pack, he closed his eyes, soaking in the comfort as the medication began dousing the fiery aches and pains.

He looked down at his hands, slowly squeezed them into fists, and opened them. He pulled the antiseptic and bandages back out of the pack and cleaned his wounds, flinching every time the antiseptic's icy bite sank into a chunk of missing flesh. The pain medication hadn't kicked in enough.

Soon, the newest wounds on Brian's hands wore dressings, and he leaned back against the door, inviting the medication to take a stronger hold. His gaze drifted to the mirror overhead. His resentment for the infernal station grew as he stewed on what it had done to his crew. The memories of the mirror plucking his comrades out of the hall and cafeteria replayed in his mind.

As Brian held his heated glare on his reflection, an overpowering feeling of calm tried to soften his simmering rage, which only served to infuriate him even more. "Oh, no, you don't! I know your tricks now," he spewed at his image.

The cafeteria door that his reflection leaned against in the mirror began sliding open, and Brian's cursings stopped short. He stared up and tried to make sense of the scene. The real door at his back didn't feel like it had moved at all, at least not from what he could tell.

He started pawing at the door behind him, trying to make sure.

Chapter 27

Brian's back was still pressed against the real door.

The cold metal didn't seem to be moving at all.

The blue-skinned alien who had sat at the bar earlier exited the cafeteria and strolled down the reflected hall in the mirror. Brian watched him travel the long corridor overhead. The door in the ceiling closed and looked like the one against his back again. "What the flib?" he muttered under his breath.

A thought drifted into Brian's mind. *Maybe if I follow him, I can find Derek's reflection.*

Brian gathered his strength and climbed to his feet. He swooned but pushed past another head rush. He began hobbling down the empty hallway, following the blue man from the bar. The most recent dose of medication held the pounding of his head at bay and dampened the intensity of his injuries. Keeping a sharp eye on the blue-skinned being, he watched for any mirror droplets forming on the ceiling and tried to hurry. The man from the cafeteria got farther and farther ahead.

As Brian hobbled down the hall, he realized his ship was in the other direction. The blue-skinned alien seemed to be headed deeper into the station—deeper than Brian ever wanted to go. He thought of the hovering platforms still waiting for his crew's return. He had to get everyone back somehow, and he concentrated on following the being in the mirror even more. His intuition told him he was headed in the right direction but needed to hurry to catch up.

Out of nowhere, something moved in the mirror, directly over Brian. He instantly crouched, and his arms defensively crisscrossed over his head. He froze in place and waited for a descending droplet to devour him, but none came.

After a moment, he peeked at the ceiling through a space between his arms. The mirror looked normal, but another being walked down the reflected hallway in the same direction as the blue-skinned man. A sense of urgency hurried Brian to follow.

Continuing down the hall at a faster hobbling pace, Brian examined the new being. The creature was hairless and had fishlike eyes that protruded from both sides of its head. He cringed at the unfortunate-looking bulges. The being wore a uniform matching all the others in the mirror. Brian tailed the two crew members in the ceiling through one of the station's plentiful intersections. He pushed himself to go faster but made little headway in catching up. As they came to another four-way, he watched the fish-eyed alien turn down the corridor on the right, but the blue-skinned man continued going straight.

Approaching the crossroads himself, Brian hesitated and eyeballed each hall. He watched both aliens slip farther away down their chosen path. Something prodded him to make a choice. He went straight, once again following the alien from the bar. The slight hesitation cost some distance between him and his prize.

He hurried to close the growing gap.

Brian's attention remained fastened to the ceiling. Even with his added speed, the being continued slipping farther away. In time, he came to another four-way. In the blink of an eye, the reflected intersection suddenly burst with activity. A crowd of aliens filled the mirror's hallways in all directions. His pace slowed as he gaped up at the sight. All of the new beings who made up the steady flow of traffic wore identical navy blue uniforms. Brian puzzled over the world flourishing overhead.

A wide array of species traveled the ceiling's hallways, moving in different directions. He searched the mirror but couldn't find the most important one in the crowd—the one he had followed from the bar. He hobbled to the center of the real intersection and stood in its empty crossroads. He caught a smidgeon of blue skin in the alien horde above and zeroed on it. A slight parting in the flow of traffic provided a clear enough view of the alien he tailed, and Brian scurried after him.

He tried to ignore the other aliens in the mirror and stayed focused on catching up with his target. Hushed whispers matching the sounds from earlier began flittering around him. The phantom-like disturbances reached differing degrees of perceptibility. He rejected the idea of understanding them. He wouldn't allow this station to drive him insane, not like it had the others. Still, the voices laced his awareness and interrupted the silence of the emptiness surrounding him in the corridor. The blue being veered to the right and entered a door down the hall. He quickly took note of which one.

"Four doors down," Brian started repeating to himself softly. Within minutes, he passed the first door, counting as he went.

The hall in the mirror overhead teemed with life as creatures of all shapes, sizes, and colors bustled about. It looked like the activity of any other ship's comings and goings. The whisperings in the back of Brian's mind picked up, and he swore there was a tangible presence every time one of the reflected aliens walked past his own reflection in the mirror. The ceiling's crew started becoming more and more like invisible phantoms brushing past him in the empty hall. The phenomena reminded him of the repelling force between same-ended magnets.

Paying more attention to his reflection, he started using it to navigate through the unseen beings surrounding him in the hall. He felt caught between two separate but somehow merging worlds. He weaved his mirror image in and out of the growing traffic in the mirror. Despite his fancy footwork, his progression toward his destination slowed.

The hushed whispers in the back of Brian's mind steadily increased. He could almost make out an actual word or two, but he didn't recognize them from any languages he knew. Bumps and shoves from the aliens in the mirror nudged him like unseen apparitions as they passed his reflection. The periodic proddings broke his concentration on the voices. Pushing forward, he battled through the horde and managed to pass two more doors. At the same time, he kept a wary eye out for any developing droplets of liquid mirror.

As he approached the door of his desire, the comings and goings of the alien crew clogged the mirror's hallway. Even with the expansive corridor, the popularity of the room beyond seemed to cause significant congestion. Brian's progress slowed even more. Squaring his shoulders, he gritted his teeth and started maneuvering through the phantom forces barring his way. He used his reflection as a guide. The door's reflected counterpart in the mirror above sat wide open, allowing the beings in the ceiling to come and go as they pleased. He looked down at the black metal tyrant in the real hall. It remained shut tight.

"This door had better open," Brian mumbled to himself.

The aliens closest to his reflection took note of his mirror image as he spoke. Brian froze and held his breath. His eyes darted wildly across the ceiling, searching for any sign of a gathering droplet. As the seconds slipped away, no ripples gathered on its smooth surface, and the aliens began ignoring his reflected counterpart once again.

He slowly let out his breath.

The beings in the mirror seemed to pay his reflection little heed, as long as he didn't make any noticeable sound. Proceeding with caution, he began pressing through the invisible presence of the alien host surrounding him. He inched toward the door, but the big, black barrier still remained closed. He stopped an arm's length away. The current of the phantom-like beings streaming around him swept him closer and closer to the door.

As he racked his brain for ideas on how to get the door to budge, the obstacle started sliding open on its own. He blinked a couple of times, trying to make sure he wasn't hallucinating. Reaching out, he placed his hands on the door. Slight vibrations of the rough metal ran underneath his bandaged fingers as the slab continued moving. He trusted his sense of touch far more than his sense of sight in this place. As the door finished sliding out of the way, Brian found himself gazing into a spacious, empty lobby. The same sweet scent from the elevator filled the air. He wondered how he could detect the smell even through the heavy packing he had stuffed in his nose.

Brian took a few steps, soaking in all of his new surroundings.

The spacious entrance lobby was well lit. As he marveled at the scenery of the deserted foyer, the door behind him started closing. He winced at the thought of the dark slab not cooperating when he wanted to leave. Glancing up, he noticed that the mirror's door remained open. Aliens continued pouring through it, and he wondered how he would get past them as well. The steady stream of the horde in the mirror parted around his reflection. The force of their invisible presence swept him farther into the room with its current.

Brian continued taking in his surroundings and found sizable, square holes that took up the bulk of the room's ceiling and floor. Glass walls outlined the enormous openings. The captivating display filled a good portion of the foyer. The swarm of aliens around his reflection thinned out the farther he moved away from the door. Their invisible presence lessened but continued guiding him forward. The picturesque scene beyond the glass walls came more into view as he approached. The openings in the ceiling and floor showcased a cross-section of the station. He could see many of the other levels, both above his and below. He gawked at the magnificence of the ship.

Slightly bending over, Brian gazed up through the glass.

The station seemed to go on forever.

He placed his hand on the transparent enclosure, and small patches of his bare skin touched the cool surface through the bandages. The sudden chill made him look at his haggard hand. Finding it difficult to accept his current predicament, he refocused his gaze on the view of the other levels. He noticed how empty this area of the real station was—just like everywhere else.

His hand slid down and returned to his side.

Remembering his search for the blue-skinned alien, Brian stepped away from the picturesque view. Taking in more of his surroundings, he found two grand staircases on either side of the glass-encased opening. The stairs on the right went up, while the stairs on the left went down. Wandering toward the staircase on the right, he noticed that the white carpeting ended at its first stair. The steps seemed to be made of the same black metal ubiquitous in the station. The handrails curved to a swirling stop that rested on top of statued end posts. The carved sentinels stood like guards over the stairs—miniature versions of the ones in the storage room. Brian ran a finger along some of their detailed groves as he walked by.

He found a colossal door in the far wall as he moved away from the staircase. It stood ajar, both in the empty lobby he occupied and in the mirror above. The alien crew strolled in and out of the room in the ceiling. A sweeping glance across the lobby revealed many similar openings adorning the other walls. The receiving area where he stood appeared to be a resting spot between the adjoining rooms and levels.

Brian headed toward the first opening he saw. On his way, he continued searching the ceiling for the blue-skinned alien. Oversized tables like the ones in the cafeteria rested along the outskirts of each room. A bittersweet recollection of Derek rolled into his mind. He remembered Derek sitting down at the bar with the alien couple. In the lobby's mirror, all sorts of beings sat at these tables as they relaxed and conversed with each other. Their chattering gnawed in the back of his mind, but the necessity of finding the blue-skinned man propelled him on.

Entering the room, he noticed different types of tables. Crowds of reflected aliens gathered around them. The place seemed to burst with energy as each group either watched or played various games. Brian inched beyond the threshold of the room full of barren tables. In the ceiling, a tall crew member juggled colorful, rectangular objects nearby. The alien's multiple sets of arms flew all around as he dealt several of the pieces to the seated participants. The creature's smooth, rapid movements conjured the very elements of speed and stealth.

Brian sensed the beginning of a game. It looked simple enough to play. He even started predicting a winner for the round. Each player took its turn until game play reached the far end of the table. An unoccupied seat, just Brian's size, seemed to appear out of nowhere. He looked down from the ceiling to the table in the real room where he stood. A matching chair sat in the corresponding placement to the one in the mirror. The legs scraped on the floor as it slid out of its own accord and faced him as though it invited him to rest from all of his troubles. He felt an urge to take a seat and gazed back up at the ceiling. The reflected chair still matched the real one's placement.

His attention drifted back to the players, and Brian watched his predicted winner lay down her crowning pieces. An eruption of jovial activity shot through the surrounding multitude. He could swear he heard a faint roar from the crowd. Some of the beings seemed to cheer, while others appeared to have lost. A smile tugged at the corners of Brian's lips. He felt a sense of pride for anticipating the champion of the hand.

The chair scootched toward him a little more.

Brian went to back away, but the dealer stole his attention by jumping to action and collecting the game pieces from the table. With rapid fluidity, the multiple-armed alien delivered a new hand. Brian watched intently and predicted the winner of that round, too. His smile grew, and he lost himself as a spectator of the game.

The urge to rest his weary limbs consumed him. The chair scooted toward him again.

Finally giving in to its request, he took a step to sit down.

Chapter 28

Agony erupted throughout Brian's lower body, and pain rushed in from every wound. He gasped for breath as he crumpled to the floor. He wondered how long he had been standing there, staring at the ceiling. His breath came in rapid puffs, and he peeled his pack off. Tremors seized his entire body, but he somehow managed to push the flap open and grab the med-gun. He fought his trembling limbs and brought the device up to his neck. His swollen, sausage-like fingers worked together to squeeze the trigger. The soft click brought its expected sharp bite.

His jaw clenched, and he curled into a convulsing heap. Waves of pressure pounded through his head. As the moments slipped by, sweet relief began to spread. His liberation came soft and slow, at first, but eventually wrenched him from torture's grasp. His body calmed, and his tremors began to subside.

Brian's shallow breaths slowed and deepened.

As the pain reliever took more of a hold and strength somewhat returned to his limbs, he crawled to his knees. He tucked the med-gun away and wiped the lathered sweat from his forehead. Slinging his pack back onto his good shoulder, he took a few steadying breaths. When he climbed to his feet, his legs almost gave out. With a few more stabilizing inhales, he began hobbling out of the room.

His eyes darted across the ceiling as he searched for the blue-skinned alien. The task felt more daunting now that he had wasted an uncertain amount of time staring at the mirror. Wondering if any of his crew might be roaming this section, too, he started keeping an eye out for them. He didn't hold his gaze in one spot for long as he staggered around in the lobby. Unsure of exactly where to go, he wandered to the closest staircase and grabbed hold of the rail. Its polished metal felt like dense rock in his hand. He lifted a heavy boot and climbed the first stair. Knowing the ascent would be more of a chore than he bargained for, he rolled his eyes and labored up each step.

He crested the lobby area at the top of the stairs. The lanterns on the walls didn't glow as brightly on this level, and the sweet scent thickened. It seemed peculiar that the fragrance was potent enough to seep through his packed sinuses so much. He touched the bridge of his nose, wondering if the gauze had somehow fallen out, but could still feel its pressure balled up inside.

Besides the dampened lighting and the stronger smell, the second story seemed to match the lower level. He glanced up at the ceiling, mesmerized by the sea of beings that flooded the mirror. Chattering whispers crept around him in the real lobby's otherwise hollow silence. The opening in the nearest wall had vibrant splashes of color that filled portions of a star-dotted landscape. The new room drew him in, and he wandered over to it. A thick cosmos blanketed its mirrored ceiling. He looked down from the galactic expansion overhead and found shiny panels covering the walls and floor.

A virtual reality room? Brian's gaze drifted back to the exquisite sight overhead in the mirror.

Out of the corner of his eye, he noticed an enormous boulder cutting across one of the dazzling nebulas in the surreal rendering of the cosmos. He wandered farther into the room and watched the asteroid cruise across the awe-inspiring solar system. One of the mirror's crew rode the large rock like a granite steed. The rider seemed to be able to move anywhere she wanted in the open landscape. The alien's bright yellow hair whipped behind her as she leaned to the side, guiding the rock in a wide turn. The asteroid blew past Brian, and a gust of wind forced him a step back.

Something else in the ceiling caught his attention. A comet streaked across the mirror, leaving a bright tail in its wake. It had a rider sitting atop it as well. "I'm winning!" a rumbling voice reverberated through the room. This alien appeared to be taunting the yellow-haired alien on the asteroid.

"I didn't know we were racing," the high-pitched voice of the first rider echoed back.

"We are now!" The second alien's words rang with more clarity.

The comet took off, and another gust blasted Brian. He stumbled as the force almost knocked him off his feet. The yellow-haired alien bolted across the vast expanse in the mirror overhead, giving chase to the taunting rider.

This isn't real. This isn't real. Brian shook his head and cupped his hands over his ears, trying to shut everything out. The riders sailing around the ceiling did very little to tie him to his senses, and he started questioning his sanity.

The ceiling's cosmos began swirling, and its stunning detail smudged into a blur. The room's lighting dimmed even more until Brian stood in complete darkness. He lowered his hands from his ears. The hushed eternal whispers quieted, and a thick silence fell around him. A light slowly started casting a soft glow on the ceiling, and a room emerged from the darkness within the mirror overhead. It appeared to be some sort of living quarters. Brian's mouth fell open as recognition of the room began sinking in. He gazed up at a perfect replica of *his* quarters back home.

His reflection stood in the middle of it.

The same cozy couches he had relaxed on so many times before sat in their usual position on either side of his reflection. A designer coffee table came up to his mirror image's knees, and a floral arrangement with accent candles garnished its top. Everything seemed to be in its place. Even the tasteful knickknacks he and Grace had picked out on their travels together adorned the rest of the room's modern décor.

Grace! Brian perked up at the thought of her and started searching the room. *Maybe she's here.*

He took a step to investigate the other rooms, but he bumped into something. Looking down from the ceiling, he found a real coffee table in front of him. Two couches sat in the exact placement as they did in the reflection in the mirror. He now stood in an identical duplicate of the quarters displayed overhead.

I'm home?

He glanced down at the coffee table and studied the photo of him and Grace. He scooped up the treasured keepsake and examined the holographic inside. The couple smiled up at him as usual. He tipped the picture from side to side, and the three-dimensional background image shifted—just like normal. *Was this here a moment ago?* He couldn't recall.

Maybe I really am home. Brian cradled the picture. "Grace?"

Scrambling around the coffee table, he headed to the adjacent room. The hushed whispers suddenly returned. His enthusiastic stride slowed to a stop. He stood there, hoping the scene wasn't just an illusion. He looked up to find the mirror still covering the ceiling. His reflection cradled its own picture and stared back at him. Brian's gaze dropped to the treasured keepsake in his hands, and his grip slackened. He dropped the photo, and it landed with a loud crack on the floor. The blow left a fracture in the panel that made it stop working. Its shiny appearance returned.

Brian turned and hobbled away.

Reentering the lobby, he watched all the beings shuffling around in the ceiling. The blue-skinned alien had disappeared somewhere in the mirror's throngs, and he felt like it would be impossible to find him—or his crew—at this point. The quiet whisperings continued interrupting the silence of the deserted station around him. He meandered to the nearest oversized table on the outskirts of the foyer and climbed onto its chair. The mirror-world above still bustled with activity while he sat. He couldn't shake the thought that his only opportunity for getting Derek and the others back was slipping right through his swollen, mangled fingers.

The rich, sweet scent saturating the air pulled at him, merging with a smell of buttery-baked goodness. His attention drifted back up to the ceiling. A steaming tower of cinnamon rolls appeared on the table in the mirror. He gazed down and peeked over the edge of the real table's top but found nothing there. He looked back up. Globs of icing drizzled down the pile of pastries as though he had just missed the application.

Brian's eyes fluttered shut, and he breathed in the intoxicating aroma right through the packing in his nose. His mouth watered, and his stomach growled. He took in another long drag of the air. *This isn't real, either.* Opening his eyes, he glared at the delicacies on the table in the mirror. He slid down from the chair and limped away.

The lobby's dim lighting flickered.

Brian clenched his swollen fingers into fists. He drifted over to the glass wall. Placing his hand on it, he gazed at the picturesque, cross-sectional view, and the lights pulsed again. He could see the disruption cascade through the other levels. The last time the lights had done that, he could have sworn he'd lost a chunk of time.

Brian braced himself for whatever would happen next.

The lights cut out altogether.

He stood alone in the lightless room. Every passing moment felt like an eternity. His pounding heart almost drowned out the whisperings crawling around him in the darkness. His thoughts returned to the ceiling. The idea of dangling droplets looming overhead—stretching down at him from the abyss—made him shrink. His breath quickened. The phantom-like presence of the aliens passing by his reflection in the mirror made the room feel small. The smell of cinnamon rolls saturated his senses with their tantalizing aroma.

Everything felt so suffocating.

The lights suddenly flickered on, blinding him with their sudden brightness. They quickly turned off, then on, then off again in rapid succession. He shielded his eyes as they flashed another time and stayed on. When he could finally look around, he found that he no longer stood in the recreation center's lobby anymore. Instead, he stood in the middle of an abandoned hall. The same decorative white lanterns hung on the walls just as they had in the other corridors, and the mirror blanketed the ceiling. An unusually lengthy hall extended out in front of him. Turning, he saw a large door behind him, ending the corridor in the distance.

No aliens moved about in the mirror here. His reflection was the ceiling's sole occupant. He breathed a little easier, being freed from the invisible weight of the alien crew members squeezing in on him. Even the smell of freshly baked rolls faded from the air, but a hint of their cinnamon sweetness still lingered.

"How did I get here?" Brian asked out loud to his reflection.

His reflection stared back, offering no answers.

Brian hung his head. "Where do I go from here?"

The soft sound of the door sliding open filled the empty hall. He turned and watched the dark slab at the end of the corridor finish moving out of the way. No one stood on the other side that could have triggered a sensor. He was growing tired of the station's antics, but his feet began moving toward the opening, anyway. He shot a narrow-eyed glance at his reflection. "What's your plan here? Lead me around until I lose my sanity?" He shuffled closer to the door and peered past the threshold.

"A docking hangar?" Brian thought of the place where they had landed their ship. This hangar looked like an exact replica. "My ship's docking hangar?"

A burst of renewed energy coursed through him, and he hurried through the open door. He continued examining the hangar as he went. It really *did* look like the same one he and his crew had landed on earlier— however long ago that might have been. He saw the raised teleportation pad and scoffed at wherever *it* might have taken him. His steps quickened even more as he tried to formulate a plan of how to get his crew back. He had no idea how he would pull it off, but his mind raced through the helpful equipment and supplies on his ship. His thoughts became a whirlwind filled with possibilities.

He ignored the pounding in his head that accompanied every footfall of his limped jog. The docking platform's symmetry provided a breathtaking view to his left, but something seemed off about it. He noticed the positioning of the hangar on which he stood. He thought back to where they had landed.

His pace slowed.

This hangar seemed to be in the middle of the upper levels, not near the bottom of the chamber, where Sivien had landed their ship. He thought back to the ceiling in the hall where they had entered the station. He remembered the hanging chandeliers. There were no chandeliers in the corridor he had just left. The new rescue plans he eagerly tried to concoct instantly dashed to pieces.

Brian stopped in his tracks.

He gingerly rubbed the back of his neck with one of his mangled hands, but his swollen digits couldn't even begin to rub this type of frustration away. He racked his brain for an escape—for any sort of solution to the insanity. A short distance away, something caught his eye. A medium-sized starship straddled a landing beacon. A red light rhythmically flashed across its undercarriage.

"Hey!" Brian's voice quickly absorbed into the thick atmosphere of the landing dock. He cupped his hands around his mouth. "HEY!"

He started waving his stiff arms as much as the swollen limbs would allow and hurried toward the ship. "I NEED HELP! I COULD USE SOME HELP! MY CREW. . ."

His steps slackened.

Chapter 29

B rian felt like someone had strapped magnets onto the bottom of his
synthetic boots.

The red beacon flashing underneath the spacecraft shone right
through parts of the ship's hull. It appeared that someone had dismantled
parts of the ship's exterior at some point. Portions of the ancient-looking
metal bent outward while other pieces littered the dock's floor. Some of
the stripped areas even revealed the ship's skeletal frame. It looked like it
had been sitting there for ages.

Brian's mind wandered to his *Gabriel*. He imagined some other voyager
approaching her as she rested over her own landing beacon. He thought
of her hull littering its hangar. The idea of someone salvaging pieces from
his ship made him fume. He remembered the station's blue force field that
had been active when they came arrived and wondered if its true purpose
was to keep people in instead of keeping people out. Considering his own
brush with the station, he didn't have to try very hard to think of reasons
this ship's crew didn't make it back to their vessel.

His rage simmered while he wandered to the nose of the ancient ship.
He noticed a gaping hole in the hull. It led straight into the bridge, or at
least what remained of it. The seats spewed their inner stuffing from splits
in their seams. None of the abundant computer consoles lit up with life,
having lost their functions to age. He continued circling the ship and
found decayed lettering—perhaps remnants of the old girl's name.

TRES . . . WILL

Brian couldn't distinguish anything else. "Sorry, old girl. I guess neither one of us really made it out of the station, did we?" He ran his haggard finger down a folded edging of the rusted metal.

The meaning of his words weighed on his mind, and his stomach growled again. His pesky hunger pains served as a constant reminder of the last time he had eaten. His crew hadn't been devoured by the ceiling back then. He almost wanted to smile as he reminisced about his friends. He wished he could rewind time, gather everyone, return to their ship, and die together with a measure of dignity. Staying on his own vessel didn't seem like such a bad idea now. "Time travel. What an idiotic notion." Brian laughed.

He looked at the ancient ship. "I bet you wish you could do that, too, don't you, girl? Go back in time and rescue your crew. The same thing happened to them, didn't it? . . . I hate to break it to you, but time travel isn't a thing. If it were, they'd have come back for you already—wouldn't they?" Brian patted the ship and rested his hand on its decayed metal.

Soft vibrations began trembling through his fingers. He placed his other hand against it, investigating the disturbance. The ship's quivering became more noticeable. Brian squinted as he gazed up at the vessel. It started visibly shaking. He could feel the tremors in his boots as the trembling spread through the floor. A rumble began accompanying the ship's quaking, and the old girl let out a deep groan followed by a high-pitched squeal from grinding metal.

Brian covered his ears.

The ship's landing gear gave out, and the vessel dropped hard onto its side. A thunderous boom echoed through the dock. More squeals cut through the air as its rusted metal continued to grind into the hangar. Brian pictured himself becoming nothing more than a messy stain underneath the ancient vessel's massive weight, and he started to back up. A portion of the hull broke away with a clank.

Brian stumbled and fell backward.

The floor shook more violently underneath him.

Just then, a titan-sized starship crested the edge of the docking platform—the apparent source of all the commotion. The giant vessel's nose
came into view as it climbed upward. Then came the engines. Heat radiated
from the ship like solar flares. The metal against Brian's back warmed to an
uncomfortable degree. He writhed from the hot wind, but the force from
the thrusters continued pinning him against the floor. His every breath
felt filled with vaporized flame. The vessel turned slightly and continued
its ascent, giving instant relief from its blazing cyclones of burning death.

Brian coughed and started sucking in the cooler air.

The starship's ascent exposed its underbelly, and its landing gear began
descending for docking. Brian wanted to jump to his feet and flag the
massive titan down, but the ground still shook underneath him, and the
heated force from the engines hadn't fully released him from its grasp. He
rolled halfway onto his side and managed to flail an arm through the remnants of the scorching breeze. The vessel continued rising. It didn't seem
to notice his pitiful warning to flee from this unholy abomination.

"HEEEY!" Brian's voice drowned under the engine's thunderous roar.

As the goliath ship continued sailing upward, the floor's quaking
calmed, and the force of the thrusters withdrew. Brian finished rolling off
his back and climbed to his feet. He hurried to the edge of the dock. The
ship began gliding up out of view and headed to land on some other level
above. He searched for a way to reach the newcomers but couldn't find
anything connecting the docks. Then an idea struck him. *The elevator lift!*
He stumbled across the floor as its residual trembling calmed, then headed
back to the hall. He needed to warn the crew on the new ship to escape
while they still could.

Somehow he needed to convince them not to stay.

Somehow he needed to find an elevator!

The shaking and rumbling faded even more. Brian pictured the ship
nearing its designated landing zone—poised over a flashing red beacon. A
solid, thunderous boom shook the dock.

The ship has touched down. Brian pushed his broken body harder. *Maybe they could even help me get my crew back.*

Brian reached the door. *Please open!* To his surprise, it did.

He thought back on his wanderings in the halls with his crew and calculated a path to the elevator. Entering the hallway, he glanced at the ceiling mirror. His reflection peered back at him. It still kept perfect timing with him as he hobbled down the long corridor. Other than his image, the rest of the mirror remained void of the blue-uniformed crew. He soon found the first intersection. A single alien dotted the ceiling. Brian slowed, but the mirror's crew member paid his reflection little heed. He hobbled past.

As he continued, more aliens peppered the reflected corridor overhead. He weaved around them but still felt their invisible presence in the real hall if he got too close. In time, he covered the distance to where he thought the lift might be. He slowed, then stopped in front of a particular door.

"Please, open," Brian whispered under his breath.

The door did.

He peered into the room and found that it matched the lifts he had already ridden. His gaze went straight up to some movement overhead. Three of the mirror's crew members stood in the ceiling. He slipped into an open spot just inside the door. It slid closed—shutting down any fanciful thoughts of escape if things went wrong.

Butterflies took flight in Brian's stomach. He leaned against the wall, settling in for the ride. He hoped he was headed in the right direction. A fiery red-skinned alien with flowing, crimson hair stood off to his right in the corner. Another being shifted nervously in place next to it. Its skin was a ghoulish green. The only eye on its face bulged out of the middle of its forehead. Wispy, black strands of hair grew from patches of its skin. The thing shifted again, and its scalp snowed white flecks onto its uniform. Brian noticed that the third crew member in the left corner was taking note of his mangled reflection. He put his head down, trying to act insignificant, but continued stealing glances at the ceiling.

The third alien's violet skin and dark, shiny eyes provided little contrast to its uniform's coloring. Its long, jet-black hair was slicked back stylishly, and it leaned against the wall. Its head tipped mischievously as it seemed to take an interest in Brian's reflection. It stood a little straighter and glanced at the other two crew members. It nodded at them, grabbing their attention.

Its gaze returned to Brian's reflection. The dark figure's mouth moved as though it spoke. At the same time, a distant, low tone drifted in and out. Brian shifted under the unwanted attention. He looked down from the ceiling, pretending that hearing the beings didn't make him feel crazier. He hoped the elevator lift would hurry.

Brian tugged at his collar and shifted in place.

The lift took ages longer than he thought it should. He peered up at the ceiling. The aliens exchanged more glances in between their stares at his reflection. The violet-skinned crew member leaned over and spoke to the red one. Hushed whispers ignited as a conversation kindled among them. Brian shuffled toward the door, and his hand inched toward the holstered gun nestled at his ribs. He rolled his eyes, remembering that his weapon didn't work on the mirror, but he would still try if the need arose anyway. He felt the weight of the aliens' stares bearing down on him, and the hushed whisperings increased. The sudden fluttering in his stomach indicated that the elevator ride would soon end.

The violet-skinned alien moved across the ceiling to Brian's side.

Brian pressed against the door.

The sweet smell lingering in the air changed to a thick, musky cologne. Brian could feel the phantom-like presence standing close to his reflection—*too* close! It pressed in even more, and a low-toned voice sounded right next to his ear. He leaned against the door, instantly wanting to transport to the other side. He closed his eyes, pretending he wasn't there.

The fluttering in his stomach stopped.

The sudden sliding of the door jerked Brian from his thoughts. Once it had opened wide enough, he bolted into the hall, not even bothering to check whether the aliens followed. He felt relieved not to find any more of them wandering the ceiling as he hobbled down the hall. He calculated where the dock would be and made turns when needed. Sweat dripped from his face as he pushed himself harder. The pounding in his head that accompanied every step made him think of re-dosing soon.

"Not yet!" Brian muttered to himself. "I have to get to that ship! I'm too close."

He found the long hallway leading to the docking hangars and hustled down it as fast as his broken body could go. He approached the door at the end of the corridor, half expecting it not to budge. Instead, it slid open with ease. Adrenalin pulsed through his veins and hurried him along to warn the new ship's crew. He searched the dock for the colossal vessel that had nearly baked him to the floor.

"Oh, no!" Brian's quickened hobbles slackened, and his shoulders fell.

The broken-down *Tress-Will* sat a little way off, tipped onto its side from its broken landing gear.

"No, no, no," Brian repeated. He cupped the sides of his head with his hands.

He combed his shaky fingers through his short hair, unsure of what to do next. He stood there for a moment, then turned on his heels, heading back to the elevator. He glared at his reflection in the mirror. "Of course, this turned out to be the wrong floor. You couldn't just send me to the right level, could you? That would be too helpful! Well, you won't stop me."

Brian hobbled down the hall. He cursed the station under his breath and thought of all the time he had wasted on this blunder. He calculated where the new crew must be by now—halfway across the hangar? Possibly wandering the halls? It all depended on where they landed, he assumed.

He took all the same turns back to the elevator and pushed through the growing complaints of his injuries. Even his stomach started throwing in more gripes. He finally made it to the right hall and glared at the mirror as he approached. The elevator door in the ceiling opened. Brian looked down to see that the real one in front of him hadn't moved an inch. He slammed into it headfirst. A fresh burst of misery exploded through him. Tiny stars dotted his vision. He staggered around, trying to stabilize his shrieking senses. Something salty trickled down the back of his throat, and his upper lip suddenly felt moist. He touched his stubble and looked at his hand. The bright red blood was smudged across his fingertips.

He began shaking off his daze, and the stars faded from his vision. Tentatively, he came within an arm's length of the door, but it didn't open. He sized up his formidable foe. "GRAAAA!" Brian slammed both his fists against its metal.

Blood gushed from his nose. The fresh pounding that ignited in his head dropped him to his knees. He slumped and watched the bright red liquid drizzle to the carpet, marring its otherwise pristine appearance. In time, his bleeding slowed. He gingerly dabbed the residual seepage with the end of his remaining sleeve, then slid his pack to the floor and carefully turned around. He rested against the cool door.

Brian fumbled around in his pack for the med-kit. When he found it, he tossed it on the floor and began picking through its contents until he found a pair of long tweezers. He pulled the blood-soaked packing out of his nose and flicked it across the hall. He knew he should repack the gauze, but instead, he hucked the tweezers in defiance. He rested against the door. Thoughts of never getting to the new ship that had just landed taunted him. He looked up at the mirror, thinking of trying a different approach.

"Please," Brian tried begging. "Please."

The station didn't respond to his pathetic plea.

"OPEN THE *REAL* DOOR!" he yelled at his reflection.

The door at Brian's back still didn't budge. He buried his head in his hands. His stomach let out a loud growl, but he didn't reach for any rations. His wounds assailed him, but he refused to administer any more medication. Brian wondered how much longer he could endure this miserable place. He cast a heated glare at his reflection. He hated it with every fiber of his being.

There's got to be a way out of this nightmare . . . Isn't there?

Suddenly, his thoughts changed direction. *Maybe I don't want to survive this nightmare.* His eyes wandered to the lantern hanging next to the door, and his seething rage calmed a little as he stared at the inviting glow of its light. His thoughts drifted to his gun, nestled in the holster at his ribs. His eyes darted back to his reflection. "I don't have to let you absorb me."

His hand moved to his weapon.

"I still have control over what happens to me," Brian whispered to himself.

He wrapped his hand around the gun's worn handle. The added pressure shot pain through his ribs. He gasped and jolted upright, glaring at the ceiling. "ARGH! That's probably what you want me to do! Isn't it, you . . . you—"

Something in the mirror on the other side of the hall silenced Brian's verbal tirade. He inspected the ceiling but couldn't quite put his finger on the abnormality. Through the fierce protesting of his body, he climbed to his feet. His head rushed, and he swooned against the door at his back. When the darkness that tried to swallow his vision cleared, he limped across the hall. He stared up at the anomaly.

A hairline crack disturbed the ceiling's smooth surface.

He wondered how he had missed the distortion his first time through this hallway. Examining it closer, he searched for its origins. The ceiling to the left smoothed out, like everywhere else, but to his right, he could see the small break traveling down the length of the corridor.

Could the mirror have a weakness after all? The question spawned new hope.

He grabbed hold of the thought and stared at the ceiling. His need to know breathed new life to explore the potential vulnerability. Perhaps the crack meant nothing at all—but what if it meant everything?

Brian hobbled back to his med-kit and rummaged through it again. With stiff, achy fingers, he wrestled a new pain-reliever vial into the med-gun. He lifted the device to his neck and squeezed the trigger. The bite and soothing sensation that accompanied it came. He jammed everything back into his pack.

He tuned out his wounds as their shrieks faded, and slung his pack onto his back. There was still a light trickle coming from his nose, but he ignored that too. He knew all of his pains would lessen soon enough. He staggered down the hall, tracking the mirror's hairline crack.

The medication soaked in with every step he took, and his physical torment subsided. As he progressed down the hall, he noted the aliens dotting the mirror again. He maneuvered around their phantomous presence in the real corridor. As time wore on, the ceiling filled with more of them, and they stopped and stared at his reflection as he passed by. Their constant whisperings crept into the recesses of his mind. He pressed forward through the hall's growing crowds and tracked the hairline crack through the expanding labyrinth of endless corridors. He could swear his reflection stepped out of sync on occasion, but every time he looked up, nothing seemed out of place. He couldn't tell which he disliked more—his mirror image or the alien crew.

So this is what it feels like to be alone in a sea of people, Brian thought with a stifled laugh.

Countless hours added up, or at least what felt like countless hours.

The only indication of the passage of time became the return of pain when his medication wore off. At this point, he almost didn't even care. The wounds on his shoulder and thigh screamed the loudest. He went to rub his shoulder, but as soon as his fingers touched the site, a sharp burn spread through it. He clenched his teeth and sucked in a reflexive breath, then moved what little was left of his tattered uniform sleeve out of the way and inspected the damage. Red, puffy skin pulled the stitches tight, and heat radiated from the surface of his flesh.

Infected? Brian flustered. *Of course, it is!*

His simmering rage fueled his pace down the hall.

Chapter 30

Torment.

Ceaseless torment assaulted Brian's existence. His skin was lathered with sweat, and his cheeks flushed hot with an elevated temperature. The fiery pain seeping from his wounds left little doubt that not only had infection set in, but that he needed expert medical attention far beyond what he could find in his pack. He wondered how long he had been wandering the halls. It could have been days or even a week—based on signs from his injuries. It didn't feel like a week, though.

He wasn't sure anymore.

Brian considered taking more medication. He knew he would have to stop soon but could handle going a little farther before he succumbed to the absolute need for another dose. The last of the vials clanked against the med-gun at the top of his pack. Given the minuscule amount he had left, Brian had little choice other than to soldier on through his misery. Still, something beyond himself compelled him forward—something almost tangible.

With a measure of what felt like supernatural willpower to withstand his agonies, Brian continued tracking the hairline crack in the mirror. In this hall, the fracture appeared a couple of inches wider. The disturbance looked more like a reflective vein that ran on top of the ceiling's smooth surface. The notion that it held some sort of special purpose kept him pressing forward. If it led to something he could exploit to get his crew back, he was determined to use it.

Few aliens showed up in the mirror in this section, so Brian didn't have to dodge them as often. After a while, he glanced across the ceiling to see that his reflection alone remained. He racked his brain for a moment but couldn't actually remember the last time he saw one of the beings. Even though the alien crew wasn't there, he swore he could still feel the weight of their stares.

Something else seemed to be missing, too, but the cogs of his mind turned sluggishly. The answer finally dawned on him: He couldn't hear the whispers anymore. At some point, they had faded away.

Silence sat thick in the air here.

He approached a four-way and slowed. At the split in the corridor, an overpowering sweetness saturated the air, and his stomach turned. The sickly sweet smell fused with the very molecules around him. He thought he could even feel it soaking into his uniform. He patted himself down as though doing so could dispel the sugary stench, but it didn't seem to help.

Brian's thoughts drifted back to his first encounter with the smell at the elevator. Back then, it made the station feel so inviting, so welcoming. Now, he couldn't stand its magnificent reek. A hint of buttery, baked goodness occasionally drifted through the air as well, tantalizing his senses. The added aroma only served to make him hate the place even more. A long growl clawed at his stomach and made him wonder if his body was aware of his hatred.

He examined the mirror's crossroads and found another reflective vein that met with the one he had been tracking. They twisted together in the middle of the ceiling and fused into one. Brian found a single, larger vein beyond their merging spot. It traveled down the corridor to his left. *Two offshoots of a primary branch, huh?* He followed the new, thicker vein.

In time, he came to a T in the hall. The sweet smell intensified as though the place bathed in it. He could even taste it in the back of his mouth. His throat dried, and a wave of nausea hit him. He gagged and held his breath. An inspection of the ceiling revealed that the vein he tracked had fused with yet another.

Brian shuffled down the corridor, following the merged veins, and the smell increased. He carefully tucked his mouth and nose in the nook of his sleeved arm. The added layer of material helped filter out a little of the pungent air, but it didn't stop it from stinging his eyes. Squinting, he wished he could just blink the acidic atmosphere away.

At the next intersection, the mirror had become overgrown with a complex network of reflective veins. Small offshoots the same size as the first vein Brian had found split from the central cluster and disappeared down the other corridors. He ignored the thinner break-offs and continued tracking the main branches. The twisted veins reminded him of the intricate braids in Callie's hair.

Brian's heart sank at the thought.

He missed his comrades.

With a heavy sigh, he followed the thick cluster of veins. Yards down the hall, they started pressing in on each other, squeezing together from lack of ceiling space. They merged into four primary bundles. Everything on their surface looked bent and distorted—everything except for Brian's reflection. His image never bowed or warped. It remained a perfect duplicate of his broken body everywhere he went.

Another dry heave pulled his attention away from the mirror. He pressed his face harder against his sleeve, hoping it would filter the air better. Unfortunately, the material provided little defense against the permeating smell. If an odor could become an actual living thing, he would put currency down for this being the one.

Brian glared up at his mirror image. He wondered if it secretly laughed at his misfortunes. His reflection's eyes peered at him from behind its arm, which draped across its own swollen face. He gagged again and gave up on using his sleeve as a filter. Slinging his pack to the ground, he eased himself to the floor. His wounds groaned at him all the way down. He flipped the pack's top flap out of the way and rummaged through his bag.

Fighting off his nausea as he choked on the sweet, foul air, he held his breath and searched for some other type of face covering. He thought back to the supplies on his ship and wished he had brought his breathing suit after all. His lungs began to complain. He fumbled through the kit faster. A particular medicine vial fell out of his med-kit, and he read its label.

He paused.

His lungs ached, and he exhaled just enough to relieve some pressure.

Brian grabbed the vial and a fistful of gauze. He placed some of the white squares on the floor, put the vial of medication on top of them, then covered it with more gauze. It looked like a pharmaceutical sandwich. He unholstered his gun and let out the rest of his breath, forcing his lungs to stay at the bottom of an exhale. He grasped the antique handle of his weapon and delivered a hearty blow to the gauze stack.

A loud crack split the air.

Brian removed the top layer of gauze. The clear liquid seeped through the fractured glass vial, soiling the bottom pads with the medication. Leaning over his little experiment, he closed his eyes and hoped it worked. He sucked in a much-needed breath. The eye-watering smell of dead fish wafted from the vial and overtook the sickly sweet one. He grabbed the soiled pads and brought them up to his face. He gulped in the putrid stench.

The medication stank, but at least it stank less.

For a split second, he thought he detected a hint of salt in the odor— as if the fishy smell brought a little of the sea with it somehow. The absurd notion faded as quickly as it came. Even though he only traded one horrible smell for another, he still claimed victory over the moment and gulped in another stinky inhale.

Brian imagined what his crew would think if they could see him now. He pictured the horror on Callie's face at the dead-fish gauze. Zella and Derek would have started concocting a plan on how to catch live fish in a stream. And Sivien would have teased him over his injuries. Thinking about his friends brought a slight smile to his face. He sucked in another disgusting breath.

"But they are not here," came a thought.

Brian's smile faded.

I shouldn't be here either.

He took another deep breath and held it as he put the stinky gauze pads back down on the floor. He rummaged through his pack. Grabbing a ration, he opened it and dumped out its crumbly, yellow contents. Then he took the cracked vial and bunched it up in the wrapper.

"You know. . ." Brian shoved the silver wad into a pocket and looked up at his reflection. "I suddenly realize how much I hate mirrors."

He reholstered his weapon.

Grabbing the stack of moistened pads, he draped them over his face. He turned to his med-gun and checked how many doses were left in the remainder of the vial he'd loaded earlier. Finding very little pain medication left but having a great deal of need, he shrugged and brought it up to his neck, delivering what might be one of his last doses. Closing his eyes, he welcomed the stinging bite. He tossed the gun back into his pack and slung it onto his good shoulder.

Brian stared up at the large silver veins on the ceiling. "You have got to go somewhere, and I'm going to find out where," he promised aloud.

He climbed to his feet, and a head rush made all his injuries pulse in unison.

Staggering to the wall, he leaned against it. His aches and pains lessened as the medication coursed through him. Gathering himself, he shoved off the wall. His legs almost gave out, and he dragged his feet for the first several steps, willing himself down the hall. With the slight improvement of smell from the dead-fish gauze draped across his face, Brian began tracking the larger silver veins once again.

His physical pains calmed with every step.

Time became a blur as he wandered down more hallways. An influence beyond himself guided him somehow. He approached a set of doors, and a pull steered him to the one on the right. He stared at it as he passed. To his surprise, it slid open. Before he knew what he was doing, he wandered over and peered inside. Everything about the new room struck him as familiar. A coffee table rested in front of two comfortable couches, and a single picture rested on the top of the table. He recognized the room as his quarters from back home. He looked up and found that the mirror ended at the room's entrance.

Brian desperately wanted to be home, and he desperately wanted to find Grace in the room. He glanced at the mirror overhead in the hall again. "This isn't my home, though. Is it? This is just another trick."

Moving away from the opening, he continued limping down the hall. The door slid closed.

In time, he found a mess of veins spewing across the ceiling. They twisted around themselves as though strangling each other for space. Some of the reflective branches were as large as tree trunks, and they drooped down from the mirror. Others resembled spiders' webbing with their delicate network of threads.

Brian weaved through the intricate system of encroaching veins, taking care not to touch any of them. The corridor's lighting dampened in the hall the farther he went. The reflective branches grew around many of the lanterns, choking out their glow.

I must be getting close to something, Brian thought.

His cumbersome footfalls made slow but steady progress. Soon, he noticed another overgrown network of veins gathering on the ceiling and walls. Thinner veins broke away from the main branches and even spread onto the floor. He moved closer to the phenomenon and found that the cluster outlined an opening to another room. It looked like someone had forced their way through the door. The metallic slab sat three-quarters of the way open. It seemed wrenched off its tracks from the inside and had a large bow in its middle. Something told him the mirror was the culprit.

Brian leaned forward, trying to get a better look inside, but the room's pitch-black interior withheld its secrets. *What kind of room is this?* he wondered in awe.

A slight creak sounded from the hall.

One of the lanterns on the wall bent and hung at a distressing angle. It looked like it couldn't handle the weight of the massive vein pressing on it anymore. Its light flickered out, and the hall darkened even more. A glass pane slipped out of its frame and broke on the floor.

Brian swallowed. He nervously opened and closed his swollen hands, and his stomach twisted in knots. *Maybe I shouldn't have come here.*

"Where else would you have gone?" came another thought.

Brian puzzled at the question and crept forward toward the room's entrance as if on autopilot. Hot, muggy air billowed around him. The humidity left steam growing on the surrounding veins. His clothes began sticking to his skin. He felt something drip onto his head, and he fell into a protective crouch. His hands shot up, shielding him from a droplet of liquid doom from the ceiling.

A few moments passed, and Brian realized the ceiling wasn't consuming him. His paralyzing fear eased, and he peeked through his shielding arms. A droplet of mirror hadn't come down to get him at all. He lowered his arms. Some of the steam must have gathered and dripped on his head. He touched his hair and started spreading the wetness around. He looked down at his fingers and rubbed them together. The liquid left behind an oily residue that was infused with the sweet stench.

Oh, great! Now, I've got it on me. Brian's fingers stiffened and began hurting again.

The medication shouldn't have worn off so quickly, but more pain raced up his arm and spread through his whole body. The oily liquid seemed to neutralize his last dose. As his agony grew, he shuffled toward the darkened doorway. The sweet stench seeped through his dead-fish gauze.

Brian gagged and held his breath.

He dug inside his pocket and fumbled for the wadded-up wrapper. Finding the cracked vial, he yanked it out and re-wetted the pads.

Brian's lungs burned from want of air.

He re-wrapped the vial, and his swollen, bandaged fingers wailed through every movement. Crumpling up the wrapper into a messy ball, he shoved it back into his pocket. He draped the re-wetted gauze pads back over his face. Desperate for air, he sucked in the putrid smell once again.

He rolled his eyes. The saturating, sweet scent still cut through the dead-fish odor. With another gag, Brian mindlessly shuffled into the dark room.

Chapter 31

Not even a sliver of light existed in the void of a room beyond the doorway.

The dim lights in the hall flickered.

"You've got to be kidding!" Brian cursed the infernal station. "What is it now? The loss of time? Am I going to find myself in a different part of the station?"

The lights flickered again and went out.

"I'm not afraid of you!" Brian shouted into the darkness.

The only sound he could hear became his own heavy breaths. The seconds felt like an endless loop of time, but the lanterns in the hall didn't come back on. Part of him wanted to find himself relocated to somewhere else already. A compelling urge made his feet start moving, but he didn't know where they were taking him.

A tiny light started shining in the distance. The pitiful glow didn't provide much visibility. For a split second, the meager beacon brightened in the darkness, then faded away, leaving the room in stilled obscurity once again. The heat of the moist air baked Brian, and buckets of sweat poured down him. His clothes clung to him even more.

He continued to move forward.

His nerves urged him to hurry to his final destination before the lights came back on and he found himself elsewhere. A dull, pink glow brightened a small area to his right, and an orange one lit on his left. They both faded back into the darkness. Other tiny, colored lights began dotting the landscape. An orchestra of eerie hues interrupted the void as they turned on and off.

Brian stared, mesmerized by the distant, star-like colors as they blinked. They created shadows that danced around silhouetted computers. He figured they were buttons on the consoles, periodically giving off a faint glow before they snuffed back out. One particular light lit up in the middle of the massive room. It started out dim but brightened more than the others—like the creation of a new sun, dotting a blanket of space a million miles away. However, its distant illumination did little to add visibility to the all-encompassing black hole of a room.

Brian drifted toward the brighter light.

While taking in what he could of the darkened chamber, recognition hit him: He was meandering through a massive bridge. From what he could tell, it seemed dozens of sizes bigger than the one on his ship. It should have been well-lit, and the place should have been hopping with a sizable crew, busy at work.

How is this station even functioning? Brian's awe propelled him forward.

The lights from the different consoles bounced off the shadows in the room. Shades of soft blue, green, and even purple continued their blinking visual symphony. They illuminated his way like fairy lights from a forgotten realm. A pathway between the computers led to the center of the bridge. As if guided by an unseen force, he maneuvered through the maze of consoles.

He felt a gnawing sensation in the pit of his stomach.

The sticky-sweet scent saturating the air seemed less objectionable, somehow. Brian's hand that held the smelly fish pads relaxed and threatened to fall to his side. In fact, his whole body felt overly calm. He couldn't sense the pressure of his broken nose or even the pain of his infected wounds anymore. The absence of his miseries made him wonder if he had taken another dose of medication, but he knew he hadn't—at least not from what he could remember.

Intense peacefulness continued engulfing Brian, yet his uneasiness grew.

He gazed down to his right as he passed another row of computers. He could see something draped across a console. In the poor lighting, he could make out the shape of another enormous vein. It looked like a tree trunk resting its felled mass across the place. In true mirror fashion, its surface reflected the flickering, colored lights of the room. The dazzling display made him pause. When one blinked out of existence, another took its place.

The stunning show held him captive. He wanted to sit down and watch the reflection of the elegant lights continue their mesmerizing dance forever, but his feet betrayed his desires. He took another step toward the center of the bridge. His attention lingered on the vein, even as he moved away. The infatuating display beckoned him to return and watch a little longer.

Getting a tenuous hold over himself, Brian approached the main attraction in the middle of the room. As the small, colored lights continued flickering their bewitching splendor around him, his attention squared on the center of the bridge. He noticed that the computers surrounding the illuminated area were overrun with a bulbous mountain of flesh. His odd dream leaped into his mind, and the similarities hounded him. Bulging folds of blubber consumed most of the consoles under their hefty weight. He couldn't tell where the disgusting mound started or ended. He glanced across the darkened expanse of the room, wondering how many computers the massive thing buried underneath its bulk.

Long, spindly threads stretched from certain portions of the fleshy mound and disappeared into the room's abyss. The strands' intricate network created a spider-like webbing. Brian's imagination ran wild with the possibility of cosmic spiders concealed within the room's gloom—advancing on *him*, their distracted prey.

Pushing his newfound fear of the dark away, he approached the bridge. A large mound of the bulbous flesh sat directly underneath the single brighter light. He kicked himself for being so inattentive. He hadn't meant to come within range of the overgrown thing, yet he continued drifting toward it. Silent alarms rang in his mind. He tried to stop and back up, but his feet propelled him forward.

Brian suddenly halted, but not of his own accord.

Gazing at the monstrous blob, he cringed. It looked more like a giant wad of discarded chewing gum than anything else. Near his traitorous feet, he found a smaller mound that came to the height of his knee. It seemed to be the same color as the antique wallpaper. The surface of the glob glistened in the dim lighting. His stomach churned as he stared at the thing. Slippery saliva filled his mouth and threatened to empty his stomach's meager contents.

A wall of sickly sweet scent slammed against him. The aroma of freshly baked bread marched in right behind it. The two smells fused, creating a compelling pull on his appetite that yanked him into his imagination. In the blink of an eye, he stood in the cozy kitchen of his childhood quarters. A tray of warm cinnamon rolls rested on the counter. Wisps of steam swayed in the air above the swirled bread, and icing dripped down the pastries' sides.

He closed his eyes and breathed in the intoxicating aroma.

His mouth watered.

Opening his eyes again, he noticed one particular roll that stood out from all the others. A large glob of the drizzly icing was accumulating on its side. His stomach growled. The droplet gathered until it looked like it would run. He reached out to catch it on his finger but hesitated.

"Just one won't hurt."

An urge to step forward washed over him, but he remembered the boulder-sized wad of blubber that rested near his feet somewhere far away. The echo of reality snapped him back out of his imagination. Once again, he found himself standing in a darkened room beneath the reach of a single light on an enormous bridge.

The bulbous mound that came up to his knees had doubled in size while he daydreamed. It swelled to the height of his chest and continued to grow. His stomach lurched again as he watched the thing's bulk churn and twist in on itself. Large bubbles inflated portions of its surface to the point that he thought they'd pop, but they never did. The pockets deflated as the rest of the massive blob folded over them.

The overpowering aroma of baked delicacies begged Brian to return to his imagination, but the mound of growing blubber consumed all of his attention. His head tipped back as he watched the mound begin towering over him. He fought to take a retreating step, but his limbs wouldn't respond. He just stood there, frozen, unable to move a muscle. His eyes remained fixed on the imposing heap of blob in front of him.

A section of the mound closest to Brian pulled back, creating some space between him and the blubber. He breathed a small sigh of relief, and the tension in his muscles relaxed slightly. The fleshy wall created a semicircular ring around him, and everything fell very still. He continued wrestling to back up but found that his efforts proved quite useless. Any sense of ease for having distance between him and the mound had been short-lived.

The wall of blubber began to change. In its center, a small dot started shining. Brian squinted as he watched the spot spread. It grew into a luminous bead that looked like glowing, liquid glass. The tiny light pierced the gloom of the room. Several other beads started sprinkling the wall like a dense, sparkling sheen of sweat.

Soon, a layer of the shimmering stuff blanketed the surface of the entire wall, making it look smooth and shiny like a crystal-clear pond. It held the brilliance of three moons—and Brian's complete attention. The bright glow lit the surrounding room, at least from what he could tell. He couldn't tear his eyes away from the spectacle to take a look around. With the dazzling sight in front of him, he almost didn't want to.

His foot took a step toward the breathtaking display. He tried digging his heels in to stop his progression but found himself moving forward anyway.

What is going on? Brian mentally shrieked, then took another step.

He went berserk and spent every last ounce of willpower wrestling with himself to retreat. His foot lifted again, and he laser-focused his thoughts in an attempt to control his rebellious limb. It slowed to a stop and hovered in midair.

Sweat poured down Brian's forehead from the mental strain.

His foot budged, ever so slightly, in reverse.

A smile—his first real smile since he lost his crew—spread across his lips over the small victory. He placed the hovering foot down, taking a step back. His thoughts flew to the hidden arsenal inside his breast pocket— the golden coin, his last-resort tool. He might not have been able to save his crew or even himself, but there could be a chance to put an end to whatever beings controlled the station and, to a large degree, the beings that apparently controlled him.

He forced his uncooperative arm to bend, reaching toward the hidden fold in his uniform. The simmering surface of the wall transformed from its brilliant, moonish glow to a soft, baby-blue hue. The color shift gave the wall a breathtaking illusion of depth. The captivating visual display almost made him forget his plan—almost. He turned his attention back toward getting his hand to his hidden breast pocket.

His fingers inched up, past his ribs.

The soft, blue glow of the wall intensified, and a horizontal divide formed. It spread like a brushstroke across the middle of the canvas, separating it into two spheres. The top half morphed into a blue horizon, and the sky became touched with pink, puffy clouds that a sun promised to kiss at any moment. The bottom half darkened and filled with sand. Brian could feel the cool granules clumping between his toes—right through his boots.

A crisp, salty breeze carried away the strong aroma of sweet pastries. The gentle wind combed through Brian's hair and cooled his feverish body as it whirled around him. The soft sound of waves playfully splashed on a not-so-distant shore. The blue sky darkened and turned a stunning shade of purple.

Mirandian's third moon? This place, again? Brian thought. *Why?*

He continued staring, transfixed by the scene that stretched out before him. Gazing at the welcoming beach, he could make out a reclining chair resting underneath a red umbrella. Another chair lay tipped backward in the sand near the first. A small, black dot suddenly started forming in the center of the remarkable landscape. Despite the serenity of the scene, the appearance of the black blotch made Brian want to run and hide. Thoughts of retreat flooded his mind. Something warned him to escape back the way he had come and never, ever return to this forbidden room.

Instead, he stood there frozen with his eyes glued to the magnificent seascape stretched out before him.

The small dot began to grow, and so did Brian's fear.

Chapter 32

The black blemish on the beach-filled canvas enlarged, and a hot burst of wind broke across Brian's skin. A sense of desperation gripped him. He began fumbling across his uniform again, trying to get to the hidden device in his breast pocket. The dot grew and turned into a thin, black line running vertically down the middle of the picturesque scene.

Brian fumbled more desperately.

WHY CAN'T I FIND THAT POCKET! he roared within himself.

His foot suddenly lifted off the floor of its own accord. "NO!" he shouted out loud, in absolute defiance.

He stopped reaching for the hidden pocket, just short of his mark, and rested his hand against his ribs. He focused all his attention on gaining control over his rebellious limb. Finding a measure of success, Brian managed to slow the foot so that it hovered in mid-air. His mind strained, and he poured even more mental effort into the undertaking. To his surprise, he leaned slightly forward and finished the step.

Panic set in.

Brian's other foot lifted to take another stride.

He wrestled even harder for control. His leg only briefly slowed in its fluid movement forward. It landed with a sense of mocking finality on the floor. The instant his foot touched down, the thin, black line thickened and elongated. It looked like a black pole: The top was rounded, but the bottom half was separated in two.

Brian took another step.

The black pole instantly doubled in size and transformed into the silhouette of a person walking toward him in the sand. His other leg lifted again, and his mind became a frenzied mess as he ransacked it for the strength to stop his forward progression. His foot touched down, and the image doubled again.

No longer just a silhouette, the newly formed shape of a man stopped and stood in the wall. The being looked like another Brian.

Brian felt his body shifting to take another step. *You've GOT to be kidding! What am I going to do? Just walk right into that thing?* he scolded his feet.

His bluster did nothing to stop him from advancing forward. The last step brought him face-to-face with his replica. He stood barely a breath away. A force pressed in on Brian from behind, making him lean closer to the wall. Thick humidity radiated from the water-like surface. Somehow, his duplicate's warm, rhythmic breath poured through the wall and down Brian's body, dumping its stinky sweetness all over him. He tried to pull away, but he couldn't move. He winced and shut his eyes, waiting for the moment of impact when his face entered the liquid, but it never came.

Realizing that he had stopped moving, he built up enough courage to peek through one eye. The colors of the sky began brightening as the sun rose on the beach's distant horizon. Brian's duplicate stood between him and the breaking dawn. They stared at each other, nose to nose.

Brian opened his other eye.

The doppelgänger's piercing gaze held Brian's stare.

Another salty, hot gust of air swirled around Brian. His lips became parched as the hot wind stole the moisture from them, making him desperate to swallow. At the same time, it also made him quite incapable of accomplishing the task.

The force holding him in place pulled him back a step.

Brian breathed a little easier from the added distance between himself and his duplicate. He sized up his replica and noticed that it wasn't quite the same as his reflection on the ceiling. Its nose showed no signs of swelling or breakage. Instead of torn, blood-soaked clothes, it wore a mirror crew's uniform. The doppelgänger seemed to be the exact opposite of his current physical state. The strong sense of confidence radiating from it made it seem more wholesome, more capable than the real Brian somehow, but an air of arrogance wafted about it as well.

The duplicate's eyes narrowed as it locked a harsh gaze on Brian.

"Not arrogance," came a thought. *"Cunning."*

Brian's heart skipped a beat.

The intrusive thought sat in the back of his mind, like extra cargo taking up precious space in a holding bay—out of the way but still large enough to notice. He couldn't shake the feeling that his last thought hadn't originated from within himself. He struggled in vain to break free from the unseen force that imprisoned him within his own body.

"You don't have to be afraid," came a soft, soothing voice.

What's going on? What's going on? Brian's mind raced.

He lacked any range of motion that would allow him to turn around to check for someone behind him. Frozen in place, he continued staring at his other self. His instincts told him the voice belonged to it, but he held the idea in reserve. His duplicate's mouth didn't move when the voice spoke. The absurd notion drifted out of his thoughts as he returned to the pursuit of his freedom.

An all-consuming wave of calm washed over him, settling him to his very core. His mind fell still, and his aches and pains started melting away. *What . . . is . . . going . . . on?* Brian's thoughts slowed, and the question hung on the last strand of his sanity.

"You are very strong." The soothing voice came again.

The doppelgänger's mouth didn't even twitch. The expression on its face remained blank. Unable to do much else, Brian continued staring at his enchanting duplicate and considered the voice's meaning. He remembered leaving Callie in the storage room while he sat on the platform of loaded fuel, Derek getting coated by the mirror near the bar, and Sivien's boot sliding from his weak grasp in the hall. The loss of his crew sat bitterly on his mind.

A stronger man would have saved his crew, Brian thought.

"Only the strongest can deal with such great loss," the pleasant voice sounded again.

The response threw him off. He started to wonder if the voice could hear his thoughts, but his attention drifted to what it had said. He had never thought about strength in those terms before.

Brian gravitated back to his original train of thought. *Can the voice hear my thoughts?*

His uneasiness grew.

Trying to brush the preposterous idea away, his frustration over his total loss of self-control simmered. Everything about his circumstances seemed to feed chaos itself. He wished he could rewind time. He imagined going back and fixing his ship's malfunction before they went into stasis. Taunting thoughts filled his mind of how he should be celebrating a welcome-home party with his crew—not drifting in some forsaken corner of space alone on a deranged station.

He envisioned keeping his crew on their ship instead of disembarking into this monstrous place. He could almost feel his crew members huddled around him as they stayed on the bridge of *The Gabriel* to die. The sound of their rapid breaths pierced his ears, and their feverish efforts to fill their oxygen-starved lungs in the thinning air consumed him. Even that would have been a better end than losing them to this infernal place.

What about regret? Brian sulked to himself. *I'm not strong enough to deal with that.*

A profound silence hushed his thoughts.

He stood staring at his motionless replica, dwelling on the tragic events that had brought him to this place. He took full responsibility for the downfall of his crew. Somehow, he should have kept them safe.

"You're right," a creamy reply came. *"You're not strong enough to deal with regret."*

An alarm blared in Brian's mind. The realization that the voice actually *could* hear his thoughts sank in. He searched for ways to stem the breach somewhere in his mind, but he didn't know how. As far as he knew, telepathy existed only in theory. *How can I fight a technology I know nothing about?*

A wry smile spread across his duplicate's lips. *"You can't,"* came another reply.

Brian locked gazes with his duplicate, and his frustration boiled. The ongoing imprisonment in his own body infuriated him even more. He tried moving his hand toward the hidden pocket on his chest again, but his fingers were pinned tightly against his ribs, refusing to budge from their useless perch. He raged inside over his inability to act. With no outlet to dispel his frustrations, his own flesh felt like a prison holding him hostage.

Another gust of hot wind blew from the beach. The sweltering breeze calmed Brian a degree, but his frustration didn't dispel completely. Being stuck in a mummified state served as a constant reminder of how little control he retained over anything.

A soft song started drifting through the air. Brian made out a single string instrument giving voice to a haunting tune. It sounded like the same song Zella had hummed earlier. A wispy woodwind stepped in for a moment, and he cringed at its off-key accompaniment. It quickly faded. The single string's voice increased in volume and rang out with more clarity. The mystifying melody calmed him even more, and he lost himself in the siren song.

Brian's eyelids felt heavy.

The song's key shifted, and the wispy accompaniment waltzed back in, but this time its off-key tune added depth and unconventional beauty. The melody sent chills racing up and down Brian's spine and pulled on his heartstrings. The memories of all his past defeats flashed through his mind in an instant. The mixture of the forlorn music and his own memories crushed him.

He wallowed in despair.

As the music continued playing, movement in Brian's peripheral vision caught his groggy attention, but he couldn't tip his head to see better. In no time, the disturbance crept close enough that he could catch a glimpse of it. Thin, reflective veins, similar to those he had tracked in the hall, edged in on the sides of the beach scene. He saw more of them worming their way toward his duplicate, who stood in the center of the gooey wall. As they encroached on the other Brian, they shimmered. The dazzling visual display reminded him of stargazing as a kid. The veins reached the doppelgänger, but they didn't touch him. Most of the beach became lost under the host of their sparkling shine.

"You're hurt. Let me help you," the soothing voice beckoned.

The duplicate's hand moved toward Brian as though it invited him somewhere. The outer membrane of the wall stretched, but the limb stayed safely encased within its goo.

Brian curled his lip at the repulsive offer.

Chapter 33

"You're the one who caused my pain," Brian countered out loud at his duplicate.

"*No,*" the voice responded. "*If you look closely, you'll find that all of this was your fault and that I have actually been helping you the whole time.*" Brian lost himself in an endless search of picking apart his actions since he woke from stasis. The idea of everything being his fault offended reason, yet he came up with different actions he could have taken. He beat himself up for asking to land on this forsaken ship, for not having Callie sit next to him on the fuel tanks, and for not getting to Derek in the cafeteria in time. He especially reamed himself for not being able to reach his hidden breast pocket—still just inches away.

"*See. This is your fault. I have only been trying to help,*" the voice cooed.

In an instant, a large measure of strength left Brian. He almost doubled over from the resurgence of his pains. His head filled with savage pounding, and the lacerations that Zella had left all over his body swelled brutally with infection. His deepest wounds, the ones on his shoulder and thigh, burned with unquenchable fire. Even his hunger clawed at him from within.

He slumped under the weight of his own suffering.

His breath quickened as shock overran his body. His mouth fell open, and a nightmarish sound split the air. He barely recognized it as his own tortured voice.

"Did you really think you could do this all on your own?" The voice laughed. *"What a valiant yet absurd notion."*

Whatever force held him in place relinquished its grasp, and Brian crumpled to the floor. Exhaustion of every kind overwhelmed him. His head flopped back, and he stared up at his double. Its hand still extended toward him. He started contemplating the offer.

"Ah, yes. Now you see," said the voice.

Brian's duplicate reached down to him. The wall's membrane stretched and thinned until its fingertips pressed through the gooey barrier and exposed a very real, very live human hand.

"Come," the voice said, *"let me take your pain away."*

The forlorn music still drifting on the breeze shifted key again. The tune morphed into an upbeat rhapsody. Brian felt bolstered by the strange, empowering song. His spirits wanted to soar, but his suffering anchored him to this miserable reality. A sluggish mental alarm prodded at him from somewhere in the recesses of his mind. He knew he couldn't trust the offer, but that didn't make it any less enticing.

Brian remembered his hidden pocket. His hand was so close. *That would end my pain, too,* he thought.

He closed his eyes.

Focusing all his concentration on the hand pinned to his ribs, he tried moving it, and it budged. He didn't stop to celebrate and pressed onward. His body started trembling as his system was overridden with shock. A faint smile spread across his lips as his fingers slid into the hidden fold of his ruined uniform.

"It doesn't have to be this way," the voice impressed upon his mind.

Brian's finger brushed against the coin, and he opened his eyes. He looked up at his duplicate. His tired smile spread further across his lips as his finger honed in on the device's detonator.

A force unlike anything Brian had ever known bore down on him, halting his progress.

"You're mighty stubborn," the voice croaked.

The doppelgänger's face scowled down at Brian from within the wall. The silvery veins inched their way onto his double, but the being didn't get buried underneath them. The duplicate moved forward, stretching the gel-like membrane thinner as it went.

Brian wanted to shrink away, but the overpowering force held him in a crumpled heap on the floor. The other Brian stepped through the watery goo and stood in front of him. The wall's membrane still clung to its back half like glue, and heat radiated from it like molten magma.

The double became a living, breathing presence.

Brian gawped at the man. The force holding Brian in place shifted his weight and lifted him into the air like a rag doll, forcing him to his feet. His hand, clinging to his chest, fell from its perch against his ribs and dangled at his side. The tips of his boots barely brushed against the floor as they dragged toward his duplicate. His body halted just inches away from his doppelgänger, where it dumped another pungent exhale down the front of him.

"Why do you fight so hard?" the voice asked, but the duplicate's mouth remained motionless.

Brian's whole body turned to the left—so far that he couldn't see the being in front of him anymore. He halted for a moment, then reversed direction, fully rotating to the other side. He got the idea that whatever entity held him captive saw him as a curious object that needed examining. The unseen force turned Brian once again until he faced his other self. His rapid breaths filled with his double's putrid, sweet exhale.

"It's a wonder you even made it here," the voice continued. *"You've lost so much blood. You should be delirious from infection and pain. I've never seen anything quite like you."*

As Brian's hands dangled at his sides, he fought to bring one of them back up to his hidden pocket, but his fingers only twitched from his efforts.

"Look at you. Even now, you don't give up. You're still trying to win—at least your version of winning. What if I told you your little plan wouldn't work? Hmm?" the voice asked.

Brian's heart sank at the thought. If he wasn't going to survive, he wanted to take this thing out with him. It was the least he could do—make it so the station couldn't keep taking in more ships and absorbing more beings into its mirror. Doubt over his plan's success began swirling in his mind. What if the voice spoke the truth? What if his plan wouldn't even leave a dent in this place? After all, his gun had proven quite useless against the monstrosity.

A sea of despair washed over him, and his will began drowning in its endless abyss. The twitching of his fingers slowed, then stopped. His thoughts wandered to his lost crew. He hadn't been able to save them, after all. His mind drifted to the other ship that had landed—he couldn't save them, either.

I've failed, Brian admitted.

"Yes, you have," the voice replied.

A bitter sting formed behind Brian's eyes. *I've failed.*

Brian met his duplicate's gaze. Floating in midair, the man stood motionless—expressionless—staring right back at him. It exhaled again, dumping more sickly sweet breath over him. Brian's spirits dampened even more, and he grew tired of his anguish. He grew tired of everything.

"It doesn't have to be this way." The voice came again. *"I can relieve you of your misery."*

Brian lost his will to keep fighting.

The thin, reflective veins wormed onto the doppelgänger's face, inching across his forehead and cheeks. The being didn't seem bothered by it one bit. A silver spark filled his eyes, which, oddly, wasn't the least bit concerning to Brian. He accepted the change. It seemed like the most natural thing in the multiverse.

An artificial relief began dousing Brian's fiery wounds, and an icy chill settled into the injuries' deepest crevices. Even the pressure from the swelling in his head eased. His resistance against the entity melted away with his pains. Ecstasy drifted in as his agony washed away.

"See," the voice cooed.

With every blink, Brian's eyes felt heavier. He labored to keep them open, but sleep beckoned to him like a lost love's embrace—Grace's embrace. At last, the nagging alarm in the back of his mind silenced, and he gained a measure of function over his limbs. He lifted his hand toward his duplicate's extended arm, finally accepting the invitation.

Through droopy eyes, he watched as the embodiment of his own perfection drew nearer, but the closeness didn't make him feel uneasy this time. As the other Brian leaned in, their noses almost touched. Another one of his exhalations filled the air with its moist scent. This time, the overpowering smell combined with the smell of baked bread and a dash of cinnamon.

Brian's mouth watered. *Cinnamon rolls,* he thought with a slight chuckle.

The doppelgänger's arms flung out wide—like he meant to wrap Brian in a hug. The shimmering veins stretched from the watery wall and twisted farther down around the being's outstretched limbs. Brian accepted whatever future the fates would bring and took one last breath. He closed his eyes and held them shut as his vein-covered duplicate leaned in.

A gel-like liquid touched the tip of Brian's nose, burning his skin. A cooling sensation, followed by a burning chill quickly covered his entire head. He felt the doppelgänger's arms wrap around him, and the scalding-ice touch engulfed his entire body. His skin tingled from the freezing fire that penetrated his very core. The sensation shook off his grogginess, but he kept his eyes closed, clinging to the extraordinary moment.

All of Brian's senses flooded with sheer euphoria. It washed over him, surged through him, and pulsed in his veins to the beat of his own heart. He could swear that he no longer stood on the bridge of a dark, horrible space station. Instead, he felt like he somehow floated in a pool of ice-cold, liquified fire. His heart continued pumping the liquid joy through his veins, and Brian lost himself in the sea of ecstasy.

Suddenly, something icy touched the back of his neck. Goosebumps streaked across his skin. The freezing object pressed so hard it began to hurt. He tried to move away, but his weak limbs wouldn't respond. The frigid thing pierced his skin, and its arctic bite stole his breath away.

He grimaced.

Freezing liquid dumped down the back of his neck and soothed the pain from the ice pick that was drilling in, but it didn't relieve any of the pressure. The thing wormed its way down between his shoulder blades. He shivered as the burrowing force settled to a stop in the middle of his back. His breath slowly returned. His body warmed again, and his mind drifted back to the ocean of euphoria he had floated through earlier.

Did I just die? Brian wondered. *Do I still exist?*

The realization sunk in that he didn't even care.

"Hello, Brian," a penetrating female voice said.

Brian fought to open his eyes.

His lids started to flutter open. As his eyes adjusted, he found himself standing in a large command center of a ship. The most exquisite creature he had ever laid eyes on floated in midair just a few feet away. A pale-blue, sheer cloak draped across her sleek, dainty shoulders. A flowing gown tightened around her elongated waist, and its hem swayed freely around her dangling feet. The female alien's pale, blue skin radiated a faint glow. At the same time, her flesh appeared slightly translucent. Some of her veins shimmered with bright liquid that pulsed to the beat of her heart. Her pasty complexion somehow complemented her dress.

"Hello," Brian whispered.

He took in his surroundings a little more and noticed the alien's thick, full mane floating and swaying around her in the air as well. Her impossibly long hair looked as if each strand had been infused with pure fiber-optics. The wispy hair covered the computers and reached to the far corners of the room—disappearing along the wall's edges. Besides the alien in the gown and her overgrown hair, Brian found no other personnel in the command center. He wondered how a ship with a bridge this size could function without a substantial crew at its helm.

"Can I help you?" the female seemed to ask, but her lips never moved.

Brian looked at the alien's face. Her high cheekbones accented her slender yet firmly set jaw, and her dark-blue lips contrasted against her pale skin. His stare drifted to her eyes, and her soulless, coal-black gaze went straight through him.

"Am . . . " Brian searched for words as he stared at the dubiously angelic creature. "Am I hurt?"

The alien searched him up and down with fierce scrutiny. She cocked a brow and tipped her head. *"I see no wounds. Are you in pain?"* Her blue lips still didn't move.

Brian looked down and inspected himself. His navy-blue uniform appeared pristinely pressed, and he patted the soft material. He'd expected to feel pain everywhere, but nothing seemed out of the ordinary. He brought his hand to his cheek. His skin felt smooth to the touch. He ran his fingers down to his chin and across the rough stubble of his well-groomed goatee. When he reached his nose, he pressed on it.

Everything seemed normal.

Brian looked back at the breathtaking alien. "Am I a captain of a ship?" He felt unsure of what the answer should be.

A smile instantly spread across the alien's exquisite features. She tipped her head back, and the room filled with her loud laughter. Brian didn't understand how, though. Her mouth never opened enough to match the sound.

The alien's laughter subsided. *"I am the* only *captain here."*

Her cold gaze fell upon him once again. Her eyes seemed to hold some sort of bizarre merriment.

Brian felt he should be concerned about something, but he couldn't figure out what it might be. "Yes . . . you are the only captain here," he automatically echoed.

The statement sounded so natural and seemed so right.

How could I have forgotten my own captain? Brian puzzled.

"You simply must get back to work," the captain insisted.

He blinked a few times, trying to remember his duties, but nothing came to mind. In an instant, his responsibilities on the ship came flooding in. He knew his section and his rank. He even remembered the location of his quarters with its cozy couches and coffee table.

Of course. How could I have forgotten all of that? Brian's gaze dropped to the floor. His cheeks flushed hot with embarrassment.

He turned to leave. With shuffling steps, he moved toward the door. The lost echo of a memory called to him from far away—a misplaced notion he couldn't quite retrieve. It hinted that something wasn't quite right, somehow.

A thought finally broke through.

Brian stopped in his tracks, halfway to the door, and turned. He looked at his captivating captain. "I greatly apologize . . . but I can't seem to remember your name." His gaze dropped to his boots on the fluffy white carpet.

"Don't worry. You needn't feel bad. It could have happened to anyone," the captain said.

Relief washed over Brian, and he looked back up at her, hoping she would give him the answer.

The captain looked him over. *"It's Terren."* Her lips still didn't move, but a wry smile formed across the soft, beautiful features of her pale face.

"Thank you, my queen." Brian gave a slight bow.

"You're very welcome," Terren replied.

Baffled by his bow and his *my queen* statement, Brian bolted for the door. Weaving his way through the computer consoles, he approached the exit. The oversized black door slid open. A thought still nagged at him like he had forgotten something—something important—but he couldn't think of what. He racked his brain for the answer, only to have his thoughts return to his list of duties on the ship.

The giant door slid closed behind him. He walked down the long, empty hallway. Decorative chandeliers hung from the ceiling, and lanterns lined the white, monotone walls. *What am I doing clear over here, anyway? It's going to take me an eon to get back to my section!* He continued scanning the hall in confusion.

Brian wished he could remember what reason had brought him all the way out here to the command center, but he just couldn't think of it. He couldn't even recall the location of the nearest teleport that would shorten his journey back. Squaring his shoulders, he quickened his step. He needed to focus on getting back to where he belonged. He hoped that luck would serve him well and that, in time, his useless memory would kick back in.

Brian gazed up at the lanterns hanging on the wall as he passed. He peered up at a chandelier dangling from the ceiling overhead. Everything seemed to be in order and felt right in his world. He started humming the uplifting tune playing quietly in unseen speakers. It bolstered his spirits and reminded him of the long-lost pleasantries he used to enjoy as a child—even though he couldn't quite remember which ones.

On his way back to his section, the hall started filling with the station's other crew members. The different types and sizes of aliens all wore the same uniform he did. He toyed with the idea of asking one of them where he could find a teleport, but he couldn't bring himself to suffer the embarrassment that the silly question would bring. He simply weaved around the growing traffic. In time, the station buzzed with activity as everyone hurried along with their routines. The commotion filled the station's busy halls with chattering.

Brian thought of himself as a tiny drop in a giant sea of navy-blue uniforms.

He knew his duty, and he easily blended in with the flow of the station.

Epilogue

The bridge door closed.

Terren sensed Brian moving down the hallway, away from her command center. She savored their intimate bond—the same bond she enjoyed with the rest of her crew. He wasn't her most difficult specimen to win over, but he had proven to be something of a thorn in her side. Still, in the end, he became one of hers. She twirled her finger in a lock of her luminous hair, mentally sifting through her connections with the others. She counted Brian's intellect like a mere piece of sand in an ocean of her incorporated beings.

Shutting out all the other crew members from her mind, Terren turned her full attention to Brian. She concentrated on him as he moved down the hall, noting his persistent mental prodding at the sphere she had created around his memories. Her perfectly arched brows furrowed. In time, he might prove to be a problem.

Most of her conquests integrated well into her society, but not all.

One way or another, she found a use for everyone—even the defects.

For now, Brian didn't fit into the category of discards. He didn't fight against the cognitive repeat—not enough, anyway. Her implant nestled comfortably inside of him. The heightened bond of the embedded link helped her know where he was in his integration process.

A grin spread across Terren's face.

Reaching up, she brushed her fingertips across her silky bottom lip—quite pleased with her ability to smile. Reveling in the satisfaction of receiving another crew member into her fold, she released her focus on Brian. Taking in a deep breath, she pulled energy from her subjects through their links, filling herself to the brim with their stolen energy. She almost swooned with lightheadedness from the pure power she absorbed.

An unquenchable urge to take in more of her subordinates' vitality consumed her, but she restrained herself from absorbing more. Devouring too much sustenance from her delicate energy sources all at once could prove disastrous. Some of her darlings wouldn't be able to handle another draw so soon. She looked down at her hands, admiring the added brilliance to her sheen.

Hunger gnawed at Terren, but with her constant food supply sitting at her fingertips like a rechargeable buffet, she waited patiently for more energy to build for another draw. Her gentle techniques left all—well, almost all of them—oblivious of her existence.

She observed her whole dimension. At the speed of thought, her mind traveled through her titanic ship and settled on a particular section. The area buzzed with activity as her crew saw to their duties—and their play. She zeroed in on her pawn. Her subject stood straighter and peered around the room. She knew her servant sensed her unseen presence.

"I'm sending you a new recruit to keep an eye on." Terren mentally sent instructions and impressed Brian's image upon her pawn's mind. *"He's not dangerous, but I'm not sure if his integration will take as smoothly as I'd like. He reminds me of some of the others who proved to be disturbers of the peace."*

"Yes, my queen," came her pawn's single, mental reply.

Terren didn't need any more of a response. She knew her servant would do as she instructed. The pathetic excuse for a being always did. She withdrew a pace and watched her dutiful servant for a moment. Her pawn went back to its work, but it took some time for its posture to relax again.

She let the section of her ship fade from her concentration. She blinked and found herself back on her bridge. She sucked in another energy draw from her subjects as though she were drinking in ambrosial nectar. Her skin shone gloriously.

Her attention turned to her newest conquest. Another starship had arrived, and more potential recruits filled the craft to its brim.

Terren's smile spread even wider.

About the Author

R. H. Deans' top interests involve the dimensions of the human mind, the depth of the psyche, and the matchless wonderment of space. She has studied psychology and holds a bachelor's degree in the marriage and family field. Besides having a flair for the psychological, finding wit and humor is top page in this author's book. She lives near Salt Lake City, Utah, with her husband, their five children, and two dogs.

A free ebook edition is available with the purchase of this book.

To claim your free ebook edition:

1. Visit MorganJamesBOGO.com
2. Sign your name CLEARLY in the space
3. Complete the form and submit a photo of the entire copyright page
4. You or your friend can download the ebook to your preferred device

Snap a photo   Free ebook   Read anywhere

CPSIA information can be obtained
at www.ICGtesting.com
Printed in the USA
JSHW032301301222
35549JS00001B/4